WHAT'S
THE
MATTER
WITH
MARY
JANE?

WHAT'S THE MATTER WITH MARY JANE?

ANOTHER POSTMODERN MYSTERY, BY THE NUMBERS

An Epitome Apartments Mystery by

CANDAS JANE DORSEY

Published by ECW Press
665 Gerrard Street East
Toronto, Ontario, Canada M4M 1Y2
416-694-3348 / info@ecwpress.com

Cover artwork and design by Brienne Lim
Author photo: © P. J. Groeneveldt

This is a work of fiction. Names, characters, places, and incidents either are the product of the author's imagination or are used fictitiously, and any resemblance to actual persons, living or dead, business establishments, events, or locales is entirely coincidental.

ISSUED AS:
ISBN 978-1-77041-556-0 (SOFTCOVER)
ISBN 978-1-77305-786-6 (PDF)
ISBN 978-1-77305-785-9 (EPUB)
ISBN 978-1-77305-787-3 (KINDLE)

This book is funded in part by the Government of Canada. *Ce livre est financé en partie par le gouvernement du Canada.* We acknowledge the support of the Canada Council for the Arts. *Nous remercions le Conseil des arts du Canada de son soutien.* We acknowledge the support of the Ontario Arts Council (OAC), an agency of the Government of Ontario, which last year funded 1,965 individual artists and 1,152 organizations in 197 communities across Ontario for a total of $51.9 million. We acknowledge the support of the Government of Ontario through Ontario Creates.

ONTARIO ARTS COUNCIL
CONSEIL DES ARTS DE L'ONTARIO
an Ontario government agency
un organisme du gouvernement de l'Ontario

Canada Council
for the Arts
Conseil des Arts
du Canada

The author gratefully thanks both the Edmonton Arts Council, whose financial assistance through its Artist Project Grants made possible the completion of this book, and the Alberta Foundation for the Arts, through its Aid to Individual Artists, for financial aid during its writing.

PRINTED AND BOUND IN CANADA   PRINTING: MARQUIS   5   4   3   2   1

MIX
Paper from
responsible sources
FSC
www.fsc.org   FSC® C103567

"To be forgiven from beyond the grave could be important
if that was the only quarter from which forgiveness could
come, which, for many of us . . . might well be the case."
                                        Alexander McCall Smith,
                                  The Right Attitude to Rain, p. 33

              Fore ðæm nedfere nænig wiorðe
              ðonc snottora ðon him ðearf siæ ˌ
              to ymbhycgenne ær his hinionge
              hwæt his gastæ godes oððe yfles
              æfter deað dæge doemed wiorðe.[1]
                             "Bede's Death Song"
                      attributed to Bede the Venerable
                  (Bǣda or Bēda; 672/673 – 26 May 735)

---

1. Loosely speaking: "Awaiting death, it's smart to ask ourselves, before
   it's too late, whether our life has been lived for good or evil, and how
   we will be judged on [or after] our death-day."

WHAT IS THE MATTER WITH MARY JANE? SHE'S CRYING WITH ALL HER MIGHT AND MAIN,

1. ONCE UPON A TIME WHEN THE WORLD WAS YOUNG . . .

During our second year of university, Priscilla Jane Gill's cat Micah died, and she had him taxidermied.

We all thought this was gross, but she said he was the truest being she'd met up to that point. She said that when she was with Micah she had been able to tune in to a special place, in touch with a purity to which she could only aspire, and that reaching for such purity gave her life a through-line of calm. She wanted to recall that clarity every day, and she thought she would do so when she looked at his effigy, posed in a lifelike facsimile of his favourite "meatloaf" lounging position.

In those days, this sort of explanation made sense.

Besides, Priscilla was a folklore major, and they were all a bit like that anyway.

I think all of us saw Priscilla a little like she saw Micah — when he was alive, of course. To us, she was a symbol of a time out of time, a pure zone between childhood and real life where we could dream of a perfection for which we would not even remember to try once we'd put our college days behind us. But Pris didn't distinguish between college life and reality, and that set her apart.

Maybe she was an early adopter of adulthood, or maybe she was a pure idealist. Either would have made her a wonder to us. We loved her evolved nature. She was an exotic, but she was *our* exotic, and long after we graduated, her image stayed with us, delicately posed in our history, perfect and without entropy, like a saint, or like Micah.

We got used to Micah's Ghost, as we called him, after a while, and some of us also were able to take Pris for granted now and again — until she breezed out of our lives on graduation day, wearing not much of anything under her graduation gown, and became one of our memories of university life, preserved in the amber of time — which is to say, idealised and mostly forgotten.

None of us had seen her since, but any time any of us encountered each other, sometime in the conversation we were bound to mention Pris, and smile, and shake our heads at our inability to match her grace and aestheticism.

The woman at my door that cold October day was tall, ascetic, and stylish, with a grey brush-cut and the hollow perfect cheekbones of a clothing retailer's anorexic display figure. When I opened my door, she was looking away down the corridor, and I saw her strong raptor profile with a mysterious thrill of buried familiarity.

"I thought I heard — someone — never mind," the woman said, turned her gaze back to me, and smiled. Then I truly recognised her, that crooked supermodel smile with the trickster underlay.

"Priscilla Jane," I said with that tone of satisfied arrival with which we greet the inevitable return of unfinished business.

2. "COME IN OUT OF THE CORNSTARCH AND DRY YOUR MUKLUKS BY THE CELLOPHANE . . ."

"Yes," she said. We stood for a moment, waiting.

"You look so different; it took me a moment," I said.

"You look just the same. I knew you right away when you went by —"

"?" I made that all-purpose noise-with-moue I've perfected in years of living with my cat Bunnywit.

"I followed you from that store down the —" She showed me where with a sharp gesture with her head. Snow particles silvered the air around her head. She often failed to finish her sentences in those days too.

"Great!" I said. "I'm glad you took the trouble. Come in!"

She looked again toward the stairway and said to it, as she dreamily edged into my hallway, "I was coming anyway but it helped to see you before you saw me. Since . . . well, I haven't been too . . . I've been . . . hmm, convalescing."

"Tea?" I held out a hand to take her snowy scarf, and she carefully folded her gloves into the pocket of her pea jacket before shaking the snowflakes from its shoulders and handing it to me. She ruffled her hair for more haloing droplets.

"You're supposed to wear that hat, not keep it in your pocket," I said. I led the way to the kitchen, Bunnywit following us with his usual disdainful curiosity, ready to make her his as soon as she slowed down enough that he didn't have to exert himself.

"Herbal," she said. "I'm trying to cut down on caffeine and sugar. Not sure it helps, but it can't hurt."

"Cancer?"

"No. And it isn't anorexia either. Make the tea."

"Fuck the tea. What's wrong? Anything I can — ?" Talk about seventy-five seconds' worth of cut-to-the-chase. I bit my tongue, but it was too late.

3

"Of course. Why do you think I looked you up after almost two decades? Make the tea." She sat down at the kitchen table in one of the sturdy oak chairs and leaned over to stroke Bun.

"Don't remind me how old I am, Pris."

"I'm older," she said. She was. It had been one contributor to her charisma.

"I'm feeling a goose walking over my grave. What are you doing here, and why do you look like death warmed over?"

"Because I very nearly *was* dead," she said. "I've spent the last year recovering from an attack."

"A physical attack?"

"Oh, yes, it was very physical."

"Who did it?"

"A guy."

"Is that why you were looking over your shoulder? They didn't catch him?"

"He's in jail. No-one follows me now — I don't think. I'm just paranoid. They say he followed me for months, learned my routine. Then when he jumped me, it was somewhere no-one could interrupt. I was stabbed seventeen times and my throat was slashed. And he broke my jaw and cheekbone. Did an after-knife kickfest."

A seriously committed attack, in both senses of the words. I busied myself readying the teapot and left the silence there. She filled it.

"Nobody knows why. I didn't recognise him. They say he's a nutbar, but he was found fit to stand trial. I have nightmares and I wear too many clothes. That part doesn't matter, the clothes, but I thought I'd get it over with."

Coming back to sit and wait for the kettle to boil, I looked her up and down. If possible, she was even more beautiful than she had been, though her beauty was a whole lot spookier for having added a shadowy echo of those too-thin mass-media clichés who throng the red carpets at award ceremonies.

3. THAT WAS THEN, AND THIS IS NOW

"I had such a crush on you twenty years ago," I said. "Well, we all did, but most of the women wouldn't admit it."

I didn't say that today she almost terrified me. Or that I wasn't necessarily delighted that she'd reached back into a place I kept in Dreamtime and brought that place into the present as if we'd never parted. Outside science fiction novels, I don't like time travel.

So: "Hmph," I said. "It's like Then is Now. Weird. I don't like time travel."

"So eloquent!" she mocked. "I'll tell you what it really is. In your head, you've kept talking to me all these years. So I show up, we have twenty-some years of friendship instead of a few years of old history."

"And you? Have *you* been talking to *me* for twenty years too?"

"I didn't have to," she said. "I knew we'd meet again. I always knew. I just . . . didn't know when."

"Why didn't you look me up, then?" The kettle whined and I got up. Bunnywit was still twining around her legs, which meant he wasn't trying to trip me as usual.

She glanced up at me sideways with that same Farmer-Pang mischievousness that had glinted out at us sometimes. Now it was sharp and clear and wicked. "Why didn't you, me?"

I laughed. "You were always in Kathmandu or Timbuktu or Mogadishu — my budget didn't run to exotic destinations." Until recently, and even then, not much, due to other decisions I will talk about in due time.

"You followed my career, though."

"Hard to avoid it. I have all your books, by the way. By the time you were back in the country, I wouldn't have dreamt of imposing on you."

She guffawed. Really. "Don't be a bloody fool!"

"Life moves," I said, grinning to try to lessen the sting. "I figured it'd moved too far. Like continental drift."

"Platypuses." She nodded. "Platypussies?" She leaned down and picked up Bunnywit. "Come here, platypussy."

4. MICAH'S GHOST

"Be careful, he bi—" I started, then watched Bun reach his front paws out and literally hug her, snuggling his head into the crook of her neck under her elegant right ear. (Her left ear was just as elegant, but he picked the right one.)

"I'll be damned. He never does that!" Even to me, most of the time.

"He smells Micah."

"You still have Micah?" Maybe I raised my voice a little. There was a catch in Bun's purr, and Pris shook her head.

"I forgot how transparent you are. I recall how Micah's continuing presence —"

"Gave me the creeps," I said flatly.

"Actually, I meant a different incarnation of Micah — a living one. I use the name over and over. This one is Five. I do keep a scrap of the original Micah's fur in my spirit bag."

"You still wear that thing?"

"Different incarnation of that too." She reached under her sweater's cowl neck and pulled at a leather thong until she had fished out a small red kid-leather bag. "Its great-great-great-grandchild by now. I make a new one every few years."

Bun purred even louder and reached out for the bag. She easily deterred him and poured him onto the floor, where he adopted the undignified gopher pose he usually uses only for salmon and craned his neck to keep the bag in sight.

"Shoo," she murmured confidentially, just to him. He dropped to a sit, washed half his face once, then quietly walked off to the living room, still purring, the little duck-tail that Manxes have twitching back and forth on his sashaying butt.

Pris dropped the bag back inside her sweater neckline and shook her head slightly. The motion was just like a preening cat.

"You are still one spooky soul, Priscilla Jane Gill."

She smiled again, looking at me comfortably and directly. I began to think I'd been craving the sight of that smile for twenty years.

I didn't want to sleep with her, exactly. It's actually pretty easy to find people to sleep with. No, I wanted her back in my life in the same way that in dreams I see my brother, who died when I was young, and want him to stay when he shows up.

As if my life might have been different all this time, in some special way, if she had stayed in it, and if she stayed in it now, her staying would retroactively make that difference real.

Schrödinger's roommate.

5. SCHRÖDINGER'S COLLEGE REUNION

I'm not a starfucker. It wasn't because she'd become famous. I'm a fan of Leonard Cohen songs, but I didn't want her to bring me tea and oranges all the way from China — or even, as in Mick Berzensky's song, "fish in a dish / from the old corner store" from which she'd followed me. But I'd always liked her a lot, and she fit into my kitchen easily. She reminded me that I'd been a better person once and that she'd liked me too.

"I didn't miss many of them, but I missed you," she said. "Not a craving, but you know, I'd be in a street somewhere, someplace I'd never been, and I'd see something I wanted to share with someone, or I'd want to talk with someone right that minute — and sometimes it was you. Those were nice moments."

I leaned back against the counter with the empty teacups in my hands.

"Yeah." I wasn't sure my tone was on the right side of sarcasm. "I liked 'em too."

"I know," she said. "I can hear myself. What a wanker, eh? All that nostalgia wasn't enough to bring me to you. It took fear, and seventeen knife scars — eighteen, really, but one was just a nick — and an article in the newspaper."

"Oh, that." A few months earlier, I'd been momentarily notorious for helping enquire into the murder of a street sex worker who was the granddaughter of a friend of mine. The situation had become worse before it was solved, and I had some scars myself to prove it.

"Yes, that," she said. "I want you to do the same for me. I want to — hire you? I have money."

I couldn't help it. I laughed aloud. Partly in disappointment, I must say, and partly from annoyance, but humour still came out on top.

She stared down her patrician nose at me as well as she could, given that she was sitting down and I was still bringing tea paraphernalia to the table. To help her with that, I sat down and assembled the cups and saucers.

"I have some money now," I said. "Money, I don't need." She kept glaring, so I went on, "You're cute when you're acting on privilege."

6. THE PEACE OF UTRECHT

I poured the tea. She breathed through her nose a couple of times, then relaxed slightly.

"I need help. Specialised help. Am I paranoid or am I really being followed? Why did someone who presented as a crazed fan but who isn't crazy and hadn't read my books attack me? I see his fucking face in my dreams. I'm fucking sick of expecting to see him for real. I came to ask you to help me. Whatever it takes."

"Time for my speech, which won't be *eloquent*," I said acerbically. "I got into that shit by accident, and I'm not getting any younger. Friends come and go. My most recent lover just ran away with the circus and maybe I won't see her again. That's okay, I'm happy for her, but between that and recovering from a few broken bones and a lot of soft tissue injuries, I'm feeling a little vulnerable. Mortal. I'm sure you can understand that."

"You sound like we're negotiating a fucking treaty. This isn't the UN. What will it take?"

"That's not the point. It's also not the point that today I was sitting here thinking about old friendships and old ties and how to renew them. Today is just because I was hungry and depressed for a long time, and I've lost the knack of having a life."

"Then it's an opportunity."

"Ha. Fuck that Newspeak. For one thing, you weren't on the renew-ties list. For another thing, I just got over being beaten to within an inch of my life — the matter is still before the courts, as they say — and you turn up out of the blue and suggest I investigate your mortal danger. You think you have any favours to call in? After all this time?"

"I don't have favours to . . . that's not what . . . Listen. I just think that if anyone in the world will get it, it's —"

"Bullshit. An opportunity. Sure."

She sighed. "Yeah. Okay. Fine. Forget it." But she showed no interest in moving. She reached out and picked up her Japanware teacup, sipped the hot jasmine tea, and then she did a small, curious thing. She licked her lips afterward as if the tea were the best thing she'd tasted in a long time. It was that little unconscious moment that got me. I'm pretty sure it was unconscious.

"That's not the point either," I said. "I just need some breathing space. It would be easier if . . ."

"If — ?"

7. JUST SAY "NIAOW"

Just then a ping-pong ball caromed into the kitchen, Bunnywit galloping after it. On his way past me, he stuck out a paw with full claw deployment and sliced at my leg, getting me right through the blue jeans. It felt as if he drew blood, and this I later confirmed.

Four cautionary little slices an inch long. Surface, really, just enough to remind me that I am not ten feet tall and bullet-proof. If he could talk, I'm sure he'd have said, "Girlfriend, what are you *thinking* . . . ? No!! She's lovely and she smells deliciously of long-dead cat, but send her away. Now!"

He did say a sharp "No!", though with his accent it came out "Niaow!"

I should have taken his advice.

AND SHE WON'T EAT HER DINNER —
RICE PUDDING AGAIN —

8. "... WHO TURNED PARADISE INTO HELL? MARBLE WALLS INTO PAPER-MÂCHÉ ..."

The best Chinese noodle house in town, Double Greeting, is across the street from a homeless shelter run by the Sally Ann and used to nestle up next to a dilapidated rooming house whose hundred-year history had transformed it from a railroad hotel (not the fancy kind, but the kind that was home to railway workers at the turn of the twentieth century) to the scummy end of the line for sad drunks and addicts, in cheap rooms above what I call "a bar of last resort".

The city had bought the hotel, though, and around New Year had solved the problem of its historical importance by bulldozing it. Dumptrucks had carted away the resulting jumbled mass of cracked heritage brick, hundred-year-old hand-crafted twelve-by-twelve beams now splintered to matchstick, filthy mattresses and rusty cot frames, and the cheap-deal doors that over the years had replaced the original Good Wood. Now to get to the Double G we cut across a series of vacant lots, the wind getting a good run at us and slicing through our overcoats, mitts, and other wraps.

My inner-city neighbourhood was undergoing "urban renewal". What that seemed to mean was "urban clear-cutting" — through the winter, old buildings kept vanishing, replaced by parking lots. I'd seen neither hide nor hair of the "renewal" part near my apartment yet, though for the first time in two decades there was new construction in the area, a few blocks north.

With my legacy from my parents last year, I'd secretly — a secret from my neighbours anyway, as I didn't want to disrupt our fragile camaraderie — bought the Epitome Apartments, the heritage brick building where I live[2].

My lawyer (for fuck's sake, "my lawyer" indeed! But my life had weirded up to the extent that I actually had a pet lawyer) had already had two developers offer to take it off my hands for a pittance, to help "renew" the neighbourhood — again, that word — by flattening one of the last heritage buildings and putting up some monstrosity of curtain-wall glass and moulded concrete. "Just say no," I told him.

I didn't have much in the way of capital left afterward, but in setting in motion the restoration of one of the hundred-year-old buildings in the inner city, I was doing my bit on the renewal front the way I wanted it done.

I'd suggested to Pris that we go have some food. To put off the inevitable conversation about what she wanted, I was explaining all this neighbourhood stuff to her as we picked our way across the snow and rubble of the vacant lots.

"You should get involved," she said.

"In what?"

---

2. My neighbours, by the way, all pronounce it "EP-ee-tome", which is part of why I love the place.

"Oh, you know. Community organisation. Heritage preservation."

I laughed. "You think I need a hobby?"

"Well, it makes you mad. So do something. Join the neighbourhood association."

Yeah. That's what my downstairs neighbour was trying to convince me to do, but back in my not-so-secret past as a social worker, I'd done a lot of unpaid time in voluntary organisations, and in the immortal words of R. A. Lafferty, that way lies rump of skunk and madness. Have you ever noticed how many paths lead to rump of skunk and madness, and how few to happily-ever-after? I would prefer HEA, and I had recently resolved to avoid the rump-of-skunk type of decision if I possibly could.

Besides, I was waiting on any precipitous decisions until the broken bones and deep tissue injuries had fully healed from the *last* time I said, "Oh sure!" to a call for help.

I tried not to let on how much pain came with my effort to get the sticking outer door of the noodle house open over the ice ridge on the concrete stoop. I still was far from rehabilitated. I held one of the mismatched inner doors for Priscilla, and she blew in on a gust of wind and laughter.

9. BLACK EGG

We shook snow off our coats and scarves. I had managed to make her wear the hat for all of half a block before she snatched it off and crammed it in her pocket, so while I was shaking snow off yards of woolly scarf and snood, Pris leaned over and shook her head like a dog. But when she straightened, she took a step sideways and grabbed my arm.

"Phew. I keep forgetting! Dizzy," she said. "Never mind, okay now."

The most efficient waitress in the world works at the Double Greeting. Mei welcomed us, gave us menus and order forms and a pen, brought me the glass of ice over which I like to pour my Chinese tea, asked after my health, replaced a dirty bowl, and added extra napkins to the table after refilling the napkin dispenser, all in the time it took Pris to slide into the seat in our assigned booth. (Pris nudged in front of me to snag the seat against the wall — facing the door, I realised after an annoyed moment, but I shook my head and let it go.)

Mei tut-tutted over our snowy coats. "I hang by hot air," she said, and swept off, greeting two other groups and directing them to tables on the way to put our wet clothing on the staff coat-hooks near the kitchen. I noticed with karma-compromising pride that the new customers' coats were referred to the customer coat-rack, over in the draught by the door.

Pris watched Mei, awed, as she supplied the newbies with menus, answered the phone and took a phone order, all whilst making a tray of red bean coolers, and delivered the coolers while telling the other waitress where to take the full tray that had just come out of the kitchen. "Gawd, look at her! Why isn't she in charge of the world?"

"My feelings exactly. If I spoke Cantonese, I'd hire her to run my real estate empire."

"No kidding! Wait, you have a real estate empire?"

"Kidding. I have the Epitome, my apartment building. 'EP-ee-tome'. That's how most of its residents pronounce it. And I ran out of money buying it, and I don't have much of an income, so I'm applying for a Residential Rehabilitation Assistance Program grant to restore it."

Pris unfolded the voluminous laminated menu. "What's good here?"

"Tendons, tripe, and spleen in broth with rice noodle?" It was my round-eye test.

14

"Sounds great," said Pris, "but get them to leave out the tripe. It's too chewy. Oh! They have black egg! I should get one for my soup."

"Okay, you win." Black egg is preserved duck egg, also known as "thousand-year-old egg", a delicacy that even some Chinese people eschew. I love black egg. I should have known not to bother with the test, given Pris's character — and peripateticism.

"What?"

"Never mind." I wrote down the soup order (#5 no tripe), with two black eggs (#61) on the side, added Hoi Nam chicken (#110) and Green Beans with XO Sauce (#236), and waved the order slip at Mei. She was on her way past with a loaded tray and the means to reset two tables, but somehow the slip vanished from my hand and a full pot of tea landed beside my glass of ice. I poured pu'er into a cup for Pris and into the glass for me. The ice crackled and dissolved, steaming. The full glass was cold, and in the humid restaurant began to gather a coat of condensation.

"How can you drink that? It's freezing out!"

"I don't know," I said.

"You always drank ice water — I remember that," she said.

"I did?" But I had. People made fun of me for it. My brother had once, when he was twelve and I was younger, drawn a cartoon of me as an ice demon surrounded by ice and empty glasses.

Lots of ice under the bridge since then.

It wasn't the most relaxing dinner. Every time the door opened, Priscilla jumped slightly. She tried to disguise the fact that she checked out every single person who came through the door. When a big group and several individuals came in at the same time, she couldn't disguise her agitation. I leaned forward and murmured, "Kwan Ying Athletic Society Board. And I recognise all the singletons — they're from the neighbourhood. Chill! Eat your tendon and spleen in noodle soup."

"No problem about chilling, with the draught from the door!" she joked, but as Mei had seated us right beside the heater we both took her remark for the smokescreen it was. She sat back slightly, however, and got slightly more serious about her dinner.

The whole evening, though, she ate like a fashion model. Which is to say, hardly at all.

10. AND IF IT WAS TRUE AS IT WAS TOLD TO ME, THEN IT IS TRUE AS I AM TELLING IT TO YOU

Here's the thing. In books, plots are often complicated — unnecessarily in many cases — by people neglecting or refusing to talk with one another. In books, so rarely in fact do people say what they mean that it's almost a shock to find a character who does, and when it happens the narrative almost seems naïve. (This is why people either underestimate or esteem the books of Alexander McCall Smith, for example, according to their natures and narrative preferences.)

There is a technical reason for this which I discovered last time I sat down to chronicle a sequence of my life's events: even if one is inclined to super-realism in literature, there is just not enough *space* in a book for all of the conversations of real life. One evening of the committed discussions of good friends, especially friends re-united after long absences and many stories, as Priscilla Jane and I found ourselves, would strain a chapter or even a whole book, if transcribed exactly.

And when one is dealing with the nature of memory, another layer is added to the difficulty of selecting from all the many exchanges and events during a certain span of time. Readers of books like this one you hold are looking for an understanding of a particular series of events represented by choices and consequences. I understand that you don't want an endless re-enactment of *My Dinner with Andre*.

Technical challenges aside, out here in the real world it is actually more common for people to try to tell each other what we mean, rather than choosing our words for dramatic effect or suspense-serving obfuscation. And yet, oddly, real life sometimes sounds like a bald and unconvincing narrative compared with literature's staged and theatrical simulations of verisimilitude.

Go figure.

So rather than the desultory-chat-analogue I have no space to record here, I will say simply that Pris and I talked intensely for hours. I told her about my adventures of the autumn[3], which had left me in a long period of healing but had brought a great Chinese-opera acrobat into my life. I learned a lot about Pris's previous and current Micahs, her recent travels, and the attack that had put her in hospital for months with knife wounds, fractures, and deep-tissue damage that still made her weak, and dizzy when she bent over.

We also compared our current levels of cynicism with our youthful ideals, discussed current and former lovers, sidelined into several examples of Internet humour during which detour she showed me how to better use the browser function of my few-months'-new mobile telephone, and I had a conversation with a couple of the board members from Kwan Ying on their way by as they left after their meal.

There were many words.

11. "I CAN'T BE NO COWGIRL'S PARADISE . . ."

I also made it clear to Pris that I wasn't the answer to her need for understanding. At least, I thought I made it clear. I even suggested she use some of her substantial earnings from famous-explorer-dom to hire a professional.

---

3. See *The Adventures of Isabel*.

She had been deeply attentive to the rest of the conversation. That part, she seemed to ignore, in part because of the interruption of the opening outer door of the restaurant.

That initial knot of people had been an anomalous rush in a usual steady-state of clientèle, and regularly, as we ate and talked for over two hours, we would hear the *clunk* of the door opening again, and I'd feel the icy breeze on the back of my neck. At first Pris would come up on point each time like a high-strung service dog, but she seemed to relax as time went on, and hardly glanced at some of the later arrivals. `

I had just made the traditional two-handed finger-writes-character-on-paper signal to Mei for our cheque when yet another customer came in. I'd turned to look for Mei, who was serving a table near the door, but my eye was held by the furtive flinch that the bundled figure, vaguely coded male by bulk and attire, made when he saw that I had noticed him.

He could have been anyone. He could have been one of the street people, whose lives tended to be one continuous furtive flinch. But he could have been caught staring at us. I couldn't tell.

Pris noticed I was watching something. But the guy had deked left, into the restrooms, and all we had caught was the olive-green, bright-green, and brown-and-grey of his back view, normal swatch-pattern for anyone bundled in winter attire of parka, scarf, cap, mitts.

"What?"

Mei zoomed past our table, with hardly a pause as she slid our cheque in front of us.

"Nothing. You've got me all paranoid."

The guy came out of the bathroom when we were halfway through paying. Later I was able to give his description to the police, but that's just because I had thought his behaviour odd. When I tilted my head to indicate him as Mei seated him across the room, and said, "Anyone you know?", she barely gave him a glance.

"Quit being weird," she said.

"Well," I said, "on the weird thing, that ship has sailed, but hey, you started it."

Pris gave no sign she was perturbed. She laughed. I could have sworn it was a real, genuine, amused laugh.

"I'm staying at the Union Bank Inn," she said. Was the weird guy close enough to hear her? Later, I was asked that.

"Want me to walk back there with you?"

"Nah, I'm fine. As you pointed out, I get weird from time to time."

"'Just because you're paranoid doesn't mean —'" I began, but her laugh cut me off.

"If you are going to help me, you have to learn when to help me and when to tell me to quit wanking," she said.

"I'm not going to help you — that way. I told you."

"Yeah, yeah, whatever."

"But now that we're back in each other's lives, let's keep it that way."

"I agree. Kindred spirits are rare enough, but kindred spirits who knew me when? Priceless." She thus proved that sometime in the past decade, she had watched some TV, somewhere. Kathmandu, probably, on some kind of solar-powered tablet device sponsored by some big Japanese conglomerate, if I properly understood how she financed all her trips to the top and bottom of the world. And by getting her joke I proved that I had also enjoyed too many commercial moments back in the day when my TV had worked.

We hugged goodbye at the door of the restaurant.

"Call me tomorrow. Let me know what you decide."

"It's still no."

"No, it isn't. Call me tomorrow."

12. ASK A POLICEMAN

Those who know me would be surprised at what I did next. Roger certainly was, when I called him.

Roger is an old buddy of mine from the bad old days. Partly as a result of covering himself in honour during that little dustup in the fall which left me with bruises and broken bones, he'd recently been promoted to head of the Major Crimes Investigation Unit.

That is to say, he is a cop.

Despite that, he is a fine fella, and I have come to be able to overlook the occasional broomstick-up-his-ass moment. Cops are like that — good cops, anyway — they come over all strict and implacable and law-and-order from time to time. Understandable I guess, given that their job is, well, law and order. Over the past little while, while keeping my disdain for the other kind, I've come to appreciate good cops.

Not that I would ever admit to Roger the depths of my conversion. Having been naked with him once or twice, many many *many* years ago, was as much disadvantage, professionally speaking, as I was prepared to accept in our collegial relationship. Well, that, and what he knew about some of my youthful indiscretions and the law enforcement attention these had received in their day.

I asked him about Pris's concerns and told him of her proposal.

"I turned her down," I said.

"You must be growing a brain," he replied in his usual friendly fashion.

"You and the horse you rode in on," I replied, equally fondly. "But I was wondering if you could kinda check it out for me. Kinda keep an eye on the situation."

"*She* hasn't gone to the police. We have privacy limits, you know."

"Okay, fine. But *I* have gone to the police. And I am making a formal expression of concern. You could at least file an incident report or something."

"Saying what? A weird guy came into Double Greeting Noodle House? A celebrity who was viciously attacked and probably has PTSD is paranoid?"

"Rog . . ."

"I'm noting it. But just sayin' . . ."

"Fine. But please note it."

And he did. As it happens, it did little good.

WHAT *IS* THE MATTER WITH MARY JANE?

13. AMBROSE BIERCE, MEXICO, 1913

Pris disappeared that night.

No, I don't mean she went back to her life and I never saw her again. I mean the other thing.

Despite my intention to stay out of it, I had called her at the hotel in the evening, and then the next morning, but I hadn't gotten an answer.

Roger called late the next evening, from outside my building. I buzzed him in, proud that the new security system still worked (this being the inner city), and he gave me the news.

"Pris went missing as of yesterday," he said.

"'Went missing'," I said. "That's the weirdest idiom. It manages to assign blame to the victim without clarifying agency. Like 'got attacked'."

"Yeah, sure," said my big tall handsome annoyed cop buddy. "Bottom line, she isn't there. Her visit. Give it all to me again."

So I told him about Pris, and Micah, and Bun.

"She left from the restaurant after we ate. That weird guy —
I'm sure he was staring at us. She pretended it didn't bother her,
but it must have. She told me to call her, and then we hugged.
She headed off across the Arctic wastes to her hotel, and I waited
to see if the guy followed her. He didn't, at least not right away, so
I mushed home in the blizzard. As far as I know, he didn't follow
me either. I must have been picking up on her jitters."

"Did you call her?"

"Not as such. Well . . . a couple of times. I left a couple of
messages. After that I figured she must have changed her mind.
But I didn't feel easy about it."

I couldn't stop obsessing about my last few minutes with Pris.
"At least I knew enough to call you. And may I say something
like 'I told you so'?"

"You didn't tell me so. You passed the burden of your worries to
me, but last I heard from you, you weren't fussing about Ms. Gill."

He let me stew for a moment, then relented. "But if it makes
you feel better, it was because of your thirteen 'couple of' unan-
swered phone calls, plus three or four by assorted other parties
and an unsuccessful visit by 'a sharp-looking guy in a fancy suit'
where they got no answer from the room, that the desk clerk
began to wonder if something was wrong. Fancy Suit insisted
there was, and insisted that the manager go up to bypass the *Do
Not Disturb* sign on the door."

"Thirteen."

"Thirteen couple of. Like dogs in the hunt. Counted by twos,
like a brace. Twenty-seven, actually, according to the call display."

"And the manager found . . . ?"

"Indications of a hurried departure or —"

"Roger! This is me, your pal, here."

"And this is me, cop, here. Indications of a hurried departure
or, at a stretch, foul play. End of answer."

"Not end of questions."

"Obviously. But my advice? Go with your original instinct. Stay out of it. Not that you ever really listen to me."

"I listen to you a lot. Especially when you are telling me something I want to hear. But now I feel — guilty. If I had said I would . . . Look, what was this 'guy in a fancy suit' thing?"

"Some dude who used to date her. He didn't have any more luck than you. Assuming he didn't make off with her himself."

"What?"

"Kidding. He has an alibi. And forget that guilt crap. If you had said, 'Sure, girlfriend,' you guys would have still said goodnight, she would have gone back to the Inn, and in the morning you wouldn't have had an answer to your calls. And you would have called me. I would have said, 'She's probably out shopping, for God's sake, so take a Valium®.' Then concern would have increased, and the manager would have been unlocking the door at exactly the same time as he did anyway."

"But . . ."

"Apart from if you had decided to stick to her like a burr, which wouldn't have guaranteed a different outcome and would have put you at the same risk — assuming there was any risk and she hasn't just gone shopping or base jumping off a skyscraper or some damn thing, nothing you did or didn't do would have made a damned bit of difference. So get over it."

"Thanks for your kind words."

"No problem. Now I have to go do my job."

When he left, Bunnywit came out from under the bathtub, where he had been playing with my grapefruit soap (his favourite), and stood by the door miaowing and foaming slightly at the mouth.

"Your own fault," I said. "You should have come and sucked up to him while he was here. Now your love is unrequited. And lay off that goddamn soap."

I washed the soap out of his mouth. That unnerved us both. To get the soap itself out from behind the claw-foot tub took heroic measures with my antique yardstick, and when I did, it was thoroughly gnawed, and furred with deeply embedded Bun-hairs.

"You, sir, are a fool and a knave," I said, as I gave up trying to save it and dropped it into the pop-top garbage can.

Bun crouched on the chrome lid of the garbage can, sulked and purred vigil over it for a good ten minutes, a triumph of kitty concentration, before ᴄoming to join me on the couch — where I was trying to concentrate myself, practising being Internet-savvy by reading the daily news on my phone, as instructed by Pris.

It was no good. Working the little buttons was driving me crazy, and my eyes squinched at the tiny screen, but I was too lazy to get up and sit at my desk with the regular computer. Too lazy and too antsy.

"What the devil happened to her?" I said to him, tossing the device onto the coffee table, where he licked the browser icon, causing odd search results to pop up.

I suppose he wanted me looking at pictures of cute cats with stupid captions, but instead I began to search out everything the Interwebs knew about Priscilla Jane Gill.

14. "... WHOLE WORLD WHISPERING / BORN AT THE RIGHT TIME ..."

I learned a lot of things about how web browsing algorithms worked (or didn't) in the next little while, but I didn't learn much about Priscilla Jane Gill that would help me — or anybody — find her today.

There were lots of paparazzi hits on her, of course. Every time she scaled another remote mountain or biked across a glacier or hugged a polar bear, there seemed to have been a photographer there — and a crowd of the Beautiful People. They would be eating something stylish in Felix Restaurant atop the Peninsula

Hotel, or accepting custom canapés served by minions on somebody's private island, or partying with the Rock, or picnicking in Antarctica, or stuff like that.

Strictly sushi all the way, while I'd been going through my lean year eating fish sticks, with Bunnywit my sole (pun unintended, but hey, I like it) complaining companion. Clearly the difference between class and underclass.

It appeared Pris never lacked for elegant and famous friends, even in Antarctica, for fuck's sake, where she was photographed surrounded — well, flanked — by a couple of rich dudes, one short, one tall, in thick, expensive parkas. The smaller one held his hand under her arm, while the tall one had his arm around her but squinted fiercely off-camera, making his pixelated face unrecognisable. Was one of these the rich guy in the fancy suit whom she had formerly dated? I couldn't tell. I couldn't find out who they were, or whom she had dated at any time. She was always getting photographed with cute millionaires and media superstars. There was a blizzard of "hits" (I only put this in quote marks because this lingo was all new to me at the time[4]) but no meat.

I did find some information about the attack on her, but nothing that had the name of the attacker, a photo, the outcome (like, whether he was still in jail), or why.

Maybe I was just a newbie at all this, but it seemed to me that I could find everything I didn't need on the Internet, and nothing I wanted to know.

You probably already knew that, dear reader, because you were an early adopter of the World Wide Web, while I was hanging out with Bunnywit in our little apartment playing Tetris on an out-of-date PC and reading real paper books and eating fish sticks.

Food of the underclass.

---

4. You do realise that time has passed since then, don't you? I am now a fucking technological star.

15. CRY WOLF?

Before I finished my research, I was interrupted by the cell phone. The display read: **PRIVATE NUMBER**. I answered cautiously.

"Hi," said a familiar voice. "How ya doin'?"

Certain pauses, the ones literature calls "pregnant", are really not so much "pregnant" as excerpts from some horror movie where the spawn of some insect monster is about to burst forth from the swollen crawling flesh of some unsuspecting human. This was one.

The voice was Priscilla's.

Pris calling me.

Asking me, "How ya doin'?"

"Um," I began.

Pause, reboot.

"Um, are you all right? Where are you?"

"I'm fine. I'm at Union Bank Inn. I changed my suite though. I wanted a better view."

"Are you aware," I said, carefully, in case I swore, "that you are the subject of a national police search?"

"Don't be ridiculous!"

"Ridiculous? You are calling *me* ridiculous? You, Ms. Missing, Blood-spatter-leaving, Possibly foul-played-upon, Preyed-upon, Sought-by-former-boyfriend-and-homicide-detectives, Doesn't-answer-her-goddamn-phone-calls-for-two-or-three-days-and-now-plays-innocent Gill? Fuck."

Oops. I swore.

I hung up.

The phone rang again.

"What?!" I said, channelling Tank Girl.

"What are you talking about?"

"About your absence without luggage, the concern of your nearest and dearest, and also of me and of the police. About a hurried departure and signs of foul play."

27

"I can explain," she said. "I guess. I had to be somewhere. So I went."

"Explain to the cops," I said, and reeled off ten digits. "Here's the number of the kindly homicide detective who is looking for your body. Rolled up, apparently, in a nice little hand-knotted Persian rug that the owner of the Union Bank Inn is pissed about losing."

"What the hell? They were the ones who took that out to be cleaned," said Pris indignantly. "Some guy with a passcard and a shirt with his name on a tag on the pocket. Assif or something. Why were people in my room anyhow?"

"Um? Because you were paranoid and you came to see me, and there was a weird guy in the Double G, and you didn't answer the phone or call when you said, and some guy in a nice suit who used to date you went looking for you and couldn't find you, and the staff at the Inn were worried, so they went into your room and there were, and I quote the police, 'signs of possible foul play'? Would that cover it for you?"

She sighed. "I tripped over my coffee table and hit my head. The dizzy thing. But I didn't hit it very hard. No big deal."

"Tell a cop who cares."

She sighed again. "Scalp wounds bleed. That's why they took the rug out. But they didn't finish cleaning? That's not like them. I'll talk to Diane about that. What was that cop's number again?"

I told her.

"Thanks. I'll call you later."

"Where the fuck did you go?"

"Never mind. I'll call you back."

"Don't bother," I said, but she had already hung up.

Cry wolf? Grrr.

I was also deeply unhappy that she hadn't given me a chance to hang up on *her* again.

"Oh, for fuck's sake," I said.

Bun jumped up and batted the phone out of my hand onto the floor, where one corner lost a tiny but definite chip at impact. "Niaowww!" he shouted.

I have to confess, I shouted back. But I will draw a veil over what I said.

Pris did not call back that evening.

WHAT IS THE MATTER WITH MARY JANE?

16. THE DOG IN THE NIGHT-TIME

Sherlock Holmes, or, as I for a minor sub-paraliterary reason tend to call him, Sherlock Hemlock, has had a number of pithy utterances move into the mainstream[5]. "The curious incident of the dog in the night-time", for instance: most people know about that. But since recently I have met someone who, no word of a lie, had never heard a single Beatles tune, even though she has lived here with all the rest of us all her life and been a teacher for a good chunk of her adult years, I will explain that what was curious about The Dog in the Night-time was that the dog didn't bark. (The dog was a watchdoggy kind of canine, you see, and there was supposed to have been an intruder, but the dog didn't make a — oh forget it[6].)

---

5. Or Conan Doyle has, I suppose. But Sherlock is so much more interesting than Sir Away-with-the-Fairies, who as far as I can tell was both stuffy and credulous.

6. Look it up.

When I answered my phone the next day, I was expecting a friend, or Pris (apologising, or Making All Clear, or even just giving me a chance to hang up on her again), or at worst someone trying to phish all my passwords by pretending to be the Microsoft® service department. I *really* enjoy hanging up on them. Occasionally I even get a call from a really nice lawyer named Dafydd Spak who takes care of bidness for me. So when the ring of the phone woke me at the ungodly hour of eight a.m., I said, "Hello?" with a blithe if somewhat groggy unconcern.

"Can you hold for Mr. Chiles?" said a precise female voice of the "cut-glass" — maybe even upmarket "cut-crystal" — type.

I allowed as how that was within the realm of possibility.

Mr. Chiles had a dark, tar-sands voice, but was also very polite. He said, "Mr. Lockwood will be expecting you at three. I am calling to offer to send the limousine around."

"Is this one of those Gold-Coast-letter scams?"

"I beg your pardon?"

"I don't know anyone called Lockwood. With or without a limo." And I hung up.

The phone rang again. This is rare for scammers. They usually just go on to the next patsy on the list.

Cut-Glass was back, saying my name, then adding, "That *is* the party to whom I was speaking, is it not?"

I allowed as how that was within the realm of possibility.

"Mr. Chiles says you were cut off."

"No, I hung up. What is *with* you people? I don't know you, and I don't want to buy anything, and I certainly don't go on dates with total strangers."

"Was Mr. Chiles not just speaking with you?"

When I was a kid, I learned a harmless but annoying prank. You and your buddies call a random phone number and ask for Bob a few times. Then the person who makes the last call says, "I'm Bob. Any messages for me?" Then you all giggle like crazy.

What possible benefit scammers could derive from a variation on this childish game, I didn't know. I sighed. "Look, I'm hanging up. And I don't want to get a call from somebody in two minutes saying 'It's Mr. Lockwood' and making some kinda dumb answering-machine joke. You can cut this out right now. It's eight in the fucking morning, for crying out loud." And I hung up.

There were no more telephone calls. When I woke up again, and after I fed Bunnywit his breakfast and had some leftover Hoi Nam chicken, I called the phone company and told them that I'd changed my mind: I wanted to sign up for that twentieth-century service they had offered my land line the week before, with the call display and stuff.

And only a couple of decades into the twenty-*first* century, at that.

I was improving.

17. COMMON SENSE: SO UNCOMMON IT'S ALMOST A SUPERPOWER

The twenty-first-century thing was not lost on either me or the person at the phone company who took my call.

She had worked there for twenty-five years, which was rare, and was talking to me from the same city, which is also rare, so we enjoyed ourselves very much as we de-Ludd-ed me into the present day. I did draw the line, pun unintended, at getting rid of the land line altogether and going with the cell only, as most people these days apparently do. It was going to cost me more per month to be nostalgic, but I decided that didn't matter. I also needed to buy a new land line phone that showed me the caller's ID, but apparently those weren't the phone company's job any more: I had to get one at a big-box drugstore. Or online, I suppose, but baby steps.

Okay, fine. I got dressed in all my layers for walking, and headed downtown. The bus got to the kittycorner stop at the same time I did, so I hopped on. It was a bus wrapped in one of those plastic ad sheaths, so it was dim, and the heater was cranked up to the max, so it was steamy and tropical and smelled of sweat socks and wet Velcro™. When I looked out between the pixels of some computer ad, the sunshine seemed watery, like the brownout during an eclipse.

Modern culture.

I picked up my new phones from two kids who clearly came from the same strange young urban techno-tribe. Each one was wearing their grad suit and the spotty bad skin of a teenager who hasn't gotten laid much yet, and each knew more about technology than I had ever learned, even though I was an early adopter of computers, though not Internets. The problem was that I was an early *adopter*, but I hadn't been an early *upgrader*. I tend to replace my computers when they are broken, or when I am shamed by sending someone something in a file format so outdated they don't own the tech to read it. Until 2005, I had had a Kaypro®, FFS, and until only the previous year my home computer had a floppy disc drive and ran Windows 98™. I only knew the world had progressed because I had had better tech at the job from which I'd been laid off a few years ago.

Also until only recently, I hadn't had a strong personal relationship with the Internet, having not participated in the online world since THE WELL, or thereabouts. So I'm pathetic: sue me.

All that was tantamount to criminality in these kids' eyes[7]. Despite the fact that I had bought a mobile phone (my first) only a few months ago, it apparently was already shamefully out of date, and in addition to a new cordless phone set with handsets for every room if I wanted them, and so many features that the

---

7. I didn't defend myself: they had never heard of the Luddites, I would have bet the remains of my bank account on it, and besides, I was there, wasn't I?

little perfect-bound instruction book was a centimetre thick, I also agreed to trade up my mobile to a new device that would cook for me, pick up my laundry, have my children and babysit them, as well as offer me seventeen call features and the ability to text-message Mars.

When I got back on the return bus, I was carrying more than just phone boxes. Reeling from the encounter at the mobile kiosk, with its fifteen-minute lesson in how to be modern, I'd been waylaid by the mall stores and bought a pair of boots that actually fit and looked nice and were warm and waterproof. I was wearing them and carrying my old boots in the new's shoebox (I would have left both at the shoe store but Bunnywit loves boots and boxes). I had been to the bookstore and bought a book called *Internet for Idiots*[8]. I had a number of things from the dollar store, many of them toys for Bunnywit, in a huge bag with improvised packing-tape handles. And I was juggling the remains of the flat box of take-out sushi I'd had for lunch.

I took my glove off to dig out my keys, and the bags hanging off my hands bashed against the wall as I flashed the fob at the new electronic lock release on the outer door. (The door worked with the old key as well, but I'd secretly paid, through the agency of Mr. Spak, a lot of money for that electronic gizmo, and I was determined to get good use out of it.)

"Crap," I said aloud, hoping I hadn't broken anything.

A gloved hand reached over my shoulder. "Here, let me help you with that." The deep voice was vaguely familiar, but not familiar enough to be a fellow tenant. I looked back — and up — over my shoulder into wide blue eyes set widely apart in a wide, windburnt, ruddy face, under a visor cap. It was a tall guy in a black suit — not

---

8. It had been in the sale bin because it was so old. Sigh. Also I had bought another book, making me statistically average for a change, because books.

a uniform, like fire or cops, but flat black — and a peaked cap straight out of the Village People[9]. He was bulky in that way that says weight room not weight problem, and from the perfectly-fitting neck of his shirt emerged not only his neck but one of those curly cords that Secret Service agents wear in movies, leading to an ear bud. There was the littlest hint of the edge of a tattoo under it. If it hadn't been for the curly cord and his ability to loom while smiling, his wide-open face might have been appealing.

Behind him, my glance took in a limousine idling at the curb. It was silver and had tinted windows. It looked like it should have a sinister master criminal, a wedding couple, or a high-school graduation party in it. With no Kleenex™ flowers bedecking it, and no cheerleaders and football players hanging out the rooftop skylight, the options narrowed in a nerve-wracking manner.

"Thanks, but I've got it," I said. "May I help you?" My thumb hovered over the coloured button on the electronic lock fob, the reason why I had bothered with this level of security for the Epi-TOME, which, face it, is as secure as a sieve. It was a button which beamed a personal call for help directly to 911 if I needed to send such a distress signal.

"My name's Chiles. Mr. Lockwood would like to know if you would join him for a brief meeting."

The voice on the phone. I was startled into honesty. "In that car? Are you *nuts*?" I stood in the doorway, blocking Chiles's entry.

Chiles became slightly human as he laughed. He stepped back and reached into his pocket. "Here is Mr. Lockwood's card. He wishes to speak with you about Priscilla Jane Gill. He will wait."

He tucked the card into the nearest shopping bag, and jogged back to the car without waiting for an answer, which was damned sensible of him, as it was really fucking cold out there and he

9. I am old, also queer, so I know who the Village People are. Were. Are.

wore no coat. One of those people who don't dress for winter because they are wearing their car. My mom used to say, "What if your car breaks down on the River Road?" If I ever got to know Mr. Chiles any better, I would ask him the same question.

I went up to the apartment slowly, in part because I was laden, but mostly because I was damned if I was going to come to heel for some rich, peremptory stranger. I was no dog.

I'm not even a dog person.

And the thing was, I hadn't even barked. I wasn't helping Priscilla; I hadn't done anything. I'd seen her just the once in years. True, I'd spent several hours with her, but if I'd been *seen* with her, it was at Double Greeting three nights ago, and who had cared enough to do the seeing? Could Chiles have been the bad-vibes guy? No — Chiles was tall, Scandinavian-fair, broad-shouldered, and would be unmistakeable in or out of scarves and winter hats.

And if she was the one who had mentioned me to someone, if she had been talking with someone about me, she hadn't said so. Not that I'd given her much chance, but still . . .

So.

Curious thing about that non-barking dog . . .

18. AN eBAY™ OPPORTUNITY

I took my time about getting my bags unpacked, digging my new cell phone out of its box and plugging it in to charge — and I gave Bunnywit one of the toys. He jumped up on the table instead and batted Mr. Lockwood's card to the floor. I put it back up. He did it again. I rescued the card and said, "Okay, fine. I'll at least look."

The card had, printed in a kind of silvery ink, only four lines: up top, larger type, in a Baskerville-Old-Face-style font, *Nathan Lockwood*. Under that: two phone numbers and a website address.

If I'd ever read *American Psycho* (or even seen the film) I'd have known more about the hierarchy of business cards, but as it was, I regarded the thick rectangle with nothing but suspicion and annoyance. It looked like a regular business card made of some kind of laid paper, but it was smoother-textured and a little heavier than regular cardboard. It was also a little oversize, about an eighth of an inch each way, which would be annoying if one were trying to fit it into a business card file of any kind.

I turned it over. On the back was a photograph of a city. My city. But reversed out of the photograph was some white type edged in red for legibility. It was a list of other cities: *Hong Kong. Yokohama. Delhi. Mumbai. Lucerne. Gaborone. Rio de Janeiro. London. Montréal.* Each one had a phone number beside it. They all had the same last four digits as the numbers on the front.

I wondered whether this guy had a pocket full of cards, each with the right phone number for the city he was in. Or maybe he had a car and a Chiles in every city, each Chiles armed with the right card.

Idly, I tapped the back of the card.

The graphic on the card changed. I almost dropped the damned thing, but held on to see the photo change to a view of Hong Kong. All the numbers refreshed like a computer screen, and suddenly my city and the local number were on the list. I turned the card back over and it had the Hong Kong number on the front, and the name and website address were repeated in characters.

I tried it a couple of times. Tapped the back, tapped the front. It worked just like my new tablet. If I tapped the front, the info I tapped got bigger. If I tapped a number on the back, the card changed to have that as its primary front listing. I ran through all the options I could think of, and got a very nice image of each place. Gaborone looked like any other downtown with glittery highrises. On that, I was kind of disappointed; I always hope our nasty example will inspire other countries to change the way they do cities, but maybe people are all just hard-wired, like termites.

I hefted the card again. Could the damn thing be some kind of "smart paper", about which I'd heretofore only read in science fiction novels? If so, and if its only raison d'être was business card, I was holding a piece of conspicuous consumption, or presumption, the like of which I'd never seen before, even when mixing with high-rollers from time to time in the course of previous work.

After a moment I called Dafydd Spak, my wonderful lawyer. He answers his own phone now, or maybe it's just when certain numbers are on the call display, in which case I'm flattered.

"Spak," he said.

"Me," I said. "But if I said 'Nathan Lockwood' to you instead, what would you say?"

There was a short silence at the other end. "Depends," he finally said. "If you are his friend, lucky you. If you are his enemy, run away. He has more money than God or Bill Gates, and he swings it around. He gets stuff done."

"His card says nothing but his name — what does he do?"

"You have one of those cards? With the photo on the back?"

"In my hand."

"Does something happen when you tap your finger on it?"

"Yep."

"You know, you can sell it on eBay™ for enough to retire on the Costa del Sol."

"On *eBay™*?"

"Someone put out a call. Anonymous offer. Swiss bank deposit for payment. Name your reserve price, starting with the high seven figures. Someone who wants the prototype, I suppose."

"It really *is* smart paper, then?"

"The El Dorado of stationery supplies. Didn't you see that feature about it last month in the *Financial Times*?"

"Get real. This is me you're talking to. To whom you are talking. So where does this guy really hang his hat?"

"Strangely enough, here."

"But I've never heard of him."

"With that much money? He doesn't need to actually exist to get things done. Not like the slightly-rich, who have to show up from time to time."

Then I called Roger. He wasn't there. I left a message. "A guy named Nathan Lockwood is taking me for a ride in a big silver limousine to talk about Priscilla Gill. If I don't come back, good luck proving he or his sidekick Mr. Chiles has done away with me. Mr. Spak tells me that this guy could buy the country. Possibly twice. I'm leaving his card on my dining room table. It's been nice knowing you. If I don't come back, sell it on eBay™ to pay for my memorial service."

I fed Bunnywit.

He said, "Niaow."

I should have listened.

Instead I washed my face, straightened my hair up, and went down to Mr. Lockwood's big silver car.

19. TAKE ME RIDIN' IN YOUR CAR, CAR . . .

By the time I went through the vestibule of the Epitome Apartments, it was sunset. Early winter sunset at latitude 53 degrees, it's true, but still, I'd kept Mr. Nathan Smart-paper Lockwood waiting for more than an hour. Beside the limousine stood two men.

Chiles had found himself one of those lush sheepskin coats with the fur turned inward and the toggles for buttons, but his ears still looked cold. So much for the River Road, but I would have to talk to Mr. Lockwood about EarCuffs™[10] for his staff sometime, when we all knew each other better. Chiles leaned against the immaculate fender with his hands in his pockets. His breath clouded the icy air.

With him stood a small, spare, elegant, intense gentleman — what other word would suffice in this scenario? — in a cashmere overcoat. I could actually tell it was cashmere from twenty paces away. Its texture manifested in a sort of aura, a penumbra of softness that extended much farther than the door of the anxious little Epitome. The patterned white silk scarf that he wore gleamed whiter than the urban snow, and his gloves looked as if they had been politely requested from the skins of the same goat kids who fed the belly hair to his coat, and the baby goats had been glad to lay down their lives for this Mr. Nathan Lockwood.

Since I wear kid gloves with cashmere linings myself, and was carrying them in my left hand at that very moment, I wasn't trying for moral high ground, just for footing on the same planet.

So far, no luck. Even the icy puffs of his breath had spectacular definition, like a CGI effect in a Spielberg film. Platonic in their perfection.

If this was not Nathan Lockwood, then Lockwood could afford to buy an extremely high class of flunky, but I was guessing that this was a demonstration of noblesse oblige. And indeed, as I approached, this vision took off his glove and presented a slender hand. His long, lean, dark face broke open into a triangular smile that revealed a lot of appealing laugh-wrinkles. I

---

10. Cute fuzzy warm ear-caps with no over-the-head strip. I've bought three sets and lost two. I'm very careful with those. But Bun likes them, so eventually I'll relax and accidentally leave them somewhere accessible, like my coat pocket or the top of the tall bookcase, and he'll kidnap them and put them with the others he has stashed somewhere. Hey, I was modern now — maybe I could get GPS trackers for them.

took his hand automatically, then wished I hadn't. With what was I shaking hands?

"Thank you for meeting me on such short notice. I'm Nathan Lockwood. Please call me Nathan. If you wish, of course."

All right. That was just too much. "And if I don't wish?"

"As you wish, I should have said. Please step into my portable office here. I'm sorry, Chiles told me what you said. It does look a bit like a Pimpmobile, but the alternatives today were either too small or ludicrous and ecologically unsupportable. So here it is."

He knew cultural references from outdated cult movies. He opened the door for me himself. What the hell did he want?

I glanced at Chiles. He was grinning. That seriously pissed me off. Not that I hadn't been annoyed before.

Curiosity killed the cat, it's said.

But it's also said that satisfaction brought it back.

I got in the car.

20. MARSHMALLOWS

Inside, the limo looked quite a lot like a movie set. That's probably because the movies is (are?) where most of us plebeians — especially those of us whose high-school grad was not a celebration, as such — get our ideas about what the inside of this kind of conspicuous-consumption car looks like. There were four leather-covered seats that swivelled just enough to make them easy to get into. I picked one near the door.

Then Nathan got in. Nathan. Ha.

Then Chiles took off his sheepskin coat and livery hat, slung them into the front seat through a gap in the carscape, and got in the back with us. That surprised me a little. Then Nathan pulled three mugs out of a little cabinet, which surprised me more, put them on a tiny shelf, and began to pour something steaming-hot into them from a vacuum flask.

"Marshmallows?" he said. Seeing my expression, he clarified, "In the hot chocolate."

"Sure, why not?" We who are about to die can have a tasty hot beverage first.

Lockwood put seven little marshmallows in Chiles's mug without asking, put the same number in mine and five in his, and topped them off with a spoonful of whipped cream from a beaker on the tiny table. He handed our drinks to us simultaneously: ambidextrous as well as everything else. We all sipped decorously. I wiped whipped cream off my lip with my index knuckle. Lockwood used a cambric handkerchief. I don't know how Chiles dealt with it.

"I suppose you're wondering why we asked you here," said Lockwood, and chuckled. Or snickered. Well, almost giggled — but in a charming and reserved way. I thought my dear lawyer, Mr. Spak, was the poster child for reserved good manners, but compared with Nathan Lockwood, he was an amateur. Of course, if smart paper and reputation were indicators, compared with Lockwood *everyone* was an amateur.

I gave my new best friend the look I often use on Roger or my friend Denis. It's effective on them, though I've tried it on Bunnywit to no avail. It's my "cut the bullshit and cut to the chase" look, and in the first bright thing about this encounter, it actually worked. Lockwood cleared his throat and looked away.

"We need your help," he said. "I would like to explain why, but if you will bear with me, I must give you a brief preface."

The minimalist shrug is done with the corner of the mouth and one shoulder. I usually use the left-sided minimalist shrug. It seemed to convey to Nathan what it conveys to the ordinary folk.

"Thank you.

"I asked Chiles to give you one of my smart cards for a reason. I'm sure you took the opportunity to check us out. I'm sure you discovered that the card is coveted technology and that we have a great deal of money. Often compared to Bill Gates, but sometimes to God or the Queen of England. None is particularly accurate."

"Did you make your money in retail?"

"No. I invented some things — software, hardware, firmware — much of it to do with resource extraction, which is how you get rich in this part of the world. They took off. But I am now heavily invested in solar and wind power and the development of sustainable technologies. My net worth has dropped a few billion as a result. God has sustainability figured out, which keeps his share prices up." He stopped for a moment. "Or hers."

"Whatever."

"Just so. Most people who meet me are impressed with my wealth in some way or another. I am impressed with my wealth myself, for the simple reason that I never anticipated it. But others: They envy it. They despise it. They wish to profit from it. It can be embarrassing. People have grovelled before me looking for funding for their charity or arts group. Or hospital. They don't know that wealth like this manages itself. I have to work hard to keep it from growing. Most of my effort for the past ten years has been spent trying to find effective ways to spend it. Or give it away. Sustainable ways. Foundations endowed with enough that the interest covers the grants. New technologies."

"Smart paper."

Chiles snorted.

"Just so," said Nathan. Ha. Nathan. "It isn't going to work, though. Smart paper. It's lovely tech, of course: so much more versatile than tablets. But it doesn't work as a sustainable replacement for a huge print industry based on diminishing old-growth forests. It creates its own resource problems, and it's elitist. We will have to look for a better option. I am delighted to report how many millions I have wasted discovering that I should be in hemp."

"Poor little rich man? Seriously? What do you want from me that you can't buy somewhere else?"

"First, let's talk about Mr. Chiles here."

His dark eyes cut to Chiles, and I looked there too, then could have kicked myself. This guy was good.

"It amuses Mr. Chiles to act as if he is my servant on excursions like this. But he is a friend, an equal, and an honoured colleague, and entrusted with a task that is very special to us."

Thinking of something I'd read in a Neal Stephenson novel, I held my mug out to Lockwood. "May I have some more, please?"

Chiles's hands twitched but remained folded in his lap. Lockwood grinned — that's really the word for a smile that fast and wide — at me and took the cup.

"Yes, you can task me. Because I am about to ask a favour. Or something like a favour. You are a strong-willed person. I have no need to dominate or control you. If you say no, I will leave you alone. Marshmallows again?"

"Absolutely marshmallows. Many. And do I believe you will leave me alone?"

"That's your problem. Ours is simpler. We are trying to ensure the safety of our dear Priscilla Jane Gill. We thought we had her protection covered."

We? I looked at Chiles. He was flushed. Blushing? Okay. Fine. Cut to the chase again.

"Against whom?"

Chiles spoke so suddenly I jumped. "That's the thing of it. That's the whole damned thing. The guy who attacked her, Mowbry? Out of nowhere. Out of fu— out of nowhere. No history. No ties. No blips on the radar. Pris's safety has been my — our — job for *years*, and he got by us. Me. And my people."

"You have a lot of resources, then."

"Of course. And we have a file on him now, but —"

"This guy, this — Mowbry? He did a lot of damage, right?"

"She barely survived."

"So where is he now?"

"Out on parole," said Nathan.

"So soon?"

"The defence was effective in suggesting mitigation, and he participated in all the required interventions in prison."

"You can buy the planet, I'm told. What on earth can *I* do, compared?"

Chiles leaned forward. "Pris wants to feel normal. She won't discuss this with us. She needs a friend who is also helping us."

"A traitor? Not a good look, on any of us."

"A friend," said Nathan, "who can call on our resources if needed. It's not suggested you would betray her confidences to us."

Chiles didn't look as sure about that.

"Do it yourselves."

"We are. We are on watch."

"In the present tense?"

"Yes."

"So she *is* being followed. By you."

"Yes. By our people."

"Does she actually know this? About you? About being . . . protected like this?"

"Well, um. Not now. Not as such."

Not *as such*?

"Why not?"

21. THE LOVE CANAL — THE TOXIC LANDMARK, I MEAN, NOT THE RUDE SLANG

Nathan was back in the game, handing me another impeccable hot chocolate. In addition to All the Marshmallows that Fit, he'd put a maraschino cherry on top.

I'd heard maraschino cherries described, years ago, as the Love Canal of candied fruit; despite their toxicity, I eat the decorative cherries anyway. I ate this one, and looked around for a place to put the stem. Lockwood took it from me and made it disappear. Almost magic. I wouldn't have been surprised if he'd put it in his mouth and quickly tied a knot in it with his tongue first. He was that good.

"Priscilla refused our help," he said. "We made a mistake. We gave it anyway. She reacted badly. Our relationship is very strained right now. But we —"

"Simply put, we love her and we are worried," said Chiles. "And we have a lot of money, so we are trying to use some of it to protect her. Without bothering her with it. You have history with her, and you like her too. We wondered if you would help. We will, of course, compensate you at whatever rate you deem reasonable."

"We would not presume on your friendship, even were it more current," said Nathan.

I looked at him. He was serious. And he had used the subjunctive in which to be serious. Which was also serious. I looked at Chiles. He was serious too. The temptation to buck the trend was whelming, but I was able to resist.

It took me a moment to untangle which thing I wanted to say first. I took a breath. Then I let it out and had some hot chocolate. I licked froth off my lip. I bought time with another long sip.

I looked across the little space at Nathan Lockwood.

Taken dispassionately, without fear, without awe, he was very beautiful. His skin was a smoothly neutral, racially-ambiguous light brown that could pass in almost every neighbourhood on the planet, at least on a superficial glance: no cops would kneel on his neck. His greying dark hair was brushed aristocratically back from strong, fine features. Like Pris, he had silver highlights in his dark hair, not red, and like Pris, had greyed so artistically that they both could have appeared in hair commercials. The fine skin around his dark eyes was crinkled with either humour or an outdoors habit, or both.

Suddenly I realised who these guys were. On the Internet I'd seen a photo of them standing by her side in Antarctica, Nathan touching her arm and looking away, Chiles with an arm over her shoulder and looking protective, as if there was a penguin stalking her or something.

I could imagine Nathan and Priscilla together. She was taller than him, of course, but he wouldn't care and neither would she. With their narrow, hooked noses and high cheekbones, their long sensitive hands, their rich swarthy skins, hers darker than his, and their wide triangular smiles, they had that similarity that many couples have who recognise their secret singular tribe in each other. They would have made beautiful children together.

I could imagine her with Chiles too, enjoying his height and athleticism, laughing at the protectiveness. But if we were picking the celebrity salt-and-pepper-shaker set, it was Pris and Nathan who would be the paparazzi's dream team — because of the overriding similarity of that gloss they had, the gloss shared by the special people of the planet, the very rich, privileged, or fortunate. The ones who have no idea how the rest of us live.

But that gloss is illusory. We all live the same way: as human. It's hard to remember that when a high-tech billionaire is carefully counting thirteen marshmallows into a cup of hot chocolate, just for you. But I managed, barely, to keep my focus.

It was the second time this week that I had been asked to help Priscilla Jane Gill with protection. Last time, I was annoyed with Pris on my own behalf. This time I was annoyed with these two on Pris's behalf.

"You made a mistake, all right," I said. "You have been dealing with employees for too long. Flunkies. Toadies. Supplicants. Poor folks like me. Even if I were still eating fish sticks, I wouldn't take your offer. You have forgotten the key element of equality in relationships."

"Fish sticks?" said Nathan.

"Fish sticks, food of the underclass," I said.

He did a very good imitation of my own raised-eyebrow, cut-to-the-chase moue. It had all the elements of a deflection, and as a former social worker as well as a big deflector myself, I had no time for it.

"Equality," I repeated, and included Chiles in my glare. "You didn't want to 'bother' her? How could you be that stupid and still make so much money? If Pris *knew* that you were on her side, and she didn't ask for help, that's her choice. Giving it to her anyway, and not telling her 'for her protection' is patronising. It says you are Big Daddy and have the right to interfere. At least you could have *told* her you didn't agree and weren't going to take no for an answer. Still as patronising as a family intervention, but at least honest."

Nathan nodded, sagely, as if thinking about it. As if.

I was on a roll. I glanced back and forth at both of them, an equal-opportunity scold. "As it is, you've just made things worse. Your shadows have probably contributed to her paranoia. After all, she *is* being followed, no matter what — by *your* guys — for years, for Chrissake — and they can't have been perfect at not being noticed."

Nathan looked at Chiles and raised an eyebrow.

Hmmm. I wondered just who was the one who put the tail on her. But nobody was getting any get-out-of-jail-free card from me. If Nathan hadn't ordered it, he'd condoned it. "Furthermore, it's just creepy. It verges on stalking. No, it *is* stalking. You have to stop, and here's what you also have to do. You have to tell her. Everything. And hope she forgives you. I wouldn't, but Pris has made a lifetime of going into different cultures and accepting what she finds. The rarefied air of the far-too-rich can't be much different from the high Himalayas."

Both Chiles and Nathan looked out different windows at the bleak winter twilight. Not much time had passed, subjectively, since I got in with them, even though we'd come a long way. Lockwood didn't speak. Chiles cleared his throat and blushed, but also said nothing.

"I don't know what either of you seriously and honestly think that *I* can do for her that the — what? Thirty-ninth? — richest guys in the world can't do. I suspect that if either of you actually were telling me the whole story, it would help me understand that. But —" I saw each of them take a breath and hurried to forestall what they might say "— not now.

"Here's the deal. If and only if you go to Pris and talk with her about what you have been doing for — years? Years? That's nuts! — and she forgives you, and you talk it over like equal grown-ups in a reasonable, adult way, and you still think there is something I can do, then come back, together, Pris and you, together and in accord, and maybe, just maybe, I might listen and consider what I can do that the three of you, with all your resources, can't."

It occurred to me I hadn't taken a breath myself in a while, so I stopped for one. I still hadn't even loosened my coat, though the car was warm inside, and I was sweating. I finished the cooled chocolate, pulled my not-so-silk scarf up around my ears, and pulled on my non-handmade gloves. When I made a feint for the door, Chiles leaned forward and reached for the handle.

"What's your name?" I said, irritated.

"Which day?" he said. I gave him the Look. "Okay. Hm. Ambrose Bierce Chiles, all right?" I glared. "My parents were weird-history buffs." His placement of the hyphen was clear.

ABC. Hmph. Truth, if it was truth, is far more annoying than fiction.

I got out of the car and turned to go.

Then I turned and leaned back in. "Only *maybe*. No guarantees. Right?"

Nathan nodded gravely. "I get it," he said. Then he grinned. "I haven't said I'll do as you ask either."

"Your choice," I said. "But if you really do love Pris, it's kind of a no-brainer."

Then I went back inside, put the smart-paper card in the secret drawer of my roll-top desk, and called Roger to say, "I'm back."

He hadn't listened to his voice mail.

"What? From where?"

"Back from nowhere," I said. "Never mind." I hung up on him.

22. SOMEONE IS WRONG ON THE INTERNET

Back at the Internet, I looked for Nathan Lockwood. That was easy and hard, same as with Pris. Easier on the new device, I had to admit.

The smart-paper business card had more information on it than all the Nathan Lockwood World (a too-cute moniker) stuff that I found smeared all over the business zones of the World Wide Web (sic: I've never believed its hype and here was proof) put together. Yes, there were websites and articles and info-sheets and articles and paparazzi blurs and articles, but nothing said what they actually *did* at Nathan Lockwood World.

Despite the mystery, everyone from Wikipedia to Boing Boing wanted to find Nathan Lockwood and get a piece of him, so there were thousands of hits. Although famously reclusive, he *had* been photographed occasionally, almost always with Chiles walking beside him, and I even found one more photo of him and Pris and Chiles together, but she was turned away from the camera.

Ignoring the glamorous draperies she was wearing, the caption read, "Nathan Lockwood and a business associate leave a meeting in Singapore", maybe because in the photo she looked about half a foot taller than him — but the built-in GPS co-ordinates on the photo (I was learning a lot) were Bangalore, which shows you how collectively smart the online brain trust is. But we've already covered that.

I cooked steak for me and Bunnywit. Then we watched a DVD of a British series called *Let Them Eat Cake*. It seemed appropriate. I had to skip the episode called "Murder" when Bun wouldn't quit with the "Niaow! Niaow!" He never has liked that episode, but still, I should have paid more attention.

I'VE PROMISED HER DOLLS AND A DAISY-CHAIN,

23. OPERATOR, OPERATOR . . .

The next morning, Pris called me back.

She had indeed called Roger, and they had had some words.

"I guess you were upset," she said.

"Duh," I said. "Where did you go? And who did you talk to about me?"

"What? I didn't talk to anyone about you. I went to see someone else. About this being-followed thing, for one. And some other stuff. Private."

"Well, if it was a therapist, you wasted your money, because you *are* being followed. Some dude named Alphabet Soup Chiles has made it his life work to see that no psychopaths ever get to you again — even though you have spurned his love and the love of his boss, the weirdest rich guy in the world — and has had bodyguards on you for ages."

"What the *fuck*!? It's *Chiles*?"

"Well, among others, I suppose. Including the extremely rich Nathan Lockwood who came over and asked me to help you, even though we'd never met. Except of course through me being with you while you were being shadowed."

"Nathan and Chiles went to see you?"

"Why not? After all, he has lots of money and invented smart paper, and he wants his girlfriend safe and happy."

"He isn't who he seems. And I didn't spurn his love. Goddammit."

"Who is who they seem? Certainly not you. And which one didn't you spurn? Enquiring minds want to know."

"I'll call you back."

She hung up again. Dammit.

She didn't call back.

Later, over sushi[11], Roger and I kicked the whole inconclusive mess around a bit, and I told him about cut-glass steno-robot-voice, Mr. A. B. Chiles, and Nathan Lockwood. I showed him the smart-paper card. He wrote down the local number in his classic little cop notebook, then tapped the card about twice as many times as I had before I tugged it back out of his hand and put it away. No crime, no problem, right? And I wish it on the record that since Roger is a public servant, and so full of ethics he can hardly bend his torso, we went dutch (and don't be a smart-ass and say "What, Dutch sushi?" or I'll tell you about the sign in Vancouver that says *Original Chinese Smorgasbord*).

Later, in the actual mail, I got a very nice card from Nathan Lockwood, on the ordinary kind of paper, saying thanks and apologising for bothering me, but I didn't get a callback from Pris that day — or that week.

---

11. You may note that having a little more money to kick around gives me access to a better class of fish, access I use as often as possible. I have not yet tired of sushi, and not for want of trying.

24. <SNIP>

There will now be a break of 3.5 months —

Imagine it, if you like, as one of those segues in an old film. Calendar pages ruffle and blow away in the wind. The city is shown in time-lapse photography flickering through days and nights and seasons.

During this time, I learned things about property ownership. It was a winter of blizzards, and we had to hire someone to clear the snow off the roof of the Epitome Apartments, but the roof leaked anyway, so we had to re-do a couple of suites in addition to the scheduled upgrades. During this process I was outed to my neighbours as the new owner. This nipped several budding friendships, but Mr. Spak, my lawyer, said that they must not have been real friends anyway. Shades of junior high school.

Having learned my dirty little secret (that one, at least), however, my neighbourhood-advocating downstairs neighbour redoubled efforts to get me to drink tea together and oh, incidentally, to get involved in civic development issues, because now, apparently, as a property owner, I had a real reason. I resisted, and I didn't need Mr. Spak to tell me that this sudden cordiality had a similar source to the sudden distrust of my other, less opportunistic neighbours — and was equally trustworthy.

With my fancy new tablet computer, I started a weblog and grew to accept that I would have to call it a blog. I realised I had nothing to say and took it down, but the experience was instructive. I took much enjoyment from the archives of xkcd, A Softer World, I Can Has Cheezburger?, and other remarkably awesome or stupid ways to waste a day online.

After a while I got over the Internet, and became a modern person.

In the real world, I went to a charmingly weird and excellent Christmas Around the World dance-and-music performance with my friends Walter, Erna, and Eva. I got my parents' piano out of storage and took a few lessons, thus becoming a person who plays the piano very badly, which was an improvement. I started going to the Little Flower open stage, resulting in me tuning my autoharp and taking up bluegrass again.

I bought a digital camera and took both a winter photography safari and a spring raptor workshop at the local zoo. I flew to San Francisco with my friend Denis for the Transgender Film Festival and a dance performance by Fresh Meat. I went to Chicago with my friend Hep and took the architecture river cruise. I also took a river dinner cruise at home, on a rickety charming riverboat, and helped organise a community conference in the Chinese community.

Mr. Lockwood's smart-card stayed in my drawer, but I renewed my library card and used it a lot —

— and in all those months, I did not see Priscilla Jane Gill.

25. FULL DISCLOSURE

I did, however, get an e-mail from her. About two weeks after she hung up on me. She said she was sorry.

26. "THERE IS A TAVERN IN THE TOWN . . ."

Tuning an autoharp takes a while, so a tuned-up autoharp is not something one wants to waste. I play mine à la Bryan Bowers, cradled in my arms so I can strum five-fingered, those fingers rendered urban-fantastic by the addition of a set of wraparound finger picks. One day in late February, Denis and Lance and Hep and I went down to the Little Flower to play a few tunes at the open stage.

Little Flower is a welcoming venue, run by Breezy, a great guitarist in a battered sequined jacket[12], and there's always someone to sit in on guitar or harmonica. I had played there a few times over the winter, never quite getting over my nerves, but having more and more fun each time.

Denis is a campy sometime-drag-queen with a secret life as a brilliant helping professional. Lance is a cop, recently transferred to Homicide and working for Roger. He's also Denis's partner. They met during the brou-ha-ha last fall, when Denis was helping me find out who killed Hep's granddaughter, and Lance was undercover as a tall, scary-looking drag queen. It's fun to watch them together. Denis has Lance wearing patterned designer shirts instead of pastels from Hudson's Bay sale tables, and Lance has Denis wearing a smile.

That night, they turned up with a particularly smug expression, and when I hugged Denis, he winced.

"What's up?" I said, concerned. "That big guy not being too rough, I hope."

"Watch your mouth, girl," said Denis. "That big guy's only rough when I let him be."

I rolled my eyes. "I never thought I'd hear you do couple-schtick," I said.

"This is nothing," he said. "We have taken couple-schtick to a whole new level. Show her, babe!"

They had gotten matching tattoos. Celtic knotwork in tasteful black and green circled their upper arms, one each, on opposite arms, or perhaps I should say on their adjoining arms. Mirror image.

Denis has known me for years, and for years we have been ragging on each other about changing our lives — from me to

12. Who runs for mayor now and again, and even if Gary is a great guy, I usually vote for Breezy.

him because for years, he lived alone in the suburban house he inherited from his mother and never dated despite an active drag career. Now he was sitting there hand in hand with a cop, goofy grins on their faces and their tattoos still red and puffy and covered with a greasy layer of, I assumed, antibiotic ointment. Denis looked slightly anxious.

"That is great!" I said. "You have gotten the ancient markings of my Celtic people[13]!"

"My people too," said Denis defensively.

"Girlfriend, I'm kidding. It's great, I mean it. When they stop looking like they were scratched on your arms with pointed twigs in a Poro Bush coming-of-age ritual, they will look fabulous, not just great."

"Is it too butch for me?" Denis fretted.

"Too late now," I said. He winced. "Oh, come on, enjoy them. They are very cool. One hell of a wedding ring."

"How did you guess?" Lance was disappointed.

I didn't say, "Because you guys are about as transparent as Denis's cellophane job." Instead, I modestly said, "Just a lucky guess, I guess," and Hep kicked me under the table.

Speaking of kicks, Hep is a kick-ass musician; she used to be a violinist but at my urging she transcended paper-training and took up the Rufus Guinchard / Amelia Kaminski style of mad, bad, crossroads-enabled fiddling. But she only ever played when I urged her: she is usually even more reclusive about her music than I am, despite being far, far better.

Hep is a tiny perfect copy of Katharine Hepburn in her prime, which is why we call her Hep. The resemblance has diminished since she cut her long hair, but it's growing back pretty fast. Her real name is Madeline Pritchard, and the business in the fall that resulted in all my injuries all started with her asking my help

---

13. Well, some of my people. I have lots of people. Peoples. People.

to deal with the death of her granddaughter Maddy. Hep had almost, especially after Chicago, gotten over feeling guilty about me getting bashed as a result, but I was using her residual guilt to get her to come out and play bluegrass with me.

Little Flower had Electric Blue Night once a month: blues and bluegrass were the only tunes allowed. No "Blowin' in the Wind", "Kumbaya", "Stairway to Heaven", or "In-A-Gadda-Da-Vida". Not even any of Jorma Kaukonen's own compositions, only the great classic blues he covered.

I may love bluegrass best, but I play and sing other stuff too. Folk music was one of the *good* things about my childhood. My parents loved it: they had met during the folk boom of the mid-twentieth century, and the highlights of our summers were long rambling trips to places where pickin'-and-singin' took place. Bean Blossom, Indiana; Cape Breton, Nova Scotia; ceilidhs in Newfoundland; successors to the Grand Ole Opry in Nashville; blues clubs in Chicago while we were in the neighbourhood, incongruous and naively Canadian in our family station wagon (this was before mini-vans); folk festival in Whitehorse; ditto North Country Fair; and, of course, our own home-town folk festival — where they proudly volunteered and my dad, once a year, gave up his tweed and elbow patches for a FolkFest T-shirt over his paunch and a pair of elderly Birkenstocks that he swore were just as comfortable as when he bought them. It was a rare foray into accessibility for him, and one doesn't have to be a psychologist to understand why my brother and I took up folk music as kids. My brother soon gave it up in favour of a garage thrash metal band, but I still enjoyed it.

Ain't got no use for your red apple juice
Ain't got no sugar baby now, lord, lord
Ain't got no sugar baby now . . .

I resonate to these old songs with their direct plaints and their stories of love, loss, and murder. Tonight I stayed away from murder as much as possible. After "Red Apple Juice" I segued into Louis M. 'Grandpa' Jones's "Eight More Miles to Louisville", changing "gal" to "guy" so I could sing it for Denis and Lance: "I'm going away this very day to win his heart and hand . . ."

Cheating a little, we segued into Geoff Muldaur's "Common Cold", with Brian and Stuart sitting in on guitar and harps, and Hep sang it. On "I'm not much younger than that old lady was", she ruffled her white hair and got a big laugh from the audience. That's not a tune on which I have much to do. I was strumming backup and looking out at the crowd. As usual, it was standing room only.

At the back, standing back against the wall under the red *EXIT* light, was a big guy in a sheepskin coat who looked a lot like Alphabet Chiles. He turned and went down toward the restrooms, and I didn't see him come back, but I got busy for a few minutes with "Turn Your Radio On" and forgot the whole thing until much later.

The last song of our set was the rollicking lament (yes, a contradiction in terms) "There Is a Tavern in the Town". We got the whole place singing along.

Fare thee well, for I must leave thee
Do not let this parting grieve thee,
And remember that the best of friends must part, must
    part . . .

I felt a draught on my left side: *my right side jump and my left begin to burn*, as the old blues song goes. Must have been the winter wind. I looked over to see a bundled-up guy of medium height paying the cover charge as the outside door closed slowly after his entry. He was unwinding a long scarf. Later I tried to remember what colour it was, and whether he consciously reminded me of the guy at Double Greeting, or only subliminally. At the time, I shrugged off the chill as the late-winter wind, and kept on playing. All that shivers-are-portents stuff was only folklore, anyway.

I should have listened.

AND A BOOK ABOUT ANIMALS —
ALL IN VAIN —
WHAT *IS* THE MATTER WITH
MARY JANE?

27. HERE'S THE THING . . .

I generally lead a pretty simple life. I don't have any Grand Plans. After my brother's suicide when we were both teenagers I went through some dramatic and tumultuous times, but lately, if it hadn't been for the need to Save the World through social justice crusades, I'd have been just as happy to settle down behind a picket fence somewhere . . . oh, maybe not.

Not the picket fence type[14].

But I certainly had been happy in my social work job until I was "downsized" after a government spending cut. That was about a year before my adventure of last fall. I lived in the Epitome with my cat — originally named Fuckwit, but whom I'd even re-named Bunnywit so as not to offend people; how normative is *that*?

The riskiest thing I'd done in a long time (aside from trust new friends and lovers from time to time, that risk of love that we

---

14. More of a picket*er*, my editor suggests.

must all do, or be lonely) was to spend most of my surprisingly-fat legacy from my parents on buying the Epitome and (unfortunately for any other plans for the rest of my inheritance) fixing its roof. I did that because I like living here, and I like the old buildings in my neighbourhood, and I like the idea of giving people nice places to live that don't cost them a mint in rent and that they don't have to buy if they don't want to.

Financially, I had just enough money left over to put in trust for myself and draw an incredibly modest income in interest and a dribble of principal. Someday soon, if I wanted to keep buying myself sushi and new technology, I was going to have to get a job, but I was waiting until my ribs healed more and the winter was gone before I started looking.

Hep had suggested I try to make more of my music, but I have friends who are Real Creative Artists, and I know the difference between them and me.

I dabble. I enjoy the concept that someone with a past as wild as mine can sit around their apartment and have hobbies. Hobbies. Like play a little music for fun. Take an art class. Take a bit part in a community theatre show. That kind of thing.[15]

I haven't quite gone as far as gluing macaroni to melted phonograph records and spray-painting them gold, something I have seen done within my extended family, though no-one speaks of it, but I have done the odd artistic craft project. (Helping Denis with his drag outfits doesn't count.) I know, however, that I have neither the talent to make a living as an artist, nor the inclination.

And for Denis, who from time to time asked me if I shouldn't just get an investigator's licence and actually be nosy for money, I had three answers. One: I don't really enjoy the concept of

---

15. Write a book about some things that happened to me. Not really a hobby, but.

being self-employed. I actually *like* having a job where someone else figures out where the money is coming from. Two: observe last fall's damage total: property damage to some of my favourite belongings, and, more importantly, bruises, contusions, and broken ribs to my favourite (and only) body — duh. Three: I am not nosy; don't be a bitch.

Oh, four answers actually: I researched what PIs really do, and it is boring and nasty and three-quarters of it involves couples who transgress standards of monogamy that I find ludicrous and incomprehensible, so there is that too.

I believe that, despite the tattoos, I am a simple, kindly, reclusive, slightly-conservative person with a desire to be left alone.

This belief seems to make all my friends laugh. Out loud.

I wonder why?

28. PARIS IN THE THE SPRING

Pris came back to town with the springtime.

Both were welcome to me.

Spring was welcome because winter had been long and RFC, and if you can't guess what the acronym stands for you haven't known me, or winters in my city, for very long.

Pris was welcome because she had been writing me e-mails, and I had been writing back.

She had started our correspondence with a message containing an apology, which after a day or two of stewing about it, and a follow-up apology from her, I decided to accept. In her second e-mail, she made a promise that on April 1, if she was still alive, she'd tell me all about it. The truth, maybe even. I didn't rise to that bait, but I did write back and allow as how I might listen.

We then spent the next three months writing back and forth about other kinds of risks, besides the danger of stalkers and not minding one's own business respectively.

I talked about my lover who had run away with the circus, and whether and how that long-distance relationship was working out (better since Jian also got a tablet and we discovered Skype, which just shows that there was at least one other person on the digitised part of the planet besides me who hadn't figured this all out with Stewart Brand).

Pris talked about her tentative reconciliation with Lockwood and Chiles (she had agreed to be protected if they would quit giving out smart-paper business cards to civilians like me, or some such deal, I gathered, though details were sketchy).

I described my friend Hep, e-mailing a few photographs, and Pris agreed that our actions in Chicago had been not only justified but about time too.

We discussed my pal Denis's new relationship with an under-cover cop and all-round arm-candy candidate, and solved all their problems abstractly, since Denis wouldn't let me discuss this with him directly.

We discussed the particular designer purses my downstairs neighbour liked (we didn't understand why, because FFS why does a purse need a first name?, but at least Pris had *heard* of these supposedly prestigious brands).

We discussed what was happening in Nepal these days (littering, including by many dead frozen Western climbers' bodies, divers belongings of divers "adventurers", and tonnes of bodily waste) and whether Pris would really be allowed to meet the Dalai Lama if she dropped by Dharamsala (he was away, so no, by default).

We planned a little side trip to New Zealand on the way to Australia — and didn't go to either place. But we did agree that Ayers Rock had been a stupid name anyway and that someday we'd like to see it under its proper moniker. (I think that discussion gave Pris the idea for a new book, going to places that had been re-named to their pre-imperialism identities and discussing their history, like Mumbai, Myanmar, Beijing, Haida Gwaii, and Maskwacis. And it would have been a great book too.)

We swapped stupid cat memes, and pictures of our own stupid cats. As might be expected, the current — the living — Micah was an Abyssinian, and every inch an aristocat — as different from Bunnywit, a raggedy Manxy tortoiseshell, as two cats could be. Pris did send me a photo of the original Micah, in his state of suspended animation, just to gross me out.

Just stuff, right? People stuff. Cat stuff. Regular stuff.

It was like digital ping-pong — it had a rhythm and momentum that added up to a nice friendship, over time, and even a higher level of trust, though I managed most of the time to remember that Pris was Very Different From Me. And she very cleverly didn't notice any of my questions about where she had gone when she "disappeared", and with or to whom, and why.

April 1 was two days away, and so was Pris. She was on a book tour for her latest book, which at the last minute had been retitled *How I Didn't See the Dalai Lama*, because the editor thought the anecdote too priceless to leave out. I didn't see why the Dalai Lama should be co-opted to make Pris lots more money, but she said that his lawyers had been consulted.

The Dalai Lama has lawyers? Go figure. Maybe Mr. Spak was not such an indulgence after all.

I admit some curiosity as the day neared. But I hid it from Pris.

Fool me once, shame on you; fool me twice, shame on me.

And all that.

I shouldn't have tempted fate by thinking of that word *fool*.

29. NO GOOD DEED GOES UNPUNISHED

When I bought the Epitome Apartments, I also bought its parking lot, in plat terms "the lot next door", and come spring we would be repairing and painting the nice old wrought-iron fence with the brick base that surrounded the lot. Developers had also offered to take that lot off my hands, in the interests of "getting rid of eyesore parking lots downtown", but the two lots were all part of the same historic package, and our tidy asphalted-and-landscaped lot bore no resemblance to the heritage-clear-cut, gravelled, weed-colonised wastelands elsewhere in the neighbourhood.

Since Pris had charged me with the challenge to get involved in fixing the neighbourhood, I had been walking around looking at what was there and what wasn't there, and thinking.

I'd even made a few calls, but only in a desultory way. I hadn't charged into full change-the-world mode. I liked to think those days were over for me.

Ha.

The phone rang about midmorning March 29.

"This is Gary."

Gary. Gary?

"As in, Mayor Gary?"

"The very one. How are you?"

He wasn't asking rhetorically. The imbroglio in the fall had started with murder, but when I started pulling the strings of its tangled web, a fraud of epic proportions emerged. I had managed to warn Gary before the city had been swindled out of $28.8 million in support money for affordable housing that wasn't going to happen. I'd risked my life to do so. He knew what injuries I'd sustained, and how.

"All healed up, mostly," I said. "And you?"

"Off my diet, but politically healthy," he said. "I have an idea for you. Why don't you collect that cousin of yours and come see me? Today at two, preferably."

"She's away at some sort of conference," I said. "Two's fine."

30. THE (SUB)PLOT THICKENS

He was talking about my cousin Thelma. Thelma is a born-again born-again Christian. No, that's not an accidental repetition. Thelma started a born-again Christian, and she used to be pretty doctrinaire, but the same brou-ha-ha previously mentioned had involved some people who used an evangelical church of already-shaky dogma to cover up some serious graft and a murder. Thelma became involved in my — well, I suppose it was an investigation, though as I keep reminding everyone, I will never have a PI licence, and I was just doing a favour for Hep — when she discovered a link to a hate organisation that was being sheltered within the fire-and-brimstone sect.

Thelma was horrified. She believes in a god of love. Without ceasing to be a born-again Christian, she was born-again as a radical, in that moment. She discovered in herself a strong sense of social justice, and started Getting On Committees. She got on the board of an inner-city housing corporation just to annoy — and keep an eye on — the Wrong-Reverend Goldring, who promoted the hate group.

Thelma was also pregnant at the time she and I got involved in last fall's adventure, and through the same case, she had also met and got involved with Vikki, a sex worker who was leaving the life, and who was retraining as a child-care specialist. Vikki lined herself up as nanny before Thelma's kid was even born. Vikki and Thel shared a love of high heels, high fashion, high hairdos, and fancy fingernails — and justice and love.

It took me until last year to appreciate Thelma, but it also took until last year for Thelma to abandon her judgmental, homophobic attitudes (about me in particular and the queer world in general), so we were even.

Her child had been born just before New Year, a lovely little morsel with a little extra genetic material, an early smile, and an outgoing personality. Who knew babies had personalities, I had thought, but this one was going to charm everyone she met. Thel resisted my pitch for a gender-unspecific name and upbringing, and called her Charlotte. I was *so* going to turn that to Charlie!

Just a few days before Mayor Gary's call, Vikki and Thelma had headed off to a conference for people with Down's syndrome, their families, and their caregivers, and Thel was going on from that to another conference on church-run affordable housing.

See?

Committees.

31. GOOD DEEDS REDUX

I was pretty sure that asking me to bring Thelma was shorthand for "listen to my new inner-city housing idea" in Gary's mind, so I brought to the meeting my tablet notebook, where I'd already jotted a few ideas, and the last year's annual report of Metropolitan Multi-Faith Foundation, known as M2F2 to its intimates (which I always had thought sounded rude), the organisation on whose board Thelma now served.

This was the organisation which had almost been defrauded of a lot of money in the same sting that almost got the city, and which I had foiled, so they had reason to be grateful, and they kept me on the mailing list.

I was right. After the necessary preliminaries, including Gary making me a hot chocolate with his very own hands, but from a packet mix, and without any of the little marshmallows and real whipped cream that the nouveaux-very-riches carry in their limos, we settled down in his office at the shiny round table that conveyed equality with the voter, and Gary got down to bidness.

"You own a parking lot," he said.

"Not selling," I said. "It has wrought iron. It's original to the Epitome."

"Want to buy another parking lot or two?"

"Can't afford it. I used up my inheritance on the Epitome. It wasn't a very large inheritance, you know. Last fall, saying I was rich during that sting we did? You *know* that was all flimflam to catch a thief."

"I know. But the city has a problem now."

I could see it coming. "Not my fault your housing plan is in the toilet. I just caught the thieves. Don't kill the messenger."

"Not your fault, but you and Thelma can help. She's on the M2F2 board. You are a property owner in the neighbourhood, and can leverage that."

"What the hell does 'leverage' mean, Gary? Is it even a verb?"

"Never mind that now, you grammar grouch. The city planned to make a deal with M2F2 to build housing on those lots. We need to keep that initiative going."

"I'm retired."

"Yeah, and I have a bridge in Brooklyn for sale."

"Really? Why not sell it and use the money to hire an executive director to do this for you?"

"Very funny. I need a community board. I need a community buy-in. I need more than M2F2 — I need local property owners. I need consensus-building. I need you to spearhead this working group."

"Why me?"

"People find it hard to say no to you."

"And I find it hard to say no to anyone."

"Well, that too."

"I'm working on my boundary issues, Gary."

"So am I. Right now, the boundary of east downtown. It's a mess over there."

"I like it!"

"I know you do. Why do you think I'm . . . oh, you were yanking my chain. Well, stop that. I like it too, old friend, but

69

I'd like it better if it were more attractive and more thickly populated."

"Up-marketed. Yuppified. NIMBYed. Gentrified."

"Densified."

"Is that even a verb?"

He gave me a look.

"Never mind. Let me go at this again. Why me? You know I'm a grouch. You said so yourself. It's been a while since my social work days."

"You were good at that."

"I did it for money."

He looked away out the window of his office, remembering perhaps when my paid job had involved his family. "Rich people are buying those lots and holding onto them," he said.

I guess I should have been flattered that we were in his office and not the boardroom, but I was edgy and chose to interpret that choice as feeling played.

"Gary, *you're* rich."

"*Really* rich people. People who couldn't spend all their money if they tried."

That sounded familiar.

He looked sideways at me. "Look," he said, "I know how you feel about rich people. I need someone up in their face. I need someone who doesn't care whether rich people like her or not. I need someone who can sashay into their offices and demand payback to the communities that made them rich, all in the name of community-building."

"You can do that. You're the mayor."

"I can't," he said. "I'm the mayor. They helped fund my campaign. I'm expected to suck up to them. They get mad when I don't. Some of them are legends in their own minds. You . . . it's possible that you have never sucked up to anyone in your life."

I couldn't help it. I started to laugh.

He actually flushed a little. "I don't mean that how . . . you know what I mean. You aren't biddable. That's your value-added, right there."

"Gary, I love you," I said between guffaws. "You are such a bullshit artist."

"Yeah, that's what my wife says," he said, grinning. "So I've got you, right?"

But he wasn't a bullshitter, of course, at least not much. That's why I liked him. He was as honest as a person can be in his position, and then a little bit extra. Which made voters like him and the Chamber of Commerce nervous. In my not-so-humble opinion that was the right order of things.

"Okay, I'll think about it," I said. "But if I do it, I'm not your creature."

"Of course. But don't think too long. I want something brought to the table by early summer. I want to have to call the planners in and say, 'Here's this citizen group. They're putting on the heat. They need us,' and then get something preliminary to Council by fall. Well, to Executive Committee."

"Fast."

"There's no point wasting time," he said. "They're not making any more of it."

"Isn't that saying supposed to be about land?"

"That too."

32. APRIL FOOL

Priscilla Gill's book event was at a big independent bookstore downtown that had stood up to the big-box threat and not only lived but thrived. It was the last remaining full-service independent since the owner of the other one in town had died, sadly too young.

All the big names came by here on their tours — those who still had in-person tours, that is. So, there was Pris's photo — a photo designed to make everyone in the world, no matter how heterosexual and/or cisgender, want to have her or be her, or both — in very fancy previews in the paper, on TV, and on social media. Other online ads too, she said, but I had become savvy and had Adblock Plus™, so those I didn't see. But I do have a radio, and every time I turned it on, some CBC or CKUA host was interviewing her. I felt like those people who think parked cars send them messages: I couldn't get away from her face and her voice.

Despite a late snowfall in the last week of March, which was still melting in gutters and under trees, April 1 was, of course[16], a balmy spring day, which means that if it had been fall I would have been shivering in gloves and a scarf, but because it was spring, I was so happy to have lived through another deep freeze that I was walking around with my coat unbuttoned, just like half the teenagers in town and three-quarters of the businessmen. (Oh, I forgot. Businessmen never button their coats anyway. All that capitalism keeps them warm.)

Pris and I were to meet for dinner beforehand, then her publicist was going to whisk her off to the store, and I would follow, a small and humble claque.

Or not so humble. But very very small, anyway.

We had arranged to meet at the sushi restaurant nearest to the bookstore. Something about spring made me think of raw fish. Well, face it, I can be convinced to think of raw fish in almost any season and any time of day. But never mind that. When I arrived at the restaurant and asked after Pris, I was ushered to a private

---

16. I mean, what are the odds in this part of the world, where April has all the spring snowstorms that January missed? But Pris always had a silver spoon up her ass, or whatever the right body part is for that idiom.

room — and discovered it had turned out to be a blind date. Pris was accompanied by Nathan Lockwood and ABC Chiles.

Despite the unseasonable high of 13 degrees Celsius, Chiles was wearing the sheepskin coat. It had a stain on the sleeve that could have been anything from hot chocolate to blood, but although it seemed weathered-in, the stain hadn't been there three and a half months ago. He didn't have the curly-corded FBI-agent earpiece any more. He grinned at me. Grinned. Fuck off, I thought but didn't say. Sometimes I am polite.

Lockwood was wearing another overcoat of a stupendous softness, less bulky than his winter one but still cashmere. I know because he hugged me. I was so surprised I hugged him back. His coat was buttoned, but in a casual way, thus respecting local culture while being more sensible than us.

I looked at them, then her.

"I know," said Pris. "It was just us. But I promised to tell you a story, and these guys are part of it. It isn't very interesting. Compared, say, to my new book, which you have read all of already, in bits. But they were coming anyway, for the launch, so whatever."

"Don't be a smart-ass," said Chiles, sounding fond.

Lockwood laughed his cute little laugh.

I blinked.

"It's kind of simple, actually," said Pris. She tucked her hand under Chiles's arm, and reached out for my hand.

"I want you to meet my boyfriend, Lockwood," she said, and joined my hand with Chiles's. "And his best friend, Nathan," and the impeccable Mr. Lockwood put out both hands and took my other hand.

This left me entangled in a mild kind of World Adventurer daisy chain, and also confused.

"I don't get it," I said. "Ambrose Bierce Chiles and Nathan Lockwood."

"Nathan Lockwood doesn't exist," said Nathan.

"We made him up," said Chiles.

"He's both of us," said Nathan.

April fool.

Me, that is.

33. WE SHARED A SECRET INSIDE . . .

I would like to think I am the kind of person who can receive a world-class secret like that with savoir-faire. "Shut *up*!" I said. "What?"

Ah, well, we all have our self-delusions.

"We are him," said Nathan. "My name is Nathan Bierce."

"And I'm actually Lockwood Chiles," said Chiles.

"But nobody knows that," said Nathan.

"Almost nobody," said Pris.

"So don't tell," said Nathan and Chiles at the same time.

Completely gobsmacked, I promised I wouldn't tell.

The even-more fool I.

I was still gobsmacked half an hour later. I'd had a large amount of raw fish and a bit of sake by then, but, unusually, sushi hadn't helped. Of course my second question had been, "Why?"

"At first it was a kind of a joke," said Chiles. Who was really Lockwood. Said Lockwood. Said the tall blond weathered one, anyway. "Nathan just looked so much more like a real millionaire. We had combined our names for the company name, but people started asking for that guy, and we'd walk in a room and they would all automatically assume he was Nathan Lockwood and I was some kind of hired help. Kind of like in that old show — *Remington Steele*?"

"Just saw that on Netflix™ or somewhere," I said.

"We were only millionaires then," said Lockwood. Who was Nathan but not Lockwood. Said Nathan. Said the short, beautiful one.

"Apparently, real millionaires don't wear sheepskin?" I asked.

"Apparently. I had already changed my name once," said Chiles. Lockwood. "Inherited wealth can be a problem if you don't like who you inherited it from."

"Tell me about it," I said. The modest financial security I had now came courtesy some seriously problematic parents. I had only momentarily been a one-point-something-millionaire, before I spent most of my capital on an apartment block, but I remembered my moral dilemma.

Priscilla, however, snickered. There was a story there — and perhaps no inherited wealth? *Never mind that now*, I thought again.

"So no big deal to change it again," he continued, "and you can call yourself whoever you like if you don't do so for fraudulent purposes."

"And I was happy to leave behind some sad stories too. So we kind of went with it. Then it became a security issue," said Nathan. "Nobody knew us as ourselves by then. Nobody we didn't like, anyway." He smiled bewitchingly at Pris, but she was feeding uni to the other, er, real Lockwood — Lock, she called him — and didn't notice.

"So who invented that smart paper?" I asked.

"He did," they said in unison, pointing their chopsticks at each other as if they were in sketch comedy, then laughing uproariously.

Pris laughed too. "They compete on things like that."

I drank some o-cha and glared at them all.

"The only problem," said Lock, "is that if you want to hang out with someone as yourself, both of yourselves have to do so. So he was always with us," gesturing at Nathan.

"And I did not think I was a ménage-à-trois kind of girl," said Pris, "so we broke up."

"And then," said Lock with commendable menace, "the asshole happened."

"And changed us *all* into people we didn't want to be," said Nathan.

34. THE TALL BLOND MAN WITH ONE BLACK SHOE

I will now return to our previous programming. Sort of.

The shorter, more glamorous one is going to be called Nathan from now on. Because everyone always calls him Nathan anyway. Because it's his name. And since Lockwood isn't Nathan's name anyway, it doesn't matter.

The taller one will be called Lock, which is his name, but sometimes Chiles if necessary in public, or maybe ABC if I get annoyed, or something else, depending on how I feel about him at the time.

And we will all know who we mean when we say Nathan. Right?

The short guy.

And we will all know who we mean when we say Lock or Chiles, right?

The tall guy.

(Of course, if anyone says Bierce we will all be confused, but that's minor.)

"So, the other question you said you'd answer is where you went when you disappeared from the Union Bank Inn. Give over."

"Sure, no probl—" Pris's gaze shifted to above my head. "Damn," she said. "Time to go."

"Hold on a minute," I began. You can't just bug out again . . ."

"No, really, time to go," she said.

"Everyone ready?" chirped the publicist from beside my elbow. I jumped.

"Sure," said Priscilla brightly. "Tell you later," she said to me quietly. Lock went over to pay the bill. Nathan helped me into my coat.

That made the glass half full, where disclosure was concerned. I looked over at Chiles and saw that despite the brown-and-tan theme of his attire, he was wearing black shoes. Reminded me of the title of a great European movie.

I hung back briefly and caught Chiles coming back from the till. "So," I said, sotto voce, "that *was* you at the folk club."

"I like to check out everyone that Pris associates with — that *we* associate with, I mean."

"Personally?"

"Well, me or my people."

"You have 'people'?"

"Of course we have people!" He grinned at me. "We have to have people."

"I mean you personally. You personally have 'people'."

"I *am* head of security," he said. "I really am. That's not a pose."

Pris came up between us and linked arms with us both. "Come on!" she said. "We'll be late!"

So off we went to make Pris just a little more famous and rich . . . and afterward to make all of our lives far more complicated and dangerous than any of us wanted them to be.

35. ". . . KNOCKIN' 'ROUND THE ZOO . . ."

There were no bars on the windows and the spoons were compostable plastic, but the launch was definitely a zoo in the James Taylor / madhouse sense of the word.

When we arrived, there were already at least a couple of hundred people in the store with copies of Pris's book under their arms — and people were still arriving. They kept arriving for hours.

Pris did a reading to a huge crowd downstairs, then they all unsardined themselves and stampeded up to pick up copies (if they hadn't already) and line up for her to sign. Pris was set up at a table between the door and the till, with her back to the window so she faced the whole store, which was teeming — I think I can use that word about what was basically an animal book — with Gillites, or Gillians, or whatever her fans would be called.

I had my free gift copy of the book signed before anybody else, with a kiss on the cheek from Pris as she gave it back, which left them all wondering who I was. Sharon and Steve, the store owners, wrangled the customers admirably, but the place was still beyond crowded, a bit steamy, slightly slushy, and loud. Really loud.

I sidled away from the lineup and circled around the very back of the store. I spent some time in Mystery, went over to Science Fiction and Fantasy, then worked my way back around the rest of the store, past the peculiar little lift they have, through Queer Culture and Gender Studies to World History. Not wanting to force my way through the scrum around Pris to get to the stairs, I went down to the lower level in the lift, which is the clanky kind they install in old churches and libraries to bring them up to code re: accessibility, where you have to hold the call button down until the lift arrives, and the floor button down all the time you are in it, or it sticks halfway) to the kids'-lit section, and looked at picture books for a while. But the hubbub from upstairs was distracting, and I wondered if I should show more support to my friend. So I ascended the main stairs into the throng, and pushed through to the back counter with the wide array of snack plates on it. One plate of goodies was gluten-free and corn-free, and one was vegan, but I stuck close to the bacon-wrapped scallops, and ate the last seven[17] that had been left[18] amid a chaos of discarded toothpicks.

----

17. Or maybe nine. Not as many as thirteen, I'm pretty sure.

18. Srsly, people, you left bacon-wrapped scallops just lying there?

Pris looked up and saw me, and made a beckoning gesture. I pushed past the line to stand behind her at the signing table, and leaned over with my ear beside her head.

She turned to whisper "Don't leave!" into my ear.

"Don't worry! They love you," I whispered back.

"There's a guy in the line I don't like the look of," she said. "He's giving me the creep-eye."

"I'll tell Lock. Er, Chiles."

"Over there behind the pillar. By that woman with the red coat. He has a tractor cap on. Green scarf, I think."

Given in what part of the world we were crammed, there were more than a few guys in tractor and baseball caps, but I dutifully told both Lock and Nathan, and stayed leaning against the New Fiction shelf as about another twelve million people, at least one-fifth of whom had some sort of beaked cap, got books signed.

The astonishing ziggurats of books around the store dwindled to zero, and by the end of the evening, despite using up another two boxes Nathan and ABC had in the trunk of their car, Pris was also signing promissory bookplates for those who hadn't snagged a copy, and looking bedraggled[19].

There was still a long line, some with books and some with bookplates.

The line took a long time to progress past the table. It was amazing how many of the people thought they had known Pris way back when. Some of them she even recognised.

Yet another guy with a cap presented a book to Pris, and she reached out for it tiredly, hardly looking up as she said, "Would you like me to sign it personally?" He leaned down and mumbled something.

---

19. Ever thought about that word? Be-draggled. Bed-raggled. It's a very sexy word.

She was already writing her name when he bent over the table. When she was done, he said something else, very quietly, then turned as he straightened up, left the book under her clenched hands, and pushed past the crowd at the till. Pris put it aside absently, then seemed to wake up. She tugged my arm, and when I leaned over her, I lost sight of him.

Pris's face was ashen.

"I think that was him — Brad Mowbry!" she whispered. "The stalker. The guy who attacked me."

WHAT IS THE MATTER WITH MARY JANE?

36. "... I'LL BE WATCHING YOU ..."

I popped up a lot faster than I had leaned down, and swivelled to scan the room. I saw a dark-haired man with his back to me, green scarf in his hand, other hand lifted to remove a cap, disappearing around the corner by the elevator as if he were browsing World Religions.

"He's lost weight . . . dyed his hair . . . but that voice! And who else would say . . ."

"Shall I call the p—"

"Lock! And get Nathan!"

But when Lock and I pushed through the crowd of autograph-seekers to the back corner of the store, no-one was there at all. The little elevator was on the lower level, and in the basement, we heard its door slam shut.

Lock pushed the button.

"Never mind that," I said. "Those things take forever. Head him off at the stairs." Lock pulled out his phone, and behind Non-fiction Bestsellers, I saw Nathan answer his. Mine, of course, was in my coat pocket, locked down in the staff office. Chiles said a few words, then I grabbed his phone, pointing to Nathan and the stairs. Nathan went down, Lock struggling through the crowd to follow, while I watched to see that no-one came back up in the elevator. No-one did during the time it took for me to call the cops. Then I heard it groan into action again. I don't know what I would have done if Mowbry had been in it, but it was Lock's blond locks I saw. He looked up at me as the lift inched upward, and shook his head. I gave him back his phone.

I pushed back to the front table, where Pris sat staring, with an open book and a quizzical fan in front of her.

I leaned down again. "Are you all right?"

"I have to go to the bathroom," Pris whispered to me as she signed and handed back the book. "Can you hold them off for two minutes?"

"What am I supposed to do, play the banjo?"

It was a joke. Besides, I didn't have my banjo any more; I sold it last year, when I was poor, and it kept me in fish sticks for a month.

She gave me A Look. Good, she was going to be able to hold it together.

Nathan came back up the stairs, and over the tops of a crowd of heads, I saw him shake his head slightly and gesture in a way that made me think he'd discovered that back door through the stock room and knew the chase had been hopeless. Lock saw too, and turned away abruptly. Alone in the crowd at the top of the steps, Nathan snapped his phone open.

"Okay, go!" I moved aside, and Pris stood up.

The remaining people in the line groaned. "Don't worry, people," I said, as Pris slipped past me and went for the stairs. I saw Nathan tuck his phone back in its case and gesture, I assumed to Lock, and heard the elevator as Lock took it back down. "Ms. Gill will be right back. She's just going to answer a call of nature. You know how she feels about nature — when it calls, she answers!"

That got a laugh, but then they began to shuffle their feet. I didn't want them heading for the door after waiting so long, so I spoke up again. "So, people, while she's gone, why don't you turn to a person near you and talk about the first Pris Gill book you read? Or that first TV special you saw? Just imagine this is a travelling book club. Don't be shy — you are all part of the family of Priscilla Jane Gill readers!"

I thought they would all give that last bit the grimace it deserved, but apparently I'd hit a chord. Soon thirty or forty people near the table were creating a weird kind of intimate hubbub-within-a-hubbub, loud but not raucous. Actually, *really* loud, but not raucous — and it was spreading. And all of them, plus the other dozens, were still carrying their armloads of books.

Sharon was standing behind me. "Nice going," she whispered. "Can I steal that idea?"

"I thought that 'all one family' bit was too much."

"I guess not," she said, and grinned.

"It's amazing what people will buy," said Nathan into my other ear.

"You should know," I said.

"Hey, I'm not in retail!"

"Yet. I thought you said you wanted to lose some money! Or were you speaking as half of Nathan Lockwood, poor little billionaire trying to divest?"

"Lock has decided he prefers farming, wind, and geothermal research for that. But he also likes his money. I've decided to go for hemp for sustainable paper, and building affordable housing."

"For real?"

"Why not?"

"I *so* have a neighbourhood for you to look at."

"Yours? I bought two parking lots there last week."

"You're joking." Ah. So Gary had heard that line from the same place I had.

"I never joke," he said, and laughed out loud.

We talked for a few minutes, and it was actually starting to seem like a good idea to build some affordable housing, but suddenly, "Where the devil is Pris?" Lock said from behind us. He was still wearing his dead sheep, buttoned up, and he was starting to look a bit stoic. He was combing back his hair with wet fingers, as if he'd just washed his hands.

"I thought you were downstairs keeping an eye on her," I said.

"I came up," he said. "Everything was fine down there. I went through the storage room and everything."

I realised Pris had been gone almost ten minutes. Had the stalker been down in the lower level after all and Lock missed him? The three of us looked at each other.

Just then Pris came up the stairs two at a time. Her cuffs were wet and there was a wet stain on one arm of her silk shirt. She was sucking at a small scrape on one hand.

"Sorry, something with the taps," she said. "They are practising to be a fountain. There's water all over the bathroom floor down there — sorry to mention it, Sharon."

"Oh, damn, they were supposed to get that fixed today," Sharon said.

"It's okay, I got them turned off," and Pris rolled up her sleeves and went back to signing. I noticed she was sweating, though the bookstore was none too warm with so many people going in and out the doors near the table. Sunny day past or not, it was still only April 1.

Over the rest of the evening, both Nathan and I also took our turn in that washroom with the leaky taps. Alone.

Which, it turned out, made us all fools — but 20/20 hindsight is a wonderful thing.

37. CILANTRO GARNISH

The crowd was gone, the staff was cashing out, the buffet plates were a wasteland of cilantro garnish and stray capers, and Pris was exhausted. She sat in the stockroom with one boot off, massaging her bare foot. I couldn't help noticing, despite my efforts not to stare, the peculiar scars there.

She saw me looking.

"Courtesy my stalker," she said.

"He stabbed your *feet*?"

"Twice each. Luckily with his blade parallel to the bones. It went in between. Only nicked one bone, and even bypassed some of the tendons. Still hurts when it's going to rain, though." She put her boot back on. "I'm heading out. I'll call you tomorrow."

She picked up her bags, and she and Lock headed back to the main store. I heard her saying, "Thanks for everything, you two!" to the store owners, and then a clatter of feet on the front stairs.

I looked at Nathan. "So. Are we on our own then?"

"I guess so. They haven't seen each other for a while. Want to get some strudel at the Bistro Praha?"

"Sure!"

"Thanks for helping with Pris up there."

"No problem. Do you think it really was the guy?"

"Maybe, maybe not. That's been the problem all along. Since he was released, she's been seeing him everywhere. Why the *hell* they gave him parole . . ."

"Before he made parole too."

"Yeah, but that was us."

"Are you sure? Just because you're being followed, doesn't mean you're paranoid. This is the woman who can face down pirates and wild predators, and remembers what to do when an alligator charges her."

"What *do* you do?" Steve came in and thumped the pile of books he was carrying down on the packing station.

"Get under the water," I said. "Then you look too big to eat and their tiny minds lose interest. Apparently. Anyway, that's what she did in that Everglades special, and it worked. But only if it's an alligator. Crocodiles don't care. Could you remember that in a crunch?"

"Not me!" Steve grinned. "Mind you, I'm not likely to be wading in a swamp in the first place."

"Wait a minute! Did Pris say it's actually going to rain? I left the top down!" said Nathan.

"I thought you came in the limo."

"Lock and Pris came in the limo. He likes that thing. I have an IQ convertible. Steve, can I get back in if I go out from down here? I'm parked at the side."

"Sure," Steve said. "Just use that brick up there to prop the door open — it locks automatically. Or you can just go out that way and come back in the front." He popped the escape bar of the lower back door, then zipped out front again, and I heard him on the shop stairs, talking to Sharon as they went up.

The back stairs were rigged with a kind of slide for deliveries, which took up half the stairs. Nathan ran lightly up the stairs beside it, and I heard the door at the top bang open. I turned back toward the storeroom.

A moment later there was a series of noises I hope never to hear again: a sliding rasp, a strangled cough, and a hard, wet thump. Something heavy hit the wooden slide and hissed down it.

Nathan's tumbling, uncontrolled form sprawled off the end of the cargo ramp and into the room. Unconscious or — I hoped, just unconscious.

He'd fallen so freely.

38. 911

My new cell phone was good for something. The 911 operator was calm, where I wasn't. By the time she had me looking at Nathan for vital signs, he was stirring and waving his legs and right arm around. By the time I'd told her the circumstances, he was trying to sit up — no, succeeding.

"Stay on the line," said the operator.

I managed to put the speaker function on, and set the phone down while I leaned over Nathan.

"Ow, fuck," he said. "Call the cops."

"Ambulance is on the way," I said.

"Cops," he said. "Somebody attacked me."

"Did you hear that?" I said to the air.

"Yes," said the operator. She added police to the mix, and asked me to report on Nathan's condition.

"I can hear you," said Nathan. "I think my left wrist might be broken. My head hurts like the devil. Everything hurts, but after my arm, my head is worst. Neck's okay so far, and I can move all my fingers and toes."

"Just stay calm, sir."

"I climb cliffs," he said. "Sometimes I fall off them. I've been through this before. In the wilderness. I am calm."

"Okay, sir. But I want you to just stay on the ground until the paramedics get there."

"I can hear a siren," I said.

"That may be them. They are nearing your location."

"Cops," said Nathan. "Tell them to be careful. The guy hit me with something big and hard." He looked at me. "And no jokes from you." Already he knew me?

I heard the siren stop outside, then another siren approaching[20].

"The emergency vehicles are in your location. They are in the alley. Have you left the scene, ma'am?"

"No," I said.

"There is only one individual there. He is on the ground. Is that you, sir?"

"No," said Nathan. "I'm inside, at the foot of the stairs, where the guy shoved me." He paused. "Down which the guy shoved me."

It was at that moment that I knew we'd sleep together. Anyone who can be careful of their grammatical structure even in a crisis was someone I could love. Or after whom I could lust, at least.

"In the basement of the store," I said.

"Ah, did you strike the attacker, sir?" said the operator.

"What? I opened the door and he — well, I think it was a he — bashed me. And when I grabbed at him, he shoved me. Last thing I remember is falling backward down the stairs."

"Well, you were certainly knocked out by the time you got down here," I said.

"And it hurts like a sonuvabitch too," he said. He was trying to stand up. I pressed down on his shoulder. Right shoulder.

"Don't! The paramedics are on their way!" I said.

"Hell with that. If I'm here, who's in the alley? Lock? Pris?"

He managed a credible rate of speed up the stairs, with the help of the right handrail to drag himself, while I followed him, still carrying the 911 operator, a reedy voice in my cell phone saying, "Sir? Ma'am? The paramedics are already —"

"I have to go now, sorry." I ended the call.

Just behind Nathan, I emerged from the stairs into the alley, and into a surreal chaos of flashing lights and urgent, cross-cutting voices. Two paramedics, three firefighters, and two police

---

20. The Doppler effect is a wonderful thing.

officers crouched around a body lying in an awkward crumple in the alley.

Behind them, near the mouth of the alley, Lock stood with an arm around Pris, who was screaming.

Screaming? Pirates in the Philippines, crocodiles in Australia, kidnappers in Liberia, a polar bear in Churchill Manitoba, hijackers in Florida, hackers in a Silicon Valley crime ring, elephants in . . . I don't know, some Rift Valley place — in any case, a person who had seen more than her share of danger, including natural and unnatural death. And she was screaming. Or maybe it was more like projectile sobbing. Loud.

Lock shook her slightly, whispered something, and whatever he said worked — partially. Pris switched from wail to laugh, until Lock grabbed her face in his big left hand and turned it to him. His forceful words this time were loud. "Pris! Pris! Calm down!"

"It's gotta be him," she said, also loudly enough that everyone in the alley could hear her. "Look at that scarf. Mowbry. Somebody stuck a knife in *him* for a change . . ."

It was a guy in a cap and a green scarf, anyway. And someone had. There was blood everywhere from the scarf down to a pool around his feet.

"Shhh," said Lock.

"It wasn't me," Pris said. "I didn't do it."

39. BLOOD THREAT

The cops were moving gingerly to avoid the blood. The others weren't. One of the paramedics sat back on his heels and shook his head. He reached over and pulled the other one's arm, and she stopped trying. The firefighters stepped back, and only then seemed to be aware that their boots were soiled with slushy blood. The paramedics began cleaning blood off, pouring some solution over each other — I assumed peroxide, to neutralise blood-borne threats.

A plainclothes cop walked around the corner and glanced at the tableau around the body. One of the uniforms shook her head and then tilted it toward Pris and Lock. Without hesitation the detective veered toward to them.

"Do you know this man, ma'am?"

Pris was still in her convulsive half-sobbing, half-giggling state of shock. Lock pulled her against him.

"She's very upset. She thinks it might be someone who . . . approached her at the book event tonight."

"Who?"

Pris pulled away from Lock, and seemed to pull herself together. He looked searchingly at her, and she returned his look and nodded. He let her go.

"I thought . . ."

"Ma'am?"

Unexpectedly, she pushed past him, walked through the EMS and cops like they were butter and she was a hot knife, reached down, and flicked the scarf away from the face.

"Fuck," she said quietly.

One of the cops grabbed her arm, but she was three inches shorter than Pris, and not a world-famous explorer. Pris drew herself up and stared the woman down. The woman let go. I'm sure that later she would be reprimanding herself, but it would have taken a stronger will than that of a rookie cop to resist that look.

Pris walked back over to the detective and said, completely composed now, "I don't know who it is. I thought it was someone who served time for attacking me with a knife, but I don't think I've ever seen this guy in my life, before tonight."

Another set of cops rounded the corner. One of them had his notebook out. Before he could speak, we heard more sirens. Another matched set of EMS responders (ambulance, fire truck) angled across the mouth of the alley, while another cop car stopped across the street. Its cops came over at a run, stopping dead when they saw the plainclothes detective.

He raised an eyebrow at them, that was all.

"Sir? We're re-responding to the assault call? Is that the victim?"

"Assault complaint?" said Eyebrow to the world at large.

Nathan was still standing beside me. He'd tucked his left hand between the buttons of his cashmere overcoat. He looked a little like Napoleon if played by Mahershala Ali, but grimacing. "That'd be me," he said. "And I could use those paramedics, here and now . . ."

We walked toward the mouth of the alley, keeping close to the wall to avoid the body and all its acolytes. I couldn't help but notice the blood spatter dripping down the wall.

Meanwhile, the detective had pointed his power-eyebrow at Notebook Cop.

"Um, stalker?" So maybe his nerves came from the ninety-minute-plus response time to our earlier call.

"That'd be Priscilla," I said, pointing to her where she now leaned against a dumpster across from us, Lock beside her.

"Come on . . ." Detective Eyebrow was about to rip some dispatcher a new one, but it wasn't fair.

"It was three cases," Lock said. "At the time."

"One and the same case now," I said. Only one cop heard me but it was the right one. From behind me, a familiar voice said, "Do not meddle in the affairs of dragons . . ."

"Roger!" That wasn't me signifying assent. It's his name. My pal Roger, chief of Major Crimes now, or whatever they call it. Homicide included.

41. "ANOTHER SCREWY ONE, LOOT?"

"What the hell are you doing at a crime scene?" Roger demanded.

"Lovely to see you too. These are my friends Nathan and, er, ah, Chiles. And you know Priscilla Jane Gill, I believe."

My pal Denis claims Roger only growls when he sees me, which Denis has from a good source, given Denis is sleeping with Lance, and Lance, as I mentioned, works under Rog's command. But I think it's something all cops learn in cop school, like maybe it's a police dog communication thing they have to practise, so Roger figured he would get some use out of it later. Or maybe they learn it from, oh, maybe bears, on those paramilitary wilderness bonding weekends the new chief goes in for. To give him credit, Roger only growled for a moment, then turned it into a cough.

"Sir?" Eyebrow gestured with his chin (which is harder to do than it sounds) toward his little coterie of constables.

"Yeah, I just happened to be driving, heard it on the radio. Sounds like a —"

"— 'screwy one, Loot?'" I said involuntarily.

Roger is also good at glaring, and apparently he has read the Frances and Richard Lockridge novels. "You took the words right out of my mouth," he said. "I asked you what the hell you are doing here."

"I heard you the first time," I said. "I'm here because Priscilla was launching her new book tonight, and Nathan and, er, Chiles over there, were with us. We called a while ago because one of the fans resembled a former stalker who attacked Priscilla a couple of years ago. Then, after the launch, when Nathan and I were leaving, someone assaulted Nathan. Pushed him down the stairs. So I called again, 911 this time. Meanwhile, Chiles and Pris found a corpse in the alley, and called it in. At least, I think it was them. Maybe it was Sharon and Steve, who own the store. Third call. Claro? Nathan thinks his arm is broken, and he may have other damage, so could we maybe change up the order of things around here?"

Eyebrow whistled — reinforcing my dog-training theories — and the new paramedics trotted over, each with a firefighter behind — to protect her? Or whatever their weird deployment model is about.

Within moments Nathan was sitting in the warmth of an ambulance, gingerly easing the coat down over his damaged arm. One of the paramedics had moved to cut his sleeves, but he stopped her with A Look. A moment later, when she took his overcoat from him, she must have understood why, because instead of dumping it on the ground, she folded it gently, giving it a little pat before she set it aside. I suspect it cost about half her annual salary. They went through the same process with the butter-suede jacket underneath. There was something wrong with the way Nathan's arm moved that had me feeling queasy as I watched. (Nauseous ≠ nauseated, by the way: it was nauseous, and I felt nauseated.) I thought because of the blood that it might be a compound fracture.

He was about to try getting out of the sweater, but by this point blood was seeping through its exquisite threads and the paramedic remembered that she was the one who was supposed to be in control.

"Stop that, sir. You have a compound fracture." Aha. Am I good? "I'm going to have to stabilise that and get you to hospital. Please lie down on the stretcher."

At this point I decided that I would rather talk with Roger than transform splinting a compound fracture into a spectator sport. I didn't want to find out the hard way that it was going to escalate in nauseousness.

"Look," I said to Roger. "It's like this —"

I was interrupted by a siren. The crime scene investigation unit had shown up. The street was getting crowded and very flashy.

"Go inside," said Roger. "I'll see you all later." He turned to Eyebrow, and pointed to me. "This one is unlikely to be guilty — of that —" he gestured toward the body "— but that doesn't mean you should leave her alone with any of the rest of them. She likes to figure things out — creatively. Using annoying bursts of initiative. So take them in the store, get them all settled, and keep an eye on them to see they don't concoct any fiction. On second thought, make some of these bozos here do it. It's a circus out here. Wait. You, I can use."

I started to walk away. "I mean *you*," said Roger. He meant me. I stopped, and the rest of the cavalcade left without me.

"What?"

"The stalker call came first," said Roger, "and it sounds like you."

"Um, yeah. Pris was busy with her fan base, and Nathan and . . . Chiles were chasing him."

"So . . . ?"

I explained the scene to Roger. I reminded him of why everyone had gotten so quickly worried in the winter when Pris seemed to go missing. I told him about the fan.

"So you saw the guy."

"Yeah. Sort of. If I had to swear to it —"

"Which you probably will," he interrupted.

"Duh. If I had to swear, it looks like the same jeans/sneakers/coat/scarf/hat combo. But I barely saw his face."

"Come here."

I knew where this was going, and pulled back, but he put an arm around my shoulders and hustled me over to the scene-of-crime truck.

"Give us some booties," he said. "I won't let her mess anything up."

Let me? *Let* me? Hmph.

The booties were slippery on the cold alley's icy pavement.

42. ". . . HWÆT HIS GASTÆ GODES OÐÐE YFLES/ÆFTER DEAÐ DÆGE DOEMED WIORÐE . . ."

An ex-person is a pitiful sight. Without the life force, their only relevant force is gravity. We tiptoed up to the head of the huddled mass now surrounded by a new batch of uniformed acolytes. Pris had already disturbed the scarf, so I could see the face. Not that I wanted to.

"Well, this guy's also Caucasian, and dark-haired. I can't see the eye colour, but I got the impression that the guy in the bookstore had kind of pale eyes. But . . . you do need to know that Priscilla moved the scarf. It was over his face before."

"Mnph. Some killers cover the face. Something about not wanting to be watched. Or he could have just fallen that way. Especially if they are going to mutilate afterward. Look at the job he — or she, of course — did on the feet . . ."

"I'd rather not, thanks. There is too damned much blood here."

"Sorry, I forgot it was you. Some people like this kind of thing. Let's get out of here, let these guys work. Take off your booties, turning them inside out as you do it, and give them to Annette here."

"Is 'guys' an ungendered word now?" I asked him as I followed instructions.

"Depends on who you ask," said Annette unexpectedly. "Some of them it bothers, but me, I figure there's a difference between 'guy' and 'guys'." She was grinning as she bagged our booties.

"Why do you do that, keep the booties?" I asked.

"Damned if I know," she said. "Ask one of those guys —" She pointed at the van.

"No, don't," said Roger. "So it's not the same guy? It is the same guy? What?"

"It's probably the same guy," I said. "Er. Person. Man? But in the interest of full disclosure . . ."

"What?" He glared. Why would he glare? I was being good.

"Pris thought she knew the guy in the store. And out here she said she'd never seen *this* guy before. And that hat looks kind of askew, and the scarf isn't actually *around* his neck, just over his shoulder, which is weird. So — any white guy in a heavy coat would look a lot like the guy in the store, if the hat and scarf got crammed onto him. And look at his feet —"

"What about his feet? Aside from the grisly obvious?"

"Have you ever seen Pris's feet?"

"Are you shitting me? Of course I haven— . . . oh, no. No. Not really?"

"Yeah, really."

He stopped with his hand on the bookstore door, held it shut while he looked at me. "Wait a minute. I notice you're not making some stupid pun."

"It's not funny," I said.

"You got that right."

"It's never funny."

"Right again."

"But you gotta laugh to prove you're alive."

He snorted and pulled the door open. "And besides, you couldn't think of one in time. Ha. I can think of five."

"Yeah, well, I'm an amateur."

"Yeah, and don't you forget it."

"'Guy'," I muttered as I followed him in. "'Don't you forget it, guy.'"

43. STAY OUT!

The others, aside from one cop sitting on the cash desk making sure people didn't come in off the midnight street and commit literature theft, must have gone downstairs to the office. Roger stopped me at the top of the stairs.

"Stay out of it," he said.

"You always say that," I said.

"I always mean it," he said. "Look what happened last time."

"That was totally not my fault."

"It doesn't have to be your fault," he said. "You just have to be there."

"Oh, come on! Just being there is too much involvement?"

"Ah, she gets it! Stay out of it means stay home. Don't call me. Don't call Annette, now that you know her name. Don't call Lance to try an end run. Stay out of it."

"In other words, not one foot over the line." Weak, and poorly timed, but I don't like dead bodies.

"'Too little too late, girl'," he said, righteously quoting one of my favourite cartoonists, and took the stairs three at a time.

I followed more decorously. Not by choice. Those stairs are steep, and he's very tall. Me, not so tall.

44. "THINGS DON'T LOOK TOO GOOD FOR MARIANNE..."

Helping the police with their enquiries, even when it's not a euphemism, is tiring. It took the rest of the night to sort out the basics.

Roger had been at the scene as part of his supervisory duties. He said he only really stayed because I was there and that made him suspicious. I think the truth is that his new, more administrative position bores him. He's great in the field.

Eventually I would get the chance to say "I told you so" about moving up a step. His colleagues are going to have to put up with a new, more hands-on management style whether they like it or not.

Eyebrow wasn't keen on it. He was about the same age as Rog and me, and I could see that "we had the same rank, and now you're my boss" vibe happening between them. It also seemed to me to have an edge of "we applied for the same job and you got it"— which, I confirmed later with Roger, was exactly the case.

Eyebrow finally convinced Roger to go home. Then he set up in the office and went through the whole routine of interviewing Sharon, Steve, the two bookstore staff members who had still been there when the red lights started flashing, Pris, Lock, Chiles, and me.

After a while he let Sharon, Steve, and their staff go home.

Pris had been exhausted at the end of the book launch. By three in the morning she looked like a very attractive limp rag. She and Chiles, whom I now had to remember to call Lock sometimes, were sitting in the back row of the chairs that had been put out for the event, and she was half-asleep, leaning against his camel-hair sweater. Apparently camels live in places where it goes down to minus 40 degrees (which is the same in both Celsius and Fahrenheit, if there are any pre-metric types in the room), and their hair is very warm. Who knew there was a camel-combing industry? And why was Lock wearing the hair of camels and the skin of sheep on a fine spring day such as April 1, now sadly history, had been? He must have no sweat glands, I thought at the time.

Lock looked half asleep too, but was tapping away on his cell phone. Apparently it was daytime in Dubai, or midafternoon in Mumbai, or buffet-time in Beijing, or something.

I had lain down across a row of folding chairs, but assuming a position of rest wasn't helping. I was just in the process of levering myself back to a sitting position when Eyebrows broke the huddle he was in with his peeps, all of them crowded into the children's-books section.

"Priscilla Jane Gill? I'd like you to come down to the station with us."

Pris looked up at him, confused.

Lock got there first. "Is she under arrest?"

"Just helping us with our enquiries."

Really. How original. The guy must watch a lot of TV.

"What's your name?" Lock said, and resumed tapping, furiously now, on his cell phone.

45. THE GROUP W BENCH

Eyebrow's name got quite the workout in the next ten minutes, while he got quite the workover.

Have you noticed that in books people call each other by name all the time, in every circumstance? But in real life, not so much, except in certain extreme circumstances. In this case, Lockwood Chiles was certainly not moaning, "Rodney! Rodney! Oh, Rodney!" so we have to go with the other explanation for bearing down heavily on a first name: he was exhibiting that boardroom dominance behaviour that probably helped him and Nathan turn their original garage-written oil-patch software into a multi-billion-dollar multi-interest multi-national.

"So, Detective Horenko, or maybe I can call you Rodney, since we'll probably be spending more time together. So, Rodney, let me understand this better. The police service, well, actually, you, Rodney, plan to take Ms. Gill here, who has had an exhausting and emotionally draining day, to the police station for questioning, when there is no proof she was in any way involved in a crime. Instead of letting her return to her hotel and questioning her there tomorrow at a decent hour."

"Assuming she's there when I get there tomorrow."

"Seriously, Rodney? Do you really think she is a flight risk? Just look at her."

We all looked over at Priscilla. She looked like some exotic raptor, even now, drooping in her chair. Particularly now, in fact, as her expensive peasant gear and trailing scarves gave the impression of ruffled feathers, while her drooping eyelids, her hooked nose, and bent posture accentuated her dangerous, predatory aura. She looked like an adventuress whose reputation had been earned, not flimflammed for her by publicists. She looked like a woman who would take revenge on an attacker by killing him the same way he had tried to kill her, foot mutilation and all.

She looked like a flight risk.

Chiles saw it too, and switched direction.

"Rodney. Let us be reasonable people together. Here is my business card. We are all staying at the Union Bank Inn —" I almost grinned. Apparently they were making amends for the winter debacle the best way rich people can make amends to a business, by putting their money overtop where the fuckup was "— and we want to go there and sleep. Ms. Gill will be available for interviewing tomorrow, after she has rested —"

"Yeah, and concocted her story with the help of some high-priced lawyers," Horenko said. I had to hand it to him. The business card hadn't fazed him, nor had the camel-hair. Mind you, if I hadn't read a Hammacher Schlemmer catalogue once, the sweater would have looked like a brown turtleneck to me, nothing special. Maybe it was the shoes that convinced me. They were pretty special. But Horenko didn't care.

Lock looked down at Horenko. He was standing a little too close to him, but Rodney didn't seem to mind. He gestured to a couple of the uniforms and pointed to Pris.

"I'll keep your card. You can come along with her, if you like. Call your lawyers too, I don't care. But Ms. Gill does what I tell her to."

Lock, of course, objected.

"You don't like it?" Rodney said. "Okay, fine."

I tried to protest too. "Look, I was here too. Why not take me?"

Horenko just looked at me and raised his eyebrow. It was a good Look, I'll have to give him that. I would have to add it to my repertoire.

"Don't make me laugh," he said. "Roger says you didn't do it, I say, 'Sir yes sir'."

"Ha," I said. "I bet. You have exactly the same grounds to arrest me as them."

"You were in sight of witnesses the whole time," he said. "Get the hell out of my way."

"So were we all," I said. "Except when we went down to the bathroom. We all did." I started to turn away. But my inner voice wouldn't. "Eat the rich, right?"

"*What* did you say?"

I explained. Oops. April fool again, though we were pushing the end of the fiscal April 1, the calendar day being long over.

I actually think what he did next was to try to both block Lock and passive-aggressively needle Roger, which is an example of how other people, often women or others perceived as low status, get used as pawns in male pissing contests.

So the media, who were by now hogging the parking spots all around the bookstore for their vans and SUVs, were treated to the sight of Priscilla Jane Gill and me — as revenge against Mr. A. B. Chiles, known associate of Nathan Lockwood, both of whom were too rich to arrest, and against Roger for getting the job Horenko thought he deserved — being escorted into two police cruisers in handcuffs.

They even did the thing to Pris where they guide the head of the person in custody into the car so it won't bump on the edge of the door. I thought that was just a TV thing. Live and learn. It's apparently because with cuffs on, people have a hard time with balance. The reason I know about the head thing is that my head also was gently muscled into the car by a young officer helping me not lose my balance despite the cuffs I also wore.

"First time I've been cuffed non-recreationally," I said to her. "I didn't like the recreational version either."

"Don't push your luck," she said, "and I'll take them off once you're in the car."

"And if I push my luck?"

She slammed the door just as I got my trailing foot out of the way.

Riding in the back seat of a car with handcuffs on is not comfortable.

46. SPRUNG

Eventually, they really do need to let you make a call, though not until Remand if they're really sticklers. But Rodney was clearly as beloved by his inferiors as he was by us, because all I had to do was ask and the cop escorting me into the temporary cells in the downtown HQ took off my handcuffs and stopped with me at the little phone kiosk in the welcome area of the cell block.

I used my call to get Roger on his cell phone and inform him of the situation. (How do I know Roger's cell phone number, when cops' cells come up private number on call displays everywhere? I'll never tell. Well, maybe sometime I'll tell, but not here and now.)

Then I went along to my cell (an unusual set of words for me, even in my misspent youth) quite contentedly, and had a nap.

Roger let us stew a long time — for him. It was almost an hour before Rodney, still smirking, let us out of the cells, Roger glowering behind him.

I knew, and Rodney knew, that the minute we were gone, Rog would rip him a new asshole, but Horenko was still strutting as he called a constable to take us out. He'd had his revenge.

Roger didn't let any of the undercurrents show, except that just before he and Horenko left us to the officer who was escorting us out, Rog leaned in close to me and murmured, "Stay out of it."

Like that was going to work, now.

I'd been handcuffed. Filmed by the TV cameras while I was being loaded into a cop car like a common — well, like a celebrity felon . . . hmmm. Celebrity felon? Maybe it wasn't so bad.

No, it was bad.

Rodney had made it bad.

So — as they say in the movies — now it was personal.

47. HOME AGAIN HOME AGAIN JIGGETY JIG

At home I met an angry cat. I had been gone one whole dark and hadn't left enough food. This was, as usual, All My Fault.

I explained about the events of the evening, and how I was one of the casualties of Horenko's pissing contest with Lock and Roger, and why that meant *I* was going to be finding out who the murderer was before Horenko, as *my* revenge.

Bunnywit raised his head from his salmon feast — an unprecedented occurrence. "Niaooow," he said. "Niaoow."

I should have listened.

SHE'S PERFECTLY WELL, AND SHE HASN'T A PAIN;

48. ENDING HOMELESSNESS IN OUR TIME . . . OR NOT

"So, as I told you, I bought some parking lots," the intercom said the next morning to me in Nathan's voice, after I figured out which end of the phone receiver was which. Takes me a few minutes to achieve binocular vision when I am wakened suddenly from a good dream. Well, a dream. It was the about eleven a.m., and I'd been asleep for four hours.

"Um . . . hi?" I said to the intercom.

"Don't we have an appointment today?" How diplomatic.

"After all that happened?"

"Especially after all that happened!" He sounded 'way *'way* too cheery. Hadn't a broken arm and hardly any sleep slowed him down? I was exhausted.

"Wait," I said, and took the phone away from my ear so I could shake my head and run my hand through my hair. I looked at my cat, and he looked back, then turned his face away.

"Niaoooow," said Bunnywit.

"I didn't think so," I said. I put the phone back to my ear. "Okay, come in, just sit down in the living room and wait. It'll take a minute . . ." I pressed the door release key and heard the buzz, then headed off to the shower. When I emerged from my bedroom ten minutes later wearing my best heavy silk-linen trousers and flowing silk shirt, Nathan was enhancing my easy chair, and Bunnywit was on his lap enhancing his cashmere coat, rolling all over it, leaving little swathes of short Manx-tortie hair.

"Bunnywit! Stop that!"

"It's okay. I invited him."

"Even so, that coat must have cost . . ." I blushed. Suddenly I had no idea how to talk with someone to whom a black cashmere coat was a purchase about on a par with — well, a box of fish sticks for me. The coat folded across his lap probably wasn't even the same one as last night. He probably went out and bought one that had no blood on it.

"You probably have . . ." I wasn't making it any better. "I mean, you got it cleaned pretty fast."

"Cold water and a pressing cloth. Does wonders." He grinned at me. I was astounded at how decorative he was, even wearing a fancy sling device on his left arm.

"You do your own stain removal?" Damned if I'd show him, even if I had put on silk.

"Always. I find you can't trust the underclass, don't you?" He laughed at my expression and got up, sliding nimbly out from under Bun and the coat, leaving them to their love-fest.

"Niaoow," said Bun, but it was clear that both Bunnywit and I were fighting a rear-guard action. We'd already lost the war.

"Don't worry," Nathan said gently. "I haven't been rich long enough to be too much of an asshole. I don't think."

"'Dear Lord, please give me the opportunity to prove that money won't spoil me'?" I quoted a desk plaque I'd seen once.

"Exactly. And if I do act like one, please tell me. But I'd be glad to give Bun— Bun— . . . ?"

"Bunnywit. It's short for Fuckwit."

"— Bunnywit this coat and all the other fine fabrics I own, just for the chance to see you blush like that again."

"I'm sure I can arrange it without you having to make that sacrifice. I have a habit of . . ."

That's how far I got before he put his good arm around my shoulders. He was the same height as me, which was going to be convenient in about three seconds.

"Thank you," he said, and kissed me.

After a while we had to breathe.

"For what?" I took the opportunity to ask.

"What? Oh, right. For last night. Help. Calling emergency. I could see that you weren't thrilled about what my left arm was looking like."

"Then. You *noticed* that? But you were . . ."

". . . not unconscious. Conscious, I notice things. And so, I think, do you."

"I notice that we are talking," I said.

"Terrible oversight," he said. We found other things to do with our lips and tongues for a bit.

After another while I said, "How the hell did you do stain removal with one hand strapped up?"

"I allowed a misapprehension. Lock did it."

"Lock is a real Renaissance kinda guy . . ."

". . . but only because I was saving my strength."

"For what?"

"For this."

Duh.

49. PILLOW TALK

I had learned a lot the year before about how to carry out amorous activities while protecting injured body parts, though then they'd been mine. I put my knowledge to good use.

Eventually we were back to talking again. Because eventually I am always back to talking again, and apparently in that we were soulmates. And of course, I asked all the questions I should have asked before we got naked.

"Nobody else waiting for you in one of those cities on the business card?"

"Not at the moment, no. I would have . . . well, maybe I would have mentioned something. You are a powerful intoxicant."

"Yeah, sure. You too, pretty boy."

"No, no-one waiting, or possessing. I have some exes and a partner who's — mostly — business."

"So does that mean you and Lock are . . . ?"

"Well, were. Sort of are. Sometimes. It's very cordial when we're not. He's kind of . . . Pris's now."

"Jealous type? Possessive?"

"Pris? A bit."

"I meant him."

"Yes. Well, yes, I guess so. Not as much as you might expect, actually. Given how competitive he is. Protective, but not too jealous? We grew up together. Well, teen years onward. Grew up as in became grown-ups. He was always bigger than me. Protective."

"And you?"

"Well, what's mine is mine. Sometimes. But that's stuff, not people. And even then . . . well, it's just stuff, you know?"

"You can always buy more?" But the minute it was out I regretted it, and said so. "Sorry. I should know better."

"Et tu, Brute?"

"Can't help it," I said defensively. "I have no idea how to deal with . . ."

But he was laughing. "Oh, don't give me that nonsense. I put my pants on one leg at a time. Or take them off likewi— . . . hmm, I guess that's wrong, isn't it?"

"The taking-off part? Yep."

"Actually, I'm not sure that I don't put them on more than one . . . oh, never mind. Come here."

"I am here."

"No, *here*."

So that was all right.

Soon it was more than all right.

50. SO . . .

The next day, Nathan tried putting his pants on both legs at a time, just to see if he could do it while standing up, and while doing so remarked: ". . . so, as I said, I bought a parking lot. Two."

"I heard you. All three times, now."

"Want to build some housing on them?"

"Personally?"

"In a manner of speaking. There would be project managers and the like."

"And what would we do?"

"Supervise for an hour every day, then come home to bed."

"Home?"

"Well, here. I like your place."

I like my place too.

Bunnywit just liked his jacket. That evening, when he came to take me out for dinner, Nathan showed up with a pillow made of cashmere.

"It's a scarf, really. I just doubled it over and sewed it up."

"Yourself?"

"Well, I borrowed the sewing machine and some thread from the tailor across from the wine store. But I had to whipstitch the edge shut after I stuffed it."

"Whipstitch? What the fuck is whipstitch? Never mind. You are some kind of Renaissance guy too?"

"Renaissance Я Us. I did it myself, honest."

He had filled the pillow with slightly-rustle-y material of some kind. It made a bit of noise if played with, not so much if slept on. I thought Bunnywit would not be that easy to manipulate. When Nathan put his folded coat on one end of the couch and the pillow beside it, Bun settled down on the coat. But the next time we surfaced he was kneading the pillow and purring, while the coat had been pushed onto the floor.

"I don't believe it," I said.

"Well, the couch is slippery. He probably just had to push a little and it slipped off."

"No, I mean I don't believe he did what you wanted him to do."

"The key to getting people to do what you want them to do is to convince them it's what they wanted to do anyway."

I filed that one away.

51. GIRLFRIENDS

"Get *out*! You and Nathan? Fan-*tas*-tic!" was Pris's opinion. We lunched at the tony restaurant in the Union Bank Inn. It was a far cry from the Double Greeting, where we could have both stuffed ourselves to immobility for the price of my appetizer at this place. But hey, she who treats chooses the restaurant. Pris was signing this to the tab on her equally tony room, which had a name rather than a number. The Hepburn, I believe. I would have to tell Hep.

"You approve, then," I said.

"Of *course* I d— . . . oh, you were kidding."

"Not entirely. You have known those guys a lot longer than I have."

"Nathan is a doll. He is a brilliant innovator, and he always believes the best of everyone, so people give him their best. It's a beautiful thing to see. I did enjoy being with him in all the ways. Back when I was."

"But you picked Lock."

"Eventually. I guess I like them . . . more dangerous. Lock has that mysterious-stranger thing going for him."

I saw Lock as stolid and taciturn, qualities that never appealed to me, but different strokes. "Mysterious?"

"Oh, his past and all that."

"I thought he was the outlier of some wealthy family."

"Only on Tuesdays. Ask him Monday or Thursday, you get a different story."

She delicately nibbled her cheese sandwich with its balsamic fig jam. The rich are not like us.

52. TUESDAYS

I had to admit, though, it was all delicious. The chef came out afterward to meet Pris. This kind of thing was obviously always happening to her. I was the mostly-invisible, possibly comic, sidekick.

We confirmed that the food had been artisan-brilliant and tasty, and were on our own again.

"Tuesdays," I reminded her.

"Oh, yes, he tells a different story every time you ask. I don't know how he keeps track, but he never repeats. What we know for sure is where and when he met Nathan, and what happened after that."

"We know that for sure, for sure?"

"Oh yes. About this stuff, he's quite happy to be accurate. After all, everything was uphill from there. Besides . . ." She nibbled more.

My mouth was full so I kicked her under the table. Nudged, only, really. We don't kick at the Union Bank Inn.

"Besides, who among us doesn't have something in their background they don't really care to have anyone know?" Her face seemed shadowed suddenly, as she hooded her eyes and concentrated a little too much on her arugula.

Despite our college association and our re-connexion, I knew very little about Pris's history, and she knew only the more visible parts of mine. "Amen to that, kiddo," I said around some mashed potatoes that tasted of lobster.

So where the hell *did* you go that time, Priscilla? But I didn't ask her. Yet. I figured I'd wait for a more private opportunity.

Alas.

Instead I went with another thing I needed to know for sure. "You don't still . . . you don't mind about me and Nathan?"

"Don't be silly. Jealousy? Me? Besides, you two are perfect together!"

After lunch, we were to meet Rodney Horenko at the cop shop. Apparently our statements needed polishing or something, though given the number of times we had been over them, you'd think he could have seen his face in them already. He claimed us at the gate and ushered us through security with a smarmy "Hello, ladies."

Ladies? For fuck's sake. "Hello, Rodney," I said, equally sweetly. "I can call you Rodney, right? Because we seem to be new best friends."

We walked ahead of Rodney toward the interview room.

"Come in with me," Pris whispered to me suddenly. "I hate that place. It creeps me out."

"That's the whole idea. They figure if you're creeped-out, you'll suddenly confess to anything to get into a nicer place. Criminals fall for that because they think cells are nice."

"We're trying to solve a murder, ladies," said Rodney from behind us. Why are people named Rodney often dicks? Some sort of anatomy/destiny thing. Naming and counting theory. You are what you are told to be.

Unfortunately, he was right this time, which is why we were there, not skiving off in the Hepburn Suite watching *Prisoners of Gravity* reruns.

"So, who was this guy, anyway?"

"What guy?"

"What a kidder you are, Rodney. The dead guy."

"Brad Mowbry. You know that."

"It wasn't him," said Pris. "It totally wasn't him. Mowbry had . . ." — she swiped her hand across in front of her face as if she were dusting off a picture — ". . . he was . . . Oh, never mind. I must have been . . ."

"She wants me to stay with her today," I said to Horenko. "She's feeling fragile."

"Fragile. She fucking wrestles crocodiles."

"It was an alligator," Pris said, "and it had a rubber band around its snout. Harmless. And they hate human flesh anyway. And I was too big. They had it all covered."

"Rubber band? Really?" Horenko said, his tough mask slipping. I imagined him at home, watching the nature channel, maybe with a wife and kiddies, or beering it up with his brother or his buddies, looking at the big bad adventuress wrestling the lizard. It made him easier to bear if I thought of him like that.

"Yeah, risk management, total control freaks. You know, there were lights and camera people and alligator wranglers and everything there. I had a lot of protection."

"And here I thought you were Crocodile Dundee or something," he said. "Geez."

No, she was just Alligator Dundee. Either way, 'way outside my comfort zone. But so was this, so clearly I have a very narrow comfort zone[21].

There was a prominent no-smoking sign in the interview room, but Horenko had one of those electronic cigarettes. He looked goofy, like a kid acting out a hardboiled detective. But he wasn't a goofy guy, and his disillusionment about Pris's heroic TV stunt just made him gruffer with her. I was glad I was there.

"Okay, let's go back to who was downstairs when you went to the bathroom. Because we haven't traced anyone who saw you down there."

"They were mostly all upstairs," said Pris. "I was pretty freaked out."

"You said that. But that was then, this is now, and Mowbry isn't stalking you any more. In fact, he's not stalking anyone ever again. So get over it and think!" When Pris hesitated, looking at him in shock, he said, "You're not a stupid woman. If you didn't do it, then whoever did was there, with you, in that basement, following Mowbry out the door. Who did you see there?"

"Ask Lock," I said. "He went down to cover Pris." They both looked at me. "I heard the elevator. And he came back later with wet hands. I thought he used the washroom too."

"Lock wasn't there," said Pris. "He was upstairs."

"Then where did he get wet hands?" I said. "There's no sink on the main floor."

"I'll ask him," said Horenko and Pris together, then glared at each other.

---

21. Unlike my Uncanny Valley, BTW, which is so shallow and wide that it may as well not exist.

I thought the glares were unfair. It was, after all, the reasonable next step. I intended to ask him too.

53. A HOUSE IS NOT A HOME

"Why are you staying in a hotel? I thought you lived here. My lawyer says you live here."

Nathan and I were eating — which was my joke — fish and chips of the frozen kind that come as fish sticks. Food of the underclass.

"Well, I sort of do."

"Sort of?"

He looked downcast. "I . . . sort of . . . I hate my house."

"What?"

"Lock's and my house, really. We bought it when we first made money. It represents . . ." He was silent for a long time.

"Come on, spit it out."

"A triumph of biddability over good taste."

"Biddable? You?"

"I was young. Younger."

"So sell it. Buy one you like."

"I can't just . . . For one thing, I leased it. Also it's jointly owned. Anyway I . . ." He flaked off three bites of fish, dipping each flake in the Kraft™ tartar sauce. "This stuff isn't half bad," he said.

"It's not half good either. Stop trying to deflect. What is going on with your house?"

"Lock talked me into it."

"Yeah, right, pull the other leg."

"We were living in it together at the time, remember? Before Pris."

"BP. The dating of the Nathan Lockwood empire. Pun unintended. Or maybe just accidental."

"It's big, it's ostentatious, and it's cold. Lock likes it. He's big."

"Why doesn't he live there, then?"

"Pris doesn't like it. She thinks it's big, ostentatious, and cold. But it does sort of . . . represent something. In our lives. And we co-own it. So as long as we do, that something . . . doesn't go away."

"It doesn't go away anyway."

"Yes, well, I get it, but this is Lock."

"Well, he can't like it that you leased it and stay in hotels."

"I did that while I was away, and the lessees are still there. That's my excuse, and I'm sticking to it. For now."

"Well, maybe you need to deal with it. You have an empire. You buy and sell neighbourhoods and mega-corporations. This is small."

"Nothing is small with Lock."

"Is he that hard to cross?"

"He has a temper." He chewed meditatively. "But it's probably me. I'm loyal."

"To a house you don't like?"

"If that's what it takes. I don't like arguments."

At the time, that seemed a virtue.

"How can you not like arguments? You're in business. Competition, wheeling and dealing, all that. Mixed message, some?"

He examined a piece of fish, then speared it on a tine of his fork and held it down to Bun.

"Niaow," said Bun, and then ate it. Mixed messages everywhere.

"How did you do that? He never eats fish sticks. We don't have to eat them either, you know. A joke's a joke. Business? Arguments?"

"Business is . . . fun. I actually make things. I talk people into helping, into using their talents for good. If there's arguing to be done, Lock tends to do it. He likes that thrust-and-parry stuff. It's a good division of labour."

He offered Bunnywit another piece of fish. Bun pawed it off the fork, then ritually scratched in front of it in the time-honoured litterbox-gesture of cat scorn.

"There, see? He says, 'Fool me twice, shame on me.' I told you he hated the things."

"I'll deal with the house," he said. "I promise. You do know why, right?"

I looked at him. I wasn't going to say it first.

"We have a future, don't we?" He suddenly looked vulnerable.

"Yes, we do."

"One hell of a future, right?"

"I think so."

"Because I love you."

"Yikes, that's fast!"

"Well? Too fast?"

I grinned and shook my head. "If it is, I'm not the one to say so. I'm finding you a bit . . . loveable too."

"So, I love you and you love me, and I want to have somewhere we can both be happy. Until then, I'd rather be here, with fish sticks from time to time."

"That's touching. But I'd like to see it sometime. Just for kicks."

"Niaow," said Bunnywit. I thought he was talking about the fish sticks.

He wasn't.

We should have listened.

54. BUILDING BLOCKS

Eventually saying "I love you" can become a habit, but at first it's a trigger for some serious physicality. If you get my drift. I would have to say it was some of my best physicality ever. There may have also been some schmaltz. I'll never tell.

At the approximate moment when an idiot would say "So, was it good for you too?", Nathan, who — as I have, I hope, established for you — was far from an idiot, said, "So, let's go talk to an architect."

Zing. He was always doing that to me. It was the "squirrel!" effect all the time when he was around. I'd say "kitten on a leash", but try Bunnywit on a leash and it's not a pretty thing, whereas this was . . . fun.

"Just any architect?"

"Short list of three."

"Is this something I want to do, or something you want me to want to do?"

"Both, I hope. Also, it's fun."

"Fun. You keep saying 'fun' like there's nothing else in life."

"Lately, feels like that, kinda. After all, making things is fun. Paying other people to make things you don't know how to make yourself is also fun. Getting wealthy from the things I made was fun. Giving presents is fun. Sharing good fortune is fun. In fact, being rich has been mostly a lot of fun. People who say money can't buy happiness —"

"— don't know where to shop!" we chorused.

"By the way, remind me and I'll take you to see my workshop later. Also we have to rent an office. And hire some people."

I was in above my pay grade.

"Nathan, what are we . . . I mean, what are you doing?"

"I'm starting a foundation to address homelessness through practical intervention. You, I hope, are advising me. Foundations need offices. They need people who aren't us to run them. They need, oh, boards and stuff."

"Stuff?"

"Technical term. Legal thing. Don't bother your pretty little head about it."

Pillow fight, then inevitable reconciliatory activities, then pillow talk again.

"Nathan, what are you doing? Really, what? Courting?" I got up and pulled on my robe, which is a vintage silk kimono with a dragon embroidered on it. I always feel patrician in that robe.

"No, I think we have courted. I'd say 'Been there, got the T-shirt', but we don't have a T-shirt. Want to have a T-shirt made? What should it say?"

"Concentrate!"

He laughed, and again I saw that resemblance to Pris, that tribal similarity.

"Was your family Armenian?" I said. "Iranian? No, wait, you have deflected me. Back to the original question."

"I am sure I have all sorts of complicated heritage, but my parents were not the kind of people who remembered all that. Functional families have history and stories; dysfunctional families have secrets and lies. As for what I am doing? I am . . . using my powers for good, not evil. I actually try to do this all over the place. Find pressure points, put some pressure on them, hope for long-term effects. It's a useful strategy."

"For getting rid of money?"

"That too. On the scale my accountants operate, this is the equivalent for me of pocket change for you. I've seen you dish out your change to the people downtown whom everyone else passes. You put a little bit where it might do some good."

"Or not. It might not, I mean."

"Yes, but how much are you risking? It's worth a try."

He bounced up and grabbed a T-shirt from the back of a chair. It happened to be one of mine. We wore the same size. I'd never had that with a male lover before. He wriggled into it as he trotted out to the living room. He came back with his briefcase. Well, with what passed for a briefcase, which was an extremely sleek leather cross-body bag just big enough to fit his tablet and a slim leather folder. And a stainless-steel woven wallet with his credit cards and passport in it. Maybe he also read the Hammacher Schlemmer catalogue. Except that he could afford to buy anything in it. And the store too.

I have to admit, affordable housing was better than those stupid pool buggies.

The folder had a number of sheets of familiar, thick, slightly oily-feeling paper: smart paper again, in slightly-bigger-than-norm size — the norm being typing paper this time. Soon we were sitting cross-legged on the bed staring at a few sheets that he had spread out, which were displaying interactive spreadsheets and very fancy son-et-lumière prospectuses. Prospecti? He had the sound off on these latter, and was shaking one piece of the paper to make it perform.

"Damn this stuff, Lock said he would do something about this bug. It has some kind of self-erasing algorithm trapped in there. *My* smart paper is far better."

"Yours?"

He gestured at the rest of the paper, lying there obediently being little computers. "Yes, Lock and I decided to have a race. We'd each have our own lab aim at smart paper. Mine is better."

"Not competitive, either, I see."

"Well, half-and-half. Something like this is kinda — teamwork. We just decided to stay out of each other's labs for six months or so, and his lab came up with the stuff just after mine did."

"Ha! He cheated, right?"

"No way! I did let a few things slip one night, but all's fair in love and drunken bets, right?"

"Hmph. He cheated."

"Well, so did I. I used all we'd done to date when I went ahead with my research. It was — er, fun, actually. It was like playing Mafia, or Thing. Have you ever played those games?"

"I used to play Mafia, but I decided it wasn't good for my soul. Cheating, deceiving with a kind face on."

"I hear you. Thing is better that way. Lock says he's trying for some kind of security wrinkle that makes it spyproof. I'm just trying for simplicity of function . . . so, look here. This is the business model for the neighbourhood revitalization. I've used it once before, on a smaller scale. It works very well."

"You know the mayor talked to me last week about this same stuff."

"Did he? I'm glad. When I saw him, he said he would make some calls."

I Looked at him. Were he and Gary playing me?

He saw my Look and divined its cause. "I tried to be subtle about it, so I didn't drop your actual name. I just said a friend of a friend bought a heritage apartment."

"Gary didn't drop your name either. He just said he knew some very rich folks were buying up land and he wanted me to keep them honest with some kind of community initiative."

"So, everyone does what they want."

"Except me. I am chivvied into action when I just want to stay at home with Bun."

"Yeah, and eat fish sticks. If I believe that, will you try to sell me a bridge in New York?"

"Funny, Gary used the same tired old joke."

He looked at me sharply. "If you're not interested, just say so. But my call is . . . you want something worthy to do. So do this."

I had to admit he was right, which I did tacitly by snatching the smart page out of his hand and looking at the budget on it.

"Holy crap. This is *pocket change*?" I took a breath, and another look. "Well, I guess it is. For you guys. But it will make a hell of a difference in *this* neighbourhood. In this *city*."

"That's the idea. Are you in?"

I looked at his lovely smile.

"Yes," I said. "I'm in. Heaven help me, but I'm in."

"Great. What are you doing Monday? I have to fly to Gaborone. Can you set up the office?"

"On Monday?"

He chose not to hear the tone in my voice, I'm sure. I'm sure it was a choice.

"Sure. I have someone from our HQ here lined up to help you, but you should pick out the furniture."

"Money no object?"

"Well, use some sense. This has to look like a place everyo— . . . oh, you were joking."

"Yeah, I was joking. Monday. Furniture. Fun."

"Get stuff delivered. I need to schedule meetings there on Thursday. A pal of mine is flying in to talk about the harm reduction component: Gabor; not to be confused with Gaborone."

"Gabor. Do you mean Doctor Gabor Maté?"

"Yeah, the doc consults on all my projects. He's a good guy. Edgy, but I like him." The foremost Canadian authority on harm reduction and addictions. Of *course* he and Nathan would be on a first-name basis.

"Yeah, 'cause with him there you aren't necessarily the smartest person in the room any more."

He Looked at me. "You know, that's probably true. But it's probably true here too."

"No, I'm not that smart. Just smart-aleck. There's a difference, you know."

He grabbed me and tipped us over.

"You're bored. That's how I know you're smart. I'm giving you something interesting to do. It's a present."

"Some people give diamonds or flowers. Or cashmere."

He laughed. "Some people are idiots. We don't have to do what they do."

I was pulling away to gather up the smart paper on the bed.

"Don't worry about that stuff. It's very durable."

But I gathered all the leaves and put them over on the night-stand where his little tablet already lay.

"Why do you still have one of these tablet things when you have this stuff?"

"Habit. It's more comfortable to type on. People expect it. Don't want the smart paper to get out there in the world just yet. Pick one or more of the above."

But soon we were busy elsewhere.

And then we went to see an architect.

Three, actually.

They were nice. Fun, one might say.

55. IT'S NOT MONOPOLY ANY MORE, DOROTHY

So I saw Nathan off to the airport in his cute little energy-efficient car — turns out the limo was Lock's idea of "fun", and rented — and all of a sudden I was running a foundation.

Temporarily, I was assured.

If I said that setting up that office was like herding cats it would be an insult to Bunnywit and other fine felines every-where. No, it was more like having a hangnail in winter. Every time you put your gloves on it catches on the lining. You can't clip it tight enough. You can't go without gloves. You can't avoid a paper-cut level of annoyance. And sometimes the gloves aren't any too warm anyway.

Okay, enough with the similes. I am trying to find an orig-inal way to admit I am just not a natural people manager. Once people have been given a job, you'd think they'd do it. But apparently not. Me believing they will is a problem.

By Tuesday I had three staff members, not counting Roma, the incredibly efficient "executive assistant" that Nathan had sent over from "HQ".

Roma was so organised that her pens were lined up by colour in a rainbow. I noticed this because mine were in rainbow order too, on the floor beside me. In my case it was for something to do while I waited on hold for the furniture people to tell me why their promised delivery hadn't shown up. I hadn't managed an improvised desk, but Roma had conjured up a piece of Good Wood, some bundled flyers, and two guys to carry it all into the empty office and set it up for her.

"You're treating them too nicely," said Roma. Did I say she wore a perfect size two suit, except possibly for the embonpoint, and was about half my age? Well, I have no idea how old she really was, but she looked twenty-one-going-on-twelve. This is how you know you are growing old, when perfectly credible people old enough to have legal sex look like preteens.

"Show me," I said, and handed her my mobile phone. She thumbed it, then waved hers over mine and gave mine back.

"Hang up," she said.

I hung up.

Turns out she had just poached all the numbers from my phone list (these may be the end times). She put her mobile on speaker so she could adjust the seams in her stockings while she waited for an answer. Seams? My *mother* had seams in her stockings. What is it with modern fashion? She then put her five-inch high heels back on. When did drag queen shoes become office wear? When Roma walked into the office in them, from my perspective, but I suspect it had happened elsewhere some time ago.

I began to feel old. Er. Older.

It took her five minutes to get the furniture delivery promised for two hours hence. She used professionalisms I had never heard and could only guess what meant, such as "someone's salty" and "I'm shook", and ones I knew, such as "Whatevs!", but gave no quarter when it came to the excuses at the other end of the line. But I wasn't salty about it; whatever works, right? (I have to say, I strongly suspect that Roma would look old to the people who sold me my phone, and that her slang was out of date. I was shook, as opposed to shaken or stirred, by this thought, but I reserved thinking on it until later. Years later, I hoped. Or whatevs.)

"I stand in awe," I said. "I'm going home. It's all yours now."

"Awesome," she said.

"That's what I said," I said. "You are now the executive director. Enjoy."

She just stared at me and adjusted her lipstick with one little finger. "Whatever," she said. "Thanks, I guess."

And that was my foray into charitable foundation administration.

I'm still on the board, of course, but that's a whole different story. On the board, you just have to show up and have ideas.

Then Roma makes them happen. Whatevs.

These *are* the end times.

56. £500 A YEAR AND A ROOM OF ONE'S OWN

"Do you still have a chequebook?" Nathan asked me the next afternoon. Back from across the world, with no sign of jet lag. The man really was made of Teflon™.

"Somewhere around here. Why?"

"I need a void cheque."

"What for?"

"The foundation."

"Why do you need a cheque of mine for the foundation?"

"Ask me no questions and I'll tell you no lies." He grinned at me. I glared at him as long as I could stand it, but I ended up giggling.

Me.

Giggling.

"Trust me. I'll tell you in a minute. It's perfectly legal."

"Why wouldn't it be legal?" I said.

He snickered. Almost a giggle.

"Hanging around with you has me not recognising myself," I grumbled as I dug my chequebook out of my shoulder bag and handed it to him.

"Well, likewise, so shut up," he said fondly, and went back to tapping his keyboard.

Two could play at that game. I had bills to pay, so after a while I went online and signed into my credit union account.

When the account balances displayed, I let out such a shriek that Bunnywit came running in from the bedroom, skidding on the hardwood as he turned the corner.

Nathan had leapt up too, and the two of them danced around each other for a moment. "What? What's the matter? Bun, look out! What are you yelling about?"

"You know damned well. What is all this fucking money doing in my account?"

He had the grace to look away, but the shit-eating grin came back.

"Expense money," he said. "For the foundation, mostly, and also to keep up with the Joneses, if you have to. Keep up with the Bierces and Lockwoods and Gills. We're an expensive habit."

"I have money."

"Yes, but not enough. And the foundation was my idea, so you shouldn't be paying for it. And if we need to stay somewhere nice, or if you want to come to Gaborone with me next time and you need to board this useless piece of fur you call a cat, I don't want you suffering financially."

I was silent for a long moment.

Finally, "I am not for sale," I said with difficulty.

He looked at me and quit grinning. "My dearest dear, I am not even trying to rent you. I am just evening things up a little. Lock would say 'levelling the playing field', but I am trying to avoid clichés. Including the cliché of money being equivalent to ownership."

I could see his point, but still — "Money was a huge issue in my family. They were always economizing, and we would eat lots of Kraft Dinner™ and fish sticks."

"Food of the underclass. You forget that I have the same kind of history."

"You do?" How could I forget what I didn't know? "How could I forget what I don't know?"

"Yes, I do, except with compulsive gamblers and fisticuffs." He stood behind me, hands lightly resting on my shoulders. Maybe it was easier to have this conversation in parallel than face-to-face.

"Really? Shit." I continued processing bill payments as I replied. "You win on agony points. My folks were just being thrifty. They accumulated a million and a half bucks or so, but did sweet fuck all for enjoyment during their lifetimes. Or ours. A few of those bucks would have eased my teen years a bit, and maybe given my brother some options besides killing himself."

As I paid my bills, the account balance overbalanced barely a whit. Only a few minor digits changed. It was scary.

"Mine were . . ." He stopped, swallowed, and his hands tightened on my shoulders. "There used to be a terrible silence in the house when they came home from the casino. We were never sure whether there would be anything left. We didn't eat fish sticks. It was that canned luncheon meat. Prem™. But yeah, Kraft Dinners™. That stuff still tastes of terror to me. We were kicked out of more rental houses . . ."

"We?"

"I have two sisters and a brother. They went . . . elsewhere. After we all were apprehended and put into foster care we were separated, and I lost track of them for quite a few years. The system is the shits that way. They were all young, and got adopted; I was a teenager and mad as hell that I couldn't keep the family together all by myself. And the bankruptcy trustee wouldn't let me have my computer — she didn't believe I bought it myself. I already had designed and sold a game a year or so before. Of course I got ripped off in the deal — I was thirteen at the time — but I could afford a really good computer, and then, boom, I was off in a group home with polyester bedspreads, religious art, and no telephone privileges."

"Hey, I know that group home!"

"Yeah, they were all pretty awful. That's when I met Lock. Fifteen or a million foster homes later, I eventually ran away and changed my name legally and became me."

"And made a lot of money being really smart. Couldn't you trace your sibs?"

"Lawyers did that, eventually. Our parents both died when I was a teenager. About three years after we were apprehended. They were flat broke by then, probably in debt to loan sharks, and they died in a fire. Suspicious circumstances but nothing proved. The sibs never knew I got the detective work done. They all have supposedly happy families — but they didn't turn out very well themselves. I'll tell you someday, maybe. Not nice. So they don't get me, they get money. Allegedly from a trust fund from the parents after a big win, or some damned stupid fiction, but it's really me."

"You might be surprised, if you met them. I have a cousin, Thelma, who sounds like a religious nut, but she turned out to be pretty cool in her own weird way. You'll meet her through the foundation. She volunteers on the board of M2F2 now."

"I'm not ready for that with them yet. I don't trust myself, and I don't trust them, either, and not just emotionally. They all have criminal records, for example. I never, in all the bad years, did anything seriously illegal. Dangerous, or wild-oatsy, maybe, but not deliberately criminal. I didn't even hustle, despite a lot of offers. They were the ones with actual adoptive homes, loving parents, all that going for them. But who knows how that shit goes down. I know it can't have been easy for them either — but I still don't like what I see. Still, I've done right by them as well as I can so far. If I were to die, they'd get a nice surprise."

"That's a good thing, though, to take care of them. Something money is good for. Someday, though, you could —"

"You're a kind, good person," he said. "Kinder than I am. Give me time."

He stroked my hair back from my face, leaned over, and kissed my forehead from above. I tilted my head back so I could see him, albeit upside-down.

"I told you true," he said. "Money is a nuisance to me. I really didn't do any of the things I did for money. They really were fun. Lock loves the money, but for me, I'd be just as happy in my workshop, fooling around making stuff."

"Well, there are cheaper and more immediate ways of making me holler, so enough with the bankroll surprises." I swung around and pulled his face down for a proper kiss. "Besides, I am not to be bought. I'm serious about that."

He allowed himself that cat-with-cream grin again.

"There will be no more. Well, it will renew magically if the balance drops below a certain amount, but that's all set up now. My work here is done."

"I certainly hope not," I said. "I had plans for later."

"I have too, but they involve the airport. Gabor is arriving, and then we all have dinner reservations."

The plane was late, so Pris and Lock, Nathan and I had dinner first instead, in a really terrible steakhouse-y place on the way to the airport. The cooks were visible through a big hatch, making a big deal out of grilling chunks of flesh over some kind of fragrant wood the smoke of which gave me a headache. Or maybe it was just the crash of the pans and knives. The supposedly-rare steaks they produced and shovelled onto trenchers for us were chewy even in their pinkish centres. They had been rendered tasty with the sort of mixed-pepper spice that gets called by name. Mrs. Dash. Uncle Dudley. Colonel Sanders. Dr. Crap. I scraped the coating off the meat and ate it with the mashed potatoes. It was salty and burnt, therefore tolerable.

"Fodder," said Nathan contemptuously.

"Food of the underclass wannabe-rich," I said. "They feel privileged because of all the fuss made over creating and serving their meal. It doesn't have to taste good."

Nathan raised his hand to call back the waiter. Lock, beside him, pulled his hand down gently, leaned in, and murmured to him, an intimate gesture neither Pris nor I missed. "It's no use, buddy," Lock said. "It's all going to be like that. Look."

At the next table the people were fighting with their alleged Fettuccini Alfredo, which appeared to be noodles as chewy as our meat with the added (dis)advantage of being insistent on clinging to their bed of congealed sauce.

"Cream of starch," said Nathan.

"Well, if you want something to chew on, chew on this," I said. I pulled out my little computer and fired it up. "If there were placemats in this damned place, I could just write this on them. We're going to talk about April first."

"We are?" said Pris.

"We are," said Nathan. "Clearly. And not a bad idea. We've all been in denial since then."

"And not a river in Egypt," Pris said. She picked at her lobster tail. "This isn't even food. It's made of rubber. It's that fake food they make for restaurant window displays."

"I'm going to set a good example," I said. "Here's my account of the evening. I started from the restaurant where we met beforehand. I wrote down everything I saw. From the time that publicist came to get us. I want you to do the same."

"Ideally, from before that," said Nathan. "If the publicist knew where we were, maybe someone else did too."

"I'm assuming that we assume that no-one here did it," said Lock, looking around the table.

"No, I don't think so." That, surprisingly, was Pris. "I don't like the idea, but if we are going to be fair . . . everyone . . ."

"Point taken," said Lock.

"Okay, then, you first," I said.

"You first first."

"Okay. To the store. People already there. Down to the stockroom place where we left our coats. Except you, Lock, didn't you keep your coat? I saw you in it later, anyway."

"I usually do keep it."

"You left it down there that night," said Nathan.

"Yeah, I remember, that's right, but my wallet and cell phone were in the pocket. So I went back and got it later. You saw me, remember? So then what?"

"Okay, then . . . I think we all went upstairs? No, I went up to say hi to that sweet guy with the glasses who works there, and you all stayed downstairs until the reading. I came back down and you were all in the back room. When it was time for the reading, Sharon introduced you, and after the reading we all went upstairs. We were kind of bodyguarding you through that throng of people. All we needed was that curly-cord earpiece you have,

Lock, and we would have looked like Secret Service agents in the movies. After that I browsed at the back while Pris signed. What were you two doing?"

"I think we all agree on the preliminaries," said Lock. "Let's move along."

"No, I think the early evening was important too," said Nathan. "If we didn't kill the guy, which we haven't actually established but I prefer to believe, then someone in that crowd did. But I certainly wouldn't have seen anything weird. There were too many people there doing too much stuff to be able to see anything at all, if you know what I mean. Any one of them could have been talking about murder instead of about Priscilla Jane Gill and how fabulous she is." He grinned at Pris to take the sting out, then went on, "Really, anyone in that place could have killed him."

"Or some random robber in the alley," said Lock. "They identified him by his prints. He didn't have a wallet. And he bought Pris's book, remember."

"He got her to sign a book," I said. "That's not the same as buying it. Some people lined up for a signature and paid for the book after. The 'random tramp' theory is out, I think. Just by Occam's Razor. And the count was out by three copies at the end, Steve said, so he probably stole it. He certainly didn't pay after he spoke to her. He went toward the back. He went down the elevator."

"Did he?" asked Pris. "He was beside it, but did he really go down in it? We didn't see him. And when Lock went down, nobody was there."

"Well, not nobody. A few people were browsing in that area in front of the stairs. There was a couple over in the kids' section, I remember, because they had this big stuffed dragon that I had to dodge to see if he was in there. And there was someone in the bargain books by the corridor to the washrooms. She hadn't seen anybody go out, but she was hunkered down reading the titles down on the bottom shelf so I didn't necessarily believe her. And nobody in the back room — I checked."

"So that's when *you* killed him," said Pris. We all looked at her. "Opportunity," she said. "Mine was just after that, when I went down to the toilet. Nobody saw me then. I came back all wet. Maybe I was washing his blood from my hands. Though from what I saw in the alley, I would have had to work hard not to get it all over me."

"Your shirt was wet," I said. "You could have washed out the stray drops. Speaking of which, Lock, your hands were wet, and you buttoned up your coat. What was that about?"

"They had some water over in the refreshments. I was going to bring some to Pris but the plastic cup was cracked and it got all over me. It was the last cup there. Probably why the locusts left it. Almost everything else was gone. So I did up my coat so I wouldn't look like I'd p— well, wouldn't look wet. But I could have got him any number of times, it's true. I was up and down those stairs like a yo-yo."

"Yo-yos go up and down stairs? Wouldn't that be 'like a Slinky®'?" I grinned, but he looked back at me with something like irritation before he smiled back. Not everyone appreciates my jokes. I get that. Hurriedly I said, "Well, I went downstairs a few times too, including after our search came up zero. I had to pee by then, and I was overheated after wrangling that crowd while Pris was downstairs."

"Yes, I heard about that," said Pris. "'The family of Priscilla Gill readers'? Pretty creative."

Nathan laughed. "Don't forget I went down to try to find the guy too. And didn't. And was out of sight. And later I went back to the washroom. And forgot about the tap, and got wet trying to shut it off. All in all, a totally suspicious bunch."

"Maybe we were all in cahoots, like in *Murder on the Orient Express*." Pris said.

"Maybe you guys were, but I don't have a cahoot to be in, and I *know* I didn't do it," I said.

"Me neither. Time to head for the airport," Nathan said. "Let's pay for this — tripe — and go."

"Tripe isn't this chewy," I said. "Hey, Pris, I just remembered. Mowbry left the book on the table. He said something to you then turned away, and you were still holding it open."

"That's right," said Pris. "I remember now. I was halfway through my signature. We found that book later and I finished signing it and sold it. Bizarre."

"What did he say?"

"He said . . . he said he had to talk to me. That he was sorry, and it wasn't what I thought, whatever that meant. And that he needed to talk."

"Twice that he needed to talk? Like you just said?"

"I think the second time he said, 'I'll talk to you later.' That's what freaked me out. Later? Like he knew where to find me? Again?"

"Okay, but what about later? When we were all closing up. Nathan and I were in the basement, in the stock room. He went up to get something out of the car, and someone pushed him down the stairs. I think that has to be legit because who would take a potentially fatal tumble down a steep set of stairs —"

"Concrete stairs, they felt like," Nathan interrupted.

"— just to establish an alibi? And the cops never really talked about who pushed him. We all assumed it was the same person who killed Mowbry. Was it?"

"I didn't see a face. Someone taller than me, in winter gear. The weird thing was that I thought it was Mowbry at the time. I have no idea why. Except, wait."

We waited.

"Maybe because of the scarf and hat? Could the killer have been wearing it, then thrown it down over the body? You mentioned it didn't seem to be wrapped around, and that seemed weird to you."

I nodded. "But does that get us any further? Pris, Lock, where were you? Next time I saw you, you were at the end of the alley, and Pris, you were screaming, or whatever that was. Some kind of panic attack."

"I was going to meet Lock."

"And I was going to meet Pris. Out back where the car was parked."

"Who got there first?" I asked.

"You did," they said in unison.

An odd thing happened next. Pris and Lock looked away from each other. After a moment, Pris spoke. "I think."

"You *think*?"

"I was pretty freaked out. I mean, you could see the guy lying there."

"Yeah, and all that blood —" I said. "It spurted as far as the wall. The knife must have hit an artery."

"So who called 911?" Nathan asked.

"I did," Pris, Lock, and I said in unison.

They all looked at me.

"Well, I did. Twice," I said defensively. "Just not about Mowbry, though. There were cops already there when we got upstairs. Somebody did."

"Me." Pris and Lock again made a ragged chorus.

"Did either of you see anyone?" I pressed on through the accidental performance art.

"I thought I did," said Lock. "But it was dark."

"It was not dark," I said. "There was enough light back there that I could see the colour of the blood. And of the scarf."

Pris nodded, and shuddered a bit. She took a long sip of the bad wine and then lapped her tongue disgustedly, like a cat.

"By the dumpsters it was dark," Lock said. "And with the body lit up, I didn't really have night vision."

Pris was watching him carefully, a sharp look in her eye.

"What?" I said to her.

"I was just thinking," she said. "I am completely sure I didn't see anyone except Mowbry's body, and Lock."

Lock shrugged. "Yeah, it's weird. It's like nobody did it."

"None of us, for sure," said Nathan.

"Let's step back for a sec," I said, "to who pushed Nathan. Could it have been Mowbry?"

"He's not tall enough," Pris said immediately.

Nathan agreed. "Mowbry was my height, at the most. Whoever it was pushed — um, down, not just across, if that makes sense." His watch chimed, and he checked a text. "Gabor's plane just landed," he said. "We'd better go."

"One last thing," I said. "Pris. You looked at his face and you said you'd never seen him before. Why was that?"

I'd seen her thousand-yard stare a few times since she popped back into my life, but this was the first time she let it show, and let it stay. After a moment she said to the upper far corner of the dining barn, "You know? After the attack I was sure I knew exactly what the guy looked like, but when they brought him in I barely managed to pick him out of the line-up. They made him speak to me, and then I was sure, but not before. Then in the trial he was always unshaven, and he looked like a crazy thug in his jail outfit. And I recognised his voice again in the bookstore. But later, under those orange lights, lying in a pool of blood, that guy looked like . . . like somebody's teenaged son, just lying there, a total blank. He didn't look like anyone I'd ever seen. Ever. Maybe that's what death does. It erases culpability."

Lock only let a short beat go by. "That's bullshit," he said. "The guy was as guilty as hell. And if it weren't that they thought one of us did it, I wouldn't give a rat's ass that he's dead."

"Healthy," I said, "but perhaps not wise."

Nathan laughed. "Who here is wise? If we were wise, we'd be on time, and we wouldn't still be hungry."

We all laughed then. Pris, still quiet, gathered up her scarves and bag. I snapped the cover over my tablet, and we went off to pick up a real wise man at the airport, and so on. The evening was far from over.

BUT, LOOK AT HER, NOW SHE'S BEGINNING AGAIN! —

58. IN THE REALM OF HUNGRY GHOSTS

Nathan and I were ambitious. We didn't just want housing, we wanted a range of housing for all the people of the neighbourhood. So we had conceived of a kind of neighbourhood fungus, a fruitbody of a foundation that would be joined under the metaphoric ground, and mushroom up in several locations. The architect we liked best had come up with some innovative and attractive designs that would eventually (we thought) make the city's architecture review board happy, and that would eventually (we thought) return the neighbourhood to its historical look. In addition to buying and restoring some more hundred-year-old structures, we planned some infill.

We were stealing some ideas about re-purposed building materials and green design — oh, yes, it was a whole new way of having fun that I had never thought I could experience, and it was heady. It also made my financially and socially risky acquisition of the Epitome Apartments seem like an amuse-bouche before a feast.

That didn't bother me, at the time. Actually, it never has bothered me. From each according to her ability, and all that.

So we were looking at the upscale version of napkin-sketches, cute drawings of cunning little Edwardian-style mini-condos with tiny yards and wrought-iron fences, small apartments with interior atriums and the look of historic buildings, and, in an area of greatest need, attractive and supportive harm-reduction housing for some hard-to-house homeless people with multiple issues of addiction and mental illness.

That's why Nathan had called in an expert. This guy had run a famous harm-reduction place in Vancouver, and now he travelled around speaking and advising. Gabor was a doll, really, in a ferociously-intelligent and more-than-slightly edgy way. But with great manners. A lot like Nathan, in fact, and it was great to watch them, and even better to work together. We got along from the moment we first saw him in the arrivals area, fidgeting as he waited for his suitcase to show up.

In the next two days, we had a whirlwind of meetings with the mayor, city planners, neighbourhood organisations, M2F2, other community groups, and the community association, and Roma had planned a series of open community consultations over the next few months.

We were the poster children for community development.

And you know what?

Nathan was right.

It *was* fun.

59. "TURN YOUR RADIO ON, AND LISTEN TO THE MUSIC IN THE AIR . . ."

Bunnywit will tell you that contrary to what I might call my public mystique — if I had a public, which I still contest isn't the case — I live a fairly abstemious life. I never smoked cigarettes, I don't drink any more (I've decided it's boring and expensive), or do drugs (ditto, which latter being boring/expensive I did find out for myself as a teenager, but I don't really have any need to back-slide, given the boring part especially), go out clubbing (as before, but with added amount of stupid), or buy a lot of new clothes (having listened to Thoreau). When I came into my parents' money, I did buy my dear old Epitome Apartments, but mostly to keep it out of the hands of developers, and I did buy a crazily-expensive grooming tool for Bunnywit, called a FURminator™, which he actually likes. I think it feels like being licked by his mom to him, or something. Anyway, he does come back for more.

Nathan introduced me to some of the pleasures of spending money, but oddly enough, he was similarly frugal on his own behalf. He did own some beautiful clothing, but not a mindless closetful of consumption. One cashmere overcoat per season. One butter-suede jacket. An astonishing red silk fringed tuxedo scarf, anywhere near which Bunnywit was not, definitely *not*, allowed. One beautiful silk tuxedo that he designed himself.

Where was his vanity?

I began to see where it was during the next while. It was in assembly. In making. Making software. Making hardware. Making deals. Making things happen. He was a Maker in the old Scots sense, or maybe the positive version of the Yiddish macher, if I understand that term right. He was — ingenious. About everything[22].

We did go over to his house, but it was mainly to see his workshop, which was in a side building. I don't know what I expected — a fancier version of my father's garage with a wall of tools hung up on a pegboard — but Nathan's workshop was a wonder. It was a combination of high-tech and hand-crafting — a 3D printer next to a box of traditional Japanese woodworking

---

22. Yes. Everything.

tools, a fabricator the size of a double refrigerator next to a hand-made workbench — and it was a mess.

I mean really messy. The centre of the floor, and the work table, were more or less clear, and there was a clever blueprint-holder that kept some huge schematics out of the dust and shavings, but I was shocked at the chaos.

"Holy fuck! This is worse than my office used to be!" Oops. Not a diplomat.

"It's a work in progress," Nathan said. "Actually, it's about seven, no, eight works in progress. That over there is the design for the new . . . hmm, better hang your coat in the hall, and I'll give you a pair of coveralls."

"Why are coveralls a pair?" I wondered as I got into them, one leg at a time. "It's one garment. It's a coverall. But they seem to come in pairs."

"It's probably regional. There's probably a part of the world where they would look at us like we were crazy and get us each one if we asked for a pair. But I'm from around here, and so are you."

"And so was my dad. I still have the coveralls he gave me when I moved out. Weirdly enough, considering how crazy he was about other things, he considered a well-equipped toolbox and a set of personal protective equipment to be a suitable and excellent graduation gift for a liberal arts major. I have to thank him for that. When I still had a car, that torque wrench was my best friend for a while. I changed my own oil and spark plugs for years."

"He gave you a torque wrench? That's great!"

"Yep. I loved it. Such a clever tool. So what is this big thing? I mean, it's a fabricator of some sort. It says so on the label. But what?"

"Well, it's excellent. You CAD something, then you put a box of these plastic beads in, laser-print the item in 3D, and then ship the box. The beads are fused selectively in all dimensions by the laser to make the item, and the ones not fused act as packing material. Blow away the spare beads, and voilà. If the person at the other end has one of these too, they tip the spare beads back into the materials bin, and round and round we go. I love shit like this. I really do."

On a shelf against the wall were a number of bricks of something oily and grey. They were oblong, a little bigger footprint than a ream of paper, but about seven inches high. Eighteen centimetres, that is. "Cripes! That looks like Semtex looks in the movies!" I said. "What is it?"

"Semtex," he said. Then he laughed out loud. "Kidding! It's moulding material. I sort of invented it. I tweaked an existing formula, but it does some cool stuff. Here, feel this."

He handed me one of the bricks, two-handed as if he were giving a business card to a Japanese person. So I took it the same way, with my two hands curving around it. It yielded to my hand in a sensual, lazy way, warming slightly in my grip. Then, suddenly, it felt cool and firm. When he took it back, it had my handprints on the sides, probably down to the detail of my skin surface. I noticed that he laid it aside on a separate shelf.

"What, you're collecting my fingerprints now?"

"It changes at a molecular level when it's handled. Did you feel it cool off? I'll make you something that fits your hands, sometime."

"What, handling it wrecks it?"

"Depends on the orders you give it. I told it to mould your hands. Usually it goes in the 3D printers and it stays malleable until it has orders from the computer. It can be coloured, and it can be told to stay flexible or to harden. It's very cool stuff."

"Cool."

"In the metaphoric sense. You can make high-impact stuff from it, or clothing. Depends on what you tell it to be. Use dyes and reagents to get the full-colour effect."

"It's smart paper in 3D."

"Sort of, yeah." He took another brick and fed the printer, then showed me the control screen. "Pick something. I'll print it for you."

I was going to take Nathan to Little Flower that night. "I forgot my finger picks at home. Can it make finger picks?"

We spent the afternoon happily making me a set of finger picks I could have bought, mass produced, for a few bucks in a five-minute transaction. It took some time. We had to 3D-scan my fingertips. We had to design the optimum grip and reach for the picks. We had to experiment with hardness for optimum sound quality. I don't like steel picks on my autoharp, even though I play in the Bowers style and I have a steel set. I like a softer sound.

The picks I ended up with fit my fingers like the tips of very expensive gloves — which they were, in a way. They were the fanciest prosthetic fingernails I had ever imagined, and about thirty-four percent more efficient than the mass-produced kind. I still have them. A patent wouldn't make me rich, but it would make a lot of string players happy.

One of these days I may let someone else touch them.

Not yet, though.

Oh, and we made a set in each of the six cartoon rainbow colours, plus a few other colour variations just for fun. I can mix and match them for any occasion. Green for Celtic night. Blue for the blues. Rainbow fingertips for Pride Week concerts. Black for murder ballads.

It was fun. Ridiculous, high-tech, first-world fun.

60. PIED-À-TERRE

The workshop was in what used to be the garage of the leased mansion. Afterward Nathan showed me a little convenience apartment above. "My pied-à-terre," he said.

It was not large, cold, or unwelcoming. It was tiny and economically fitted, like a boat. And it had a very nice bed. We tested it a bit and decided we would come back there after the folk club.

We met Pris and Lock at the café beside the Little Flower venue. Pris had brought a tambourine. She held it up. "I'm a little flower child," she said. "Pun intended!"

"Where have you guys been?" said Lock once we'd established ourselves at a table in the club where the open stage was held.

"Workshop," said Nathan.

"You went to the house?"

"No, just the workshop and the flat."

"Are those people still living in the house?"

"Yes, until August."

"Damn. I miss that place."

"I don't," said Nathan. He was looking away toward the stage at the time. "It's time to move on."

"I thought you liked it."

Nathan heard the tone and smiled at his friend. "I did, Lock. I do. But it's the past. I need something different now. Something cozy."

"Cozy," said Nathan.

"Something downtown, I think. I never did like all that freeway driving to get out there."

"I miss those days."

"Do you? Really? All that pizza and canned soup and adrenaline?"

"Sort of, yeah. The adrenaline part. Nothing these days gives me that kind of kick. We were really on the edge of so much."

"The edge is where you make it," Nathan said. "This year, smart paper. Next year, schools for girls in sexist danger zones."

"Yeah," said Pris. "That would be fun. Someplace with a chance of getting shot at."

I almost laughed. Then I realised she meant it.

"I could go for that," said Lock. He meant it too.

"You're both crazy," I said.

"It's fun," said Nathan.

"Correction. You're all crazy."

Nathan grinned at me. "Pot," he said. He meant the pot was calling the kettle black.

I had to grin back. It *was* fun.

But they were still crazy.

61. "SEND ME DEAD FLOWERS ..."

For some reason it was death night at the open stage. Some earnest kid sang a lugubrious acoustic version of the Stones' "Dead Flowers". Someone else did a wistful banjo-accompanied "Banks of the Ohio" and had us all sing along on the chorus of the classic jealous-lover ballad about the guy who killed his love object because she wouldn't agree to be his love object:

Then only say that you'll be mine
In no other's arms entwine
Down beside where the waters flow
Down by the banks of the Ohio

"I never understood this jealousy stuff," I said quietly to Nathan.

"You are such a hippie," said Pris, overhearing.

"You can't push the river," I said sententiously.

"Amen to that, sister," said Nathan.

"If I'm your sister, we're in a Greek play by now," I said.

Pris and Nathan laughed. Lock didn't. "I get jealous," he said. "I don't like losing something."

"People aren't things," said Pris.

"Point," said Lock. "But you know what I mean. When a business deal doesn't work I get pissed. I understand how someone could feel like that about love. If they thought of love as a commodity, and felt like they deserved to have it."

"The way you feel about money," Nathan laughed.

"Yeah," said Lock. "Pretty much."

"Sounds a bit sociopathic," I said.

"If that's what sociopathy is, then count me in," said Lock. "I like money, and I like having a lot of it."

"To do stuff with," said Nathan.

"Because it's mine," said Lock.

When it was my turn, I was sick of the slow tunes, but just for the fun of it I kept to the theme, so I laid out "The Bold Fisherman", "Unfortunate Miss Bailey", and, finally, "Poor Howard", which is a good singalong blues with the usual downbeat lyrics and upbeat music:

Poor Howard's dead and gone
Left me here to sing this song . . .

By the end, we had the joint rollicking.

We went back to Nathan's distant flat, just because we'd said we would, but I was glad in the end, because I got to experience his red cashmere bathrobe and his rich-guy plumbing (not a euphemism. I'd already had a lot of experience with that. I'm talking about the deluxe bathtub. And the bidet. Bidet. For Chrissakes.).

Rinse. And repeat.

62. A HOUSE IS NOT A HOME REDUX

In the morning — the late, late morning — well, the afternoon, but only just barely — we walked through a fringe of designer trees and up to The House That Nathan Lockwood Built.

"I really don't like Lombardy poplars," I said. "I understand their design utility, but they are so uptight."

"Well, they suit this place," said Nathan.

That was true. The house stood on the highest point of the property, overlooking the river on one side and a cluster of other mansions on the other. It was an austere collection of glass blocks, like a miniature Urban Brutalist art museum. We walked through a beautifully-designed garden as austere as the place itself. The house's public spaces were open to view, protected only by their invisible glass curtain walls, so that even in the daytime it was like watching Rich-Folks-TV. In the dark it would blaze spectacularly into an almost-empty landscape, controlled by design and urban plantings into a secret safe space for conspicuous consumption. The rooms were big, with discreet post-modern furniture, dotted with sculpture and papered with huge colour-field paintings.

"Art by the yard," I said. I like my Mendelson Joe. "Sorry, I should think before I blurt. I've seen abstract art that I like, just not this kind. Olitski and company. The Clement whassisname — Greenberg? — school of ingredients-only art. I like my art to have a subject, I guess."

"Don't worry, I wouldn't be offended even if I did like them. But they wouldn't be my choice now. There *are* two in the bedroom that I like. They're a little less . . . neutral. That one really is a Jules Olitski." Nathan, pointed through the "great-room" window. "Lock bought it. An investment."

"And you rent it out as part of the fitments? What the hell is the security deposit on this place?"

"The kind of people who rent a house like this," Nathan bitched, "don't pay security deposits. Their lawyers and our lawyers have lunch. It's a fucking racket."

"You hardly ever swear," I said. "What's the matter?"

"I guess I'm saying goodbye, in a way. Not to the house. To something else. To my . . . youth? To being stupid?"

"You have never in your life been stupid, I can pretty much guarantee."

"No, but I've been naïve," he said. "That amounts to the same thing, and can do just as much damage."

63. NOT A JOKE

Nathan had a meeting with his business guys, so we hopped into the little pod of a car and I went home to spend quality time with Bunnywit for a few hours before dinner. We were to dine with Pris and Lock again, at the Unheardof.

It was a difficult dinner despite all the efforts of the wonderful gourmet chefs there, because over our soup, Nathan brought up the house issue.

"The tenants want to buy it, Lock. They even want some of the art. And I want to resolve it. It's been hanging over our heads for years now, and it's time to make a decision."

"We built that house together." Lock was quiet, but I could see his jaw was tight.

Pris could too. She put a hand on his arm, but he edged his arm away.

"I know we did, and that's why I've held off so long. A lot of good things happened in that house. We had a lot of great life there. But we've moved on."

"You never liked it, the whole time." Lock's voice was flat.

"I liked it then. But I don't like it now, that's true," said Nathan gently. "I've grown up, Lock. When we built that house, we had no idea. We were kids with a new toy. We thought we had all the money we would ever need."

"Speak for yourself."

"I am, love," Nathan said. "I am. But we made mistakes, Lock. We built a monument to everything we said we didn't want to be. We bought art worth millions, while kids go hungry and people are homeless. It sounds pretentious to say so now, sitting here wearing these clothes and eating this food, but I'm working on changing *how* I am rich."

"That's my house. I love that house."

"I thought you might say that. So I'm signing my interest in it over to you. House and contents. Except for one of the paintings in the bedroom. You know the one."

When Lock blushed slightly, I wondered what exactly those paintings were like. Nathan hadn't said, and perhaps they were more representational than I had assumed.

Lock spread his hands out in one of those slow, carefully-unthreatening gestures that large men — large people, I suppose — learn to make instead of the rapid, fiery gestures we small- or medium-sized people can get away with. "I don't want —"

"Lock, I don't want to argue about it. You know how I feel. The house isn't us any more, and we're not the house. You know I love you, and I'll always remember everything that we had there, but we have something else together now."

"Don't you remember how —"

"Lock. Not everything about living in that house was a dream. We were kids. We played at being grown-up, being rich. We were damned lucky that we were solid enough together to survive that phase. When I think of some of the things we did, I still quiver in my boots. If you'd been caught with that file-transfer thing that time, we'd probably both still be poor, if not in jailhouse duds. We walked away alive, with each other, and with this company that we have built together. That has to be enough for you. We can't go back."

"I wasn't playing."

Nathan could have been more patient, I grant that. "Of course you were. Of course *we* were. We were lazy and irresponsible. I'm changing that for myself. I've been setting up a foundation to change the way I use most of my money. I'll still put the same amount into the company, R&D, all that, but this hellacious big balloon of obscene overabundance is going back to the community. Not just this city. The world. Starting with the places we made our money. There's plenty to do. It's a drop in the bucket. But it's what I can do."

"Don't think you can make me ashamed of being rich," said Lock. "I worked hard to get what I have, and I'm not done yet. I like it. I like everything about it. I like having new shirts and handmade shoes. I like that house, and I like that art. I *will* keep it, with thanks, and I'll live in it again too, if you haven't spoiled it for me. And I'm moving this company forward, too, with you or without you."

Listening to the edge in Lock's voice, I would have recommended the latter course, but Nathan gave him a surprisingly sweet smile. "With me, of course, my dear friend," he said. "That's never been in question. Just give me this. I have to go with my conscience."

"Your bloody conscience. We'd have twice the money to devote to good works if you didn't insist on making business decisions with your conscience too."

"We've been through this too," Nathan said. "How much good does blood money do? Our factory people don't throw themselves off buildings. How much money do we need?"

"All of it," said Lock.

Priscilla laughed reflexively, then put her hand over her mouth, equally as reflexively. Something in her knew laughing at that point was dangerous.

Nathan had chuckled too.

After a moment, Lock grinned back at them.

But I saw the effort it took.

He hadn't been joking.

I hadn't made a sound, hoping that Lock would forget I was there. I had experience with the dangers of being a witness to the humiliation of powerful people.

But Lock hadn't forgotten. He turned his head to me. "Pay attention," he said. "I keep what's mine."

"Not a necessary tone, dude. I have no designs on your money."

"Your money, or your life," Nathan made it into a bandit joke, with a pointed finger and a Dirty-Bodine[23] growl.

I grinned. "Seriously, you guys!"

"I am serious," said Lock, but he smiled as he said it.

Nathan ruffled his hair. "Too serious," he said. "Have some fun with us!"

"Sure," said Lock. "It's all fun until —"

"One hundred percent safe until the moment of impact," I said involuntarily.

"What?" said Nathan.

"Just a saying. All I mean is, it's not worth fighting over. Are you both good here?"

"Fine," said Nathan and, a moment later, Chiles.

Pris seemed oblivious to the undertones. "Well, I'm glad you two finally settled that. Now can we talk about our next trip?"

Trip?

"I want to go climbing," she said, "and conditions are great around Jasper right now. I don't have anything to do for the book for a whole week, and that detective has finally said we can leave town. So let's."

"Sure," said Lock. "What climb do you want to do?"

"Your call," she said. "Something that gives us a bit of a workout. Something high. I'm damned sick of climbing walls in warehouses."

"I can't do much with this arm still bunged up," said Nathan.

"No way," I said. "You can't climb rock faces with one bad paw. No way."

---

23. Westerns: "I'ma comin' ta get you, Dirty Bodine!"

"Oh, don't worry," said Pris. "We'll do the climbing and then haul him up on the end of a rope."

"Yeah, I have a lot of practice pulling his weight," said Lock sourly.

"Don't be like that," said Nathan. "It's only a house. We're still us whether we live there or not."

He and Lock exchanged a long glance, and it was Lock who looked aside first. "I guess," he said. "Give me some time to get used to it."

Nathan clasped his hand briefly. "You'll be fine," he said.

"Sure you will," said Pris. "We'll build a better house."

Dinner improved after that. Around the dessert stage, I said to Pris, "You promised to tell me where you went when you left the Union Bank Inn that time."

"I did, didn't I? I'll tell you when we get back."

"Oh, for goodness' sake."

"Seriously. Look, here's the crème brûlée. You can't tell stories over crème brûlée. It's a sin not to give it one's complete attention."

"Nice deke."

"You know I'm right. Look, we'll have lunch as soon as I get back. The Tuesday after. Unless you want to come with us. Go up a mountain?"

"I get dizzy on a ladder. You couldn't pay me enough to climb thousands of feet up a vertical wall."

"That's the difference between you and us," said Lock.

"One of the differences," I said.

"What do you mean by that?"

I broke the perfect surface of my dessert with a tap of my spoon. "I'm not tall," I said.

64. DARWIN RUNNER-UP?

Later, at my place, feeding Bun:

"You're kidding. You're really, seriously going — *climbing*? With a broken wrist? What, you are trying for, a Darwin Award?"

"I've already contributed to the gene pool. I'm not eligible."

"You have a kid?"

"Maybe." At my double-take, he said, "When I was studying at MIT, I made money by donating to a sperm bank."

"You're kidding."

"I never kid. Well, I may have kidded, unbeknownst and anonymously, but none of them has come after me for child support."

I gave him the Look. I tried to raise an eyebrow to go with it but I decided I'd have to practise in front of a mirror, because he just laughed.

We leaned against the kitchen counter, arms around each other. "Seriously, I'm worried. I feel like I should go and watch over you, but I wouldn't be any good on a mountain. You sure I can't talk you out of the climbing thing?"

"I promise to be the passive party."

"You? The quintessential top?"

"Only in some things. And, as you know, I share the honours."

"If you weren't so pretty that look would be described as a leer."

"And since I'm so pretty?"

"Oh, pretty much a leer."

We were so damn pleased with each other.

"I am beginning to think I will love you forever," Nathan said quietly.

I backed off until I could see his face more clearly.

"You're not kidding, are you? You're that certain."

"From the moment I saw you, pretty much," he said. "Scary, isn't it?"

"Well, not if it's reciprocal."

"And is it reciprocal?"

"I'm beginning to think so," I said. "Though I may have waited until you gave me thirteen whole marshmallows in that hot chocolate before I knew."

He kissed me.

"Well, that's all right, then," he said.

"Niaow," said Bunnywit.

We should have listened.

WHAT *IS* THE MATTER WITH MARY JANE?

65. 20/20 FORESIGHT

In the morning Nathan called me to say they had arrived safely in Jasper, and we talked for a few minutes, but his call-waiting beeped before he could get me the privacy code I needed to get through to their suite at the hotel. Rich-people security.

"Code!" I blurted.

"I don't remember it. Dammit! I'll call back. But I really need to get this call. I love you, dear one." I thought I could get used to hearing that — or never would get used to it. The weeks hadn't taken the shine off. And as was becoming usual, we'd practised it a lot the night before.

"I love you too," I said. But the click of a lost signal happened on "too".

He didn't call. Priscilla didn't call. None of them called me.

All day.

It didn't feel right. Sure, you think I can say that now, with 20/20 hindsight, but in fact, I said it to both Hep and Denis when they showed up for the afternoon and to cook dinner with me. I was uneasy in a way I usually never am.

"What's the problem?" Hep said.

"Yeah, use your words," urged Denis.

"You know that old blues about 'my right side jump and my left begin to crawl'? It's like that, except it's not about something as inconsequential as non-monogamy."

"That song's not about non-monogamy, it's about infidelity," said Denis. "It's about fear of betrayal. Fear. Dread, even."

"That's what I'm feeling. Dread. A killer is out there somewhere."

"They're up on a mountain. Who's going to be able to get them there?"

"Anyone. If it's a stranger who killed Mowbry, they wouldn't recognise him — or her — from two feet away. And if not . . . they're off on a mountain together, and it could be one of them."

"Not Nathan? Come on. You think the sun shines out of his backside," said Denis. "You don't seriously think he's the killer."

"Well, not unless he's a complete cold psychopath — but those do exist, you know. Lock is a better contender. He's possessive, he has a temper. But how could he have done it and not even been dishevelled?"

"That leaves Pris. She was out of sight the longest." Hep loved Pris's books, so she was just playing devil's advocate.

"Ditto with Pris. How? It's a total mystery to me. But it's weird . . ."

"Oh no," said Denis. "Don't tell me. 'I feel like I know something, if I could only put it together?' That's what they say at this point in the detective shows on TV. And then it turns out that a candy wrapper or an obscure reference to mushrooms was the key to everything."

"No, I was going to say — I can think of a few ways it could have been them, but they all depend on something being found that the cops haven't found. Protective clothing. Gloves. That sort of thing. And the cops have been thorough."

"How do you know?"

"I asked Horenko. — What? He called me in for another interview, so I asked."

"I thought you were staying out of it," said Hep.

"I mostly am. I am. Staying out of it. Really I am."

"Why don't I believe you?" Denis grinned.

I don't know why. At that point, it was more or less true. Sure, I'd showed a bit of curiosity, but I'd been distracted by Nathan's and my new enthusiasm. That was as unlike me as giggling, but hey, it was early days for the love train. Nathan would be back, we'd get into a routine, and I would have plenty of time for both, I thought.

Suddenly I felt a cold draught down my back and everything in the apartment seemed very far away. I shivered, and I felt tears stand in my eyes.

"You cold, pet?" said Hep.

I blinked, and everything was fine again. "No," I said. "I don't know. Maybe." I got up to check the thermostat, but the temperature was as just as usual.

"Never mind," I said. "Let's get the baking started."

"Ouoa naouw," said Bunnywit.

He meant, "Oh no," but I didn't understand his accent.

66. THE GHOST AT THE FEAST

While I was prepping the sausage pie for the oven, I saw a flicker at the edge of my vision that I thought was Nathan coming in in his overcoat. I had started to turn before I realised it was Bunnywit hopping off the couch and into the kitchen. He'd somehow created himself a shadow that climbed the wall briefly before disappearing.

He kept sliding into my peripheral vision all evening.

Nathan, that is, but when I'd turn, it was Bun again, on a chair or table, walking across the back of the couch, and once, as we sat having our Vietnamese coffee (which is dessert and coffee and excessive taste sensation all in one glass), just sitting there on his cashmere-scarf pillow.

I wished for Ativan™.

I wished for Nathan.

"Cut that out!" I said to Bun.

Hep and Denis looked at me. "What?" said Denis.

"Nothing," I said.

"Niaow! Oooaow!" said Bunnywit, and flounced off to the closet to lie on his red leather drag boots, his extreme comfort zone.

67. OH.

The whole time Hep and Denis were with me, which was from about three to nine p.m., I had been antsy about the silent telephone. They urged me not to worry, and told me a gazillion reasons why I shouldn't. I pretended to believe them.

After they left I had nothing to distract me.

By midnight I had gone from deeply worried to seriously pissed off and back a dozen times. Had the other shoe dropped, or was this typical Pris again? But Nathan wasn't like this. Usually.

I called the Jasper Park Lodge, but without the code I couldn't get through to Nathan's room (because his privacy was being guarded in the usual rich-people manner), or Lock's (ditto), or Pris's (ditto). I left messages there and on their cell phone voicemails. I went to bed, but I couldn't sleep.

I blamed the Vietnamese coffee. But I knew it wasn't the coffee.

68. NO.

Turns out, Pris couldn't call me because she was dead.

She was dead.

Lockwood Chiles, who never would have called me anyway, was presumed dead.

And Nathan, lovely Nathan, couldn't call me, because he was dead.

69. NO, NO.

Roger showed up at my door about three in the morning. He knew I didn't watch TV or listen to radio, where the news was already spreading because of who they were. The news was this:

Around midafternoon, Pris and Lock had been up on a rock face with two other climbers and a couple of guides. Nathan had been down at the bottom of an icy section. Because of his healing arm, he was waiting for them to do whatever rope thing climbers do to anchor themselves so they could help hoist him up. He was talking to some other guides and climbers, and another group was waiting a few metres away on a different part of the slope.

Something happened. Nobody knew exactly what yet.

Down came climbers, mountain and all.

It was the survivors of that slightly-distant group who gave shaken statements to rescuers and media. Roger and I watched the TV host interview a ruddy-faced guide with blood in his blond hair, wearing a bloodstained blue parka.

"There was yelling up top. I could see Andy and one of the tourists up on the snow already. The big guy and the woman in red were swinging out on the rope. The big guy pulled himself up over the ceiling, and just then the woman fell. But then there was a crack, and the whole overhang came down. It just . . . came down. Just . . . I actually felt someone bang into me — I knew it wasn't just more snow and rock because I felt his rigging. They dug him up . . . Andy . . . right beside me . . ." He broke off, and sobbed into his bent arm, and someone pushed the camera away.

Bodies and unconscious people were still being recovered from under the snow — those who had been sensible enough to wear avalanche alarms. At the time we turned on the TV Lock and one of the other climbers up top were still unaccounted for. One of the guides up top had been anchored to a tree, and was hanging from the edge, unconscious but alive; it took ages to get him down because they were afraid a helicopter would set off another avalanche. They medevac'd him straight to the city and he was still in ICU. In his limited moments of consciousness, he remembered nothing of the day.

Down below, one of the guides was alive. Some of the other climbers were alive. Some were not.

Priscilla and Nathan were not.

It seemed she had fallen directly onto him: their bodies had already been found, tangled and battered under the weight of snow and rock.

WHAT IS THE MATTER WITH MARY JANE? I'VE PROMISED HER SWEETS AND A RIDE IN THE TRAIN,

70. HOW IT WORKS

Jasper is in Alberta, Canada. In Alberta, the system of coroner's death enquiries was replaced in 1977 by a system of Medical Examiner's death enquiries. The idea was to separate the circumstantial investigation and the public hearing in a case where an enquiry into a death must be held. If you are interested, just under a third of deaths in that jurisdiction are investigated — "all unexplained natural deaths and all unnatural deaths" — and Alberta was the first jurisdiction in North America to make the Chief Medical Examiner a forensic pathologist and hire people with medical training as their medical investigators. Eat your heart out, Quincy and Wojeck.

That means there are no coroners here. Medical examiners investigate, helped in far-flung areas by "a network of some 130 fee-for-service medical examiners, all of whom are physicians, [who] investigate the remaining cases with the assistance of the

RCMP, municipal police forces, and hospital-based patholo-gists", and if, on the basis of their report on "the identity of the deceased and the cause, manner, and circumstances of death", the Fatality Review Board decides the case should go to a fatality enquiry, this hearing is held in public before a provincial court judge.

"The OCME is responsible for the investigation and certi-fication of all deaths in Alberta caused by violence, as well as all unexplained and some unattended natural deaths . . . Violent deaths are not just limited to homicides, but are actually all deaths not caused by natural diseases . . ." So says their own 2003 annual report — old, but not inaccurate for all that. Their fatality reports are available to next-of-kin and other interested parties who are willing to pay.

Having money in the bank is a benison at times of great trial.

"Roger," I said, "What do senior cops — investigators — do on their days off?"

"What?"

"Cops. Say, really good forensic technologists. When they aren't watching *CSI*?"

"They don't watch *CSI* . . . what the fuck?"

"I'm serious. I seem to have access to a lot of money, tempo-rarily. Off-duty officers do private security on fee-for-service. I've seen them at rock concerts and street parties. What about more senior police members? Can I use some of the money Nathan gave me to hire some off-duty Annettes and Rogers, take them up to Jasper so they can help the Medical Examiner's Investigator be the best he or she can be?"

Roger actually stopped to think.

He began to speak. Then he stopped again, tilting his head like a Pomeranian. "Um, I can't actually think of a reason why not."

71. POOR NATHAN'S DEAD AND GONE

His face was almost unmarked, and with his body laid out and covered with a sheet, the extent of his injuries (grievous, instantly fatal, everyone knew that by now) didn't show.

I had told them I had to see him, and in honour of a relationship to which Roger attested on my behalf, they allowed me to be the official identifier.

The doctor who was acting as Medical Examiner's Investigator had her hand under my arm, but I wasn't going to fall down. I had turned to stone.

"It's him," I said. "For the record."

But it wasn't him. He was gone from that yellow-grey shell.

"'Left me here to sing this song,'" I murmured.

"Hmm?" said the doctor.

"Come on," said Roger. "There's nothing for you here any more."

The pathologist glared at him, but Roger has known me a long time, and he was right.

72. THE HUNGRY GHOSTS

The worst part was that I kept seeing glimpses of them in the periphery. It was the standard grief thing. Pris in the hotel restaurant would turn out to be another woman in a red coat, resembling her not at all. When we searched Nathan's room, for a split-second he was coming out of the bathroom, but when I turned it was his scarlet bathrobe on the back of the door. Lock lurked behind a potted palm in the lobby, but when I turned it was really dark-haired Horenko in a sheepskin coat who walked across and sat down stolidly on a couch.

73. ". . . AND THANKS FOR ALL THE FISH."

Horenko? Well you might ask.

In the end it had been Annette and Dan (a former member of her team, a forensic anthropologist who had been a pathologist before he went back to teach at the university), Staff-sergeant Lance (Denis's fiancé), and Rodney Horenko who came with Roger and me. I didn't like Rodney much, but the murder behind the bookstore was his case, and I thought he deserved to be there. But this time, I was paying[24]. Their expenses, in the case of the homicide detectives, because they are public servants, can't take gifts, and their cases overlapped — but it was enough to keep me in the loop.

Which is how I knew what the investigators found: that Pris's rope had been cut; that the climbing rig they thought was Lock's was damaged too; that Pris's body had a knife halfway through one hand, which could mean she was using it or someone was using it on her.

Some bodies were still unrecovered — it had been one hell of a big avalanche — including Lock's, but some of the blood on the snow and Pris's rope had his DNA. And, peculiarly, on Nathan's rig too. Andy the guide, in hospital, still remembered little of the day and could tell us nothing about why Pris and Lock had been twisting in midair, nor about how Lock's gear came to be anchored so much farther up the slope than the others had been.

And if Nathan hadn't been at the bottom to be avalanched upon, he'd have been at the bottom not long after he began his climb, because his gear, too, had been cleverly sabotaged.

The afternoon that the DNA results came back, we all sat in the stuffy little hotel meeting room we were using as an office

---

24. Well, indirectly, Nathan was paying, but that wasn't their business.

and stared at each other. What the hell went on up on that rock ceiling — during the "incident", as police love to call these catastrophes, and before?

There were as many scenarios to explain this as there were players in the case, and relationships between them, plus one.

Did Pris cut the rope? Did she try to cut Lock's? Did Lock cut her rope, and she tried to stop him and got the knife in her hand? Did Nathan set it all up like a suicide pact? Did each of them have a separate plot against the others? Did two of them plot together against the third, and who were the plotters and who the third? Did someone else, someone murderous, go up that mountain with them and set it all up, only to perish in the unexpected fall of that ceiling or survive among the innocents? Andy was under guard, ostensibly in case he said anything useful, but also in case he said anything incriminating. Three bodies were missing despite excavations still ongoing. Had anyone actually survived, and if so where were they?

"I can't think any more," I said. "There are too many ways to slice this."

"Don't bust your head over it," said Lance. "It's just the beginning. These investigations can take years sometimes."

"Lance is right," said Roger. "It goes to the Mounties now. There's enough to suggest criminal intent on somebody's part."

"Our report will so find," said the Medical Examiner's Investigator. The rôle this time was filled by a wild-haired, comfortable Woman of a Certain Age who wore leggings and lumpy sweaters, but people still damn near saluted when she ambled past. "There will be a fatality enquiry, and probably someone will press to have it sooner rather than later." She smiled tiredly at us. "And I have to say, thanks for the help. You-all's work speeded up the results, which I gotta appreciate, and more eyes are always good. RCMP will keep up the momentum, don't worry. Meanwhile, I'd appreciate if you'd keep everything under your hats until we do our thing. We've already bent the process enough."

"Sure thing," said Rodney. We all looked at him. "Just sayin'," he said defensively.

It was at this point that Rodney proved exactly what he was made of: he went straight out of the room with his notebook in his pocket, hastily called a news conference — which was pretty easy to do given that half the world's reporters and paparazzi were hanging around the ski hotels drinking on their employers' tabs and waiting for a story — and told the media that he had headed the special team that had discovered all these things.

While he was at it, he told them all about who Nathan Lockwood really was. Or were.

Then he advanced his theory, which was a love triangle gone wrong. He blamed the murder in the alley on Pris, citing unbalanced mind and revenge, and suggested she'd offed herself and her lover and set Nathan up to fall too, out of jealousy. "Case closed," he said.

Then he quit his job (or, well, was fired) and (not necessarily in this order) sold his exclusive story and notes to the highest bidder — which was pretty high.

Way to go, Rodney.

Thanks.

74. THE TRUTH WILL SET YOU FREE . . . BUT FIRST IT WILL MAKE YOU MISERABLE

In the next few days, Pris became the demon of the world media, and Nathan Lockwood became the most famous case of false identity on the planet. It was hard to parse which the media thought was more of a crime, mass killing (unproven) or pulling the wool over the eyes of gossip columnists everywhere (proven, and, to the columnists' chagrin, universally successful).

As far as I could see, deceiving the international gossip machine was winning as the worst transgression — in the opinion of the international gossip machine. Shades of the Hinton body bag[25].

What Nathan Bierce and Lockwood Chiles had done was not criminal, because they never tried to defraud anyone, and people can call themselves whatever name they want. And because it transpired that on all the documents that mattered, their legal signatures were both there, clearly — and confidentially. But outraged media all over the world dissected their "deception", as it was being called by the most conservative of the media: you don't want to know (though you probably remember) what Fox News and the worst of the tabloids were saying.

Known Associates sold blurry "candid" shots to tabloids for big bucks. Trusted Employees leaked details of "secret" meetings that were simply day-to-day doings-of-business. Nathan's name change became public, after which some people appeared claiming to be his surviving family, loaded for bear, discovered their legacy trust funds, regrouped, and swore they'd sue for more (but that was later). The physical resemblance was striking, though they were nothing like Nathan otherwise — so at least they were *attractive* sharks.

No family surfaced for Lock. Sometimes he had styled himself the black-sheep scion of a wealthy family, other times the successful

---

25. I'd say "Look it up" but the story's hard to find these days, except in Brian Fawcett's book *Cambodia: a book for people who find television too slow*. In 1986 at a huge train wreck near Hinton, Canada, media had camped out at the scene, hampering investigation, clamouring for the "money shot" — a body being brought out. So investigators put rubble in a body bag and took it out past the cameras: the media got their shots — then were furious when they found out it was a decoy. Briefly, the indignant media flurry was larger than the reporting of the disaster. (Laughably, these days if you look up the disaster online, you see the fake photo without any note that it's fake.)

escapee of an abusive poverty, but no one was left to confirm any story: he left a remarkable lack of history. No-one ever knew his original name.

Pris's parents and friends valiantly defended her innocence, but in the media Pris was tried, convicted, and pilloried post-mortem. Even though the Mounties were still investigating, even though three bodies, and much evidence, were still putatively buried under tonnes of rock and ice, and even though there was absolutely no evidence to suggest she killed Mowbry, Horenko had spun them a good story.

Back in Jasper, I discovered later, Horenko had arrived at a deal with Roger moments after Roger furiously hauled him bodily off the dais at the media conference. Horenko would take his tabloid-sourced payment, a.k.a. retirement fund, which was in the low seven figures, and resign effective immediately, and Roger would agree not to hang him upside-down by his nuts in a closet in the cop shop.

Or something like that.

After he was gone, Roger was cleaning out Rodney's desk and found the card Lock had given Rodney early in his investigation. Whether intentionally, as a big Fuck You, or by accident, it was one of the smart-paper ones.

To Roger's delight, Rodney had never figured it out.

Roger brought it to me.

"This isn't evidence, so I don't have to keep it," he said. "If I leave it there, someone will figure it out, and what they could get for it makes Horenko's blood money look like chump change. How come bad cops are so damned stereotypical?"

"Never mind, Rog," I said. "We'll always have Paris."

"What the hell are you talking about?"

"We know," I said, waving the card. "We know he didn't have a clue what this is."

"Yeah. When I think he almost had this job. He would have been my boss."

"Well, there's a reason he didn't get it. Duh."

"Thanks, kiddo," he said. "Look, let me say . . . I'm damned sorry about your pals. Pris, and your . . . Nathan. You know that."

"Yeah, Rog, so am I," I said. "So am I. But what the fuck can we do about it now?"

"Nioowww," echoed Bunnywit. He had it all figured out, but we weren't listening.

75. THE BOX

Nathan had left me some things in his will. For a guy who was not planning to die, he was pretty thorough. His lawyer said he updated his will before car trips, plane trips, rock climbing — so I had to go downtown one lovely June morning and see said lawyer. I took Mr. Spak with me, ostensibly for legal advice but really for moral support.

Nathan left me his cashmere overcoat and twelve other garments, including his butter-suede jacket and the scarlet cashmere dressing gown. (I'd worn the latter when I slept over at his place after the workshop tour. "This is to die for!" I'd said. "Yes, isn't it?" he had replied, then creatively removed me from it over the next hour, culminating in a little death for each of us, which we hadn't intended would foreshadow anything but more fun later.)

He left me the ongoing income he'd set up for my foundation work. It was enough to live on comfortably but not richly, just as I preferred. I was so mad about that I could spit, but he wasn't there to argue with.

He left Bunnywit a silk scarf and a pair of fine leather boots to sleep on.

And he left me a box. I was to take it home before I opened it.

At home, I left the box on my bed while I carefully made a meal for Bunnywit and one for me.

I took my plate, put on the cashmere dressing gown, and went to bed. Bunnywit came to join me. It wasn't exactly unprecedented for me to go to bed at noon, but usually in that case I hadn't been alone, so he was curious about the break in routine.

I had tried to explain to him that Nathan, Pris, and Lock were dead, but his "Niaow" had sounded less like a despairing cri de cœur than like a demand to produce them right now, right then; that I could not do so was in the same This Is All Your Fault category as fish sticks and vet visits. In this case I knew how he felt (times about a million), but saying "No!" hadn't worked for me either. Also, he was easily distracted by cat food, and ignored me once he had some. Cat food didn't work for human-on-human loss. So Bun hadn't been much comfort up to now.

In bed, I put the box on my lap and my plate on the box, and ate the crab sandwich and the spinach salad. I put aside the plate. Bun began to lick it while I examined the box.

It was a lovely box: filigreed and inlaid wood with no visible lid. It was about thirteen by ten by seven inches, whatever that is in metric, and had a slight fragrance of sandalwood, cedar, and sawdust. Getting it open was easy. The side and top had hollows that fit my hands. Now I understood the wood shavings on one of Nathan's workbenches, and that elaborately casual effort in his workshop to get me to hold that block of fancy modelling clay. This box had been well underway by that point. Nathan had made it himself, by hand, for me, as our relationship developed.

The last time we were together he had said to me: "I knew I loved you the moment I saw you. Anything gradual about our courtship was the artifice of an essentially shy man."

"Gradual?" I had joked, and that was that, but he had told me true.

76. ". . . HERE IS MY BOX; I NEVER TRAVEL WITHOUT MY BOX . . ."

In the box was all the smart paper in the world.

All. His *and* Lock's versions. A stack of blank, slightly oily, reproachful paper. And two tiny data storage sticks.

And a letter. Written on the topmost piece of smart paper, in Nathan's tiny, tidy, calligraphic handwriting. Maybe even with his fingertip, as a pen wasn't necessary on this stuff. I could see him doing it.

That's what ghosts are. They are memories so strong they have imprinted themselves on our smart little brain cells, and they pop up unbidden.

I tapped the paper and the paper began to read me the letter — in Nathan's voice. "Beautiful best-beloved . . ." it began. I couldn't bear it, and tapped it for silent reading.

Much of the rest is private. There are a few passages I had to show Dafydd Spak, and I may feel moved to share some of them from time to time, if circumstances demand. I read the whole letter out loud to Bunnywit, when I could speak for crying. I can cry in front of Bunnywit; he puts a paw on my shoulder and licks my face. I know it's self-serving of him, but a little anthropomorphism at a time like this is necessary.

The letter ended: "As for the contents of this box, as far as I know it's all the smart paper there is. Do as you will with it. Make a lot of money out of it, or keep it a secret. It's up to you. Nobody knows you have it, so it doesn't matter."

"Naiaooow!" said Bunnywit. Nathan should have listened, but he was beyond 20/20 hindsight now.

But — I was still alive, and I should have listened.

AND I'VE BEGGED HER TO STOP FOR A BIT AND EXPLAIN —

77. IN THE EVENT OF MY DEATH

I sat on the bed with the box in my hands for some time.

Nathan came through the door twice, in little flickers of memory, and lay beside me in other flickers.

I don't know how much longer I would have sat there, thinking, or what would have happened if I had been able to follow my impulse, close the box right then, and put it on the top shelf of my closet until I could bear to look at it.

But while I still sat staring at the wall, Bunnywit got bored, as usual. He put his paws on the edge of the box, and his weight tipped it over. The smart paper and the tiny thumb drives slithered out onto the bed. Bun pursued one of the drives under the paper, scrabbling at one of the sheets to get it out of the way. His paw triggered its contents, and Nathan's voice spoke into the room.

"In the event of my death . . ." he said.

"Niaow!" shrieked Bunnywit, and jumped up, back, and sideways, two feet each way. Which meant he fell off the bed.

". . . take all this paper to your lawyer. Be careful. Don't activate any of it until you can record it, just in case Lock has his security bug worked out. That's why I haven't even looked at some of it . . ."

Bun, trying to pretend he had meant to fall, hopped back on the bed and landed on the paper. Nathan's voice stopped.

Now I was the one to yell "*NO!*", as violently as if Bunnywit had killed him again. I swatted at Bun and he made himself very scarce, leaping across the spilled paper, launching himself off the bed, and skidding out of the bedroom and down the hall. His paws started all the paper they touched.

I sat there in a tiny cacophony of secret messages, in several voices: Nathan, Lock, Pris, and others I didn't recognise.

"Where did she go? Who did she see? Find out, Mr. Chi— . . ."

"Rodney — I can call you Rodney, can't I? . . ."

"I can't believe he really was stalking me. Lock says he had to keep an eye . . ."

"Memo: lab to Mr. Chiles . . ."

"Hey, I have the results of that forensic audit. Call me."

In a panicky flurry, I slapped them out.

No way of knowing if Bunnywit had triggered some kind of *Mission: Impossible* auto-erase.

I sat in silence for a while, and thought too much.

Then I disguised the box as much as possible inside an eco-conscious grocery bag, put my digital camera in my pocket, called a cab to the back alley, went out the apartment's back door for a change, and took the box directly to Dafydd Spak's office.

There, we activated, recorded, and photographed every piece of smart paper we could. Including the card Lock had given to Horenko and the one he had given to me.

There were some surprises, which I will duly reveal, don't worry. The most interesting was another piece of paper with Pris's voice on it, saying sadly, "I won't turn him in, but I'm going to have to leave him. I'll tell him after we get home ..." It was Lock's paper she was using, which we would later discover mattered.

There were some "aha!" moments.

There were some questions. Lots and lots, actually, but we deferred every question that wasn't relevant to the mystery of their deaths.

There were some that stayed stubbornly blank. Had they always been blank? I didn't hear Pris's voice complete that incomplete sentence on any of the sheets, so Bun had messed up at least one. Damned cat. His name *used* to be Fuckwit, a year or so before, and I was tempted to backslide on that.

There were also some actual surprises who showed up at the door, but they went away when I called Roger. Then I had to explain about the paper, so I arranged with Roger to meet at Spak's office the next day.

Nathan had been a devious man.

But then, they all three had been devious.

The jigsaw puzzle had started to make more sense, but key pieces still weren't there.

Spak locked away the box and the camera in his safe, and I went home to feed the cats.

78. THE CATS

Notice that plural slipped in there? That's not accidental. Just as I was leaving Dafydd Spak's office, he got a call. I waved goodbye, but he shook his head and pointed to the chair I'd just left. I sat down in my own warm spot.

"As it happens, she's right here," he said. "We've been going over some things."

He waited while the other end talked, which came across to me as a faint scratching at a distant door.

"Oh yes?" he said politely.

The other party talked some more.

"That's correct," he said. I saw that he was smiling slightly.

"Thank you so much. I'll convey that information to her."

By now I was actually almost curious, almost distracted from my funk about hearing Nathan and Pris and Lock's voices over and over again.

Spak gently placed his telephone receiver back in its cradle.

"Was that about me?" I said, redundantly.

He nodded.

"Why didn't you put it on speaker?"

He looked at his telephone, and then did something I had never yet seen him do. He laughed. He laughed out loud.

"What?" Someone laughing at a secret joke is one of the annoying paper-cuts of life. I glared at him and he ramped it down to a chuckle.

"I was protecting you," he said.

"Protecting me?"

"From a charge of . . . oh, perhaps uttering threats?" He had another moment of silent laughter, then pulled himself together, back to the calm, serene, unflappable Mr. Spak I knew.

"You have been left a small legacy," he said. "That was Priscilla Gill's lawyer."

Oh no.

"Oh, no!"

Oh, yes.

"Oh, yes. She has left you . . . her cats."

"Her cats — plural?"

He was still having trouble with the laughing, doing that silent shoulder-shake that people do when they don't want to laugh during a funeral.

"You mean . . . Micah."

"Both of them. The living one and the . . . dead one. They're being delivered to your apartment right now. They'll be there when you get there."

I looked at him helplessly.

He smiled. His shoulders shook a bit more. He shook his head.

"It's never boring," he said.

"No, it isn't," I said, and took my leave.

79. "I WISH I HAD HER FINGERS."

It was a nice spring day, and I decided to walk.

My cell rang when I was halfway home.

It was Roger.

"News," he said. "They've found part of Lock. A glove, a couple of fingers. Blood. Some mangled gear. There's a bunch of rock in the way of anything else. They're keeping me posted."

"Sounds like deus ex machina to me," I said. "Can you find out more?"

"Maybe. It might cost more of Mr. Bierce's money."

"Fine by me. Do it."

"Don't get used to giving me orders," said Roger.

"Roger that," I said.

He hung up.

80. WHERE DID SHE COME FROM, WHERE DID SHE GO?

That voice had said, "Where did she go? Who did she see?" They were talking about Pris, on that particular smart page, but the questions reminded me of that old folk song I'd been playing at the folk club.

Where did he come from, where did he go?
Where did he come from, Cotton-eyed Joe?

I'd heard enough about Nathan to start tracking his childhood. But not Chiles.

Chiles had shown up in that foster home where Nathan had been stuck as a teen, calling himself Lockwood Chiles and saying he was fifteen but mighty big for his age. Had he been telling a different story every day of the week, even then? Had he been flying under the radar for some youthful transgression?

I called Roger back.

"I've been thinking. Can we get into the juvenile system and find Nathan and Lock?"

"No. Those records are sealed for a reason."

"I don't believe you."

"Let's put it this way," said Roger. "Guys, now dead or presumed dead, and who when living had more money than God, have made sure that those records have been sealed, redacted, probably fictionalised, and for all we know rendered non-existent. I already tried. There is nothing about the youthful Nathan Bierce and Lockwood Chiles that couldn't safely be leaked to tabloids, hasn't been, or, from what I can gather from the people I asked, soon will be."

"Ah."

"Ah indeed. See you tomorrow."

And for that matter, where *did* she go? Who did she see?

I would be following up on some of the smart-paper recordings later to find that out. Right now, I had Pris's Revenge waiting for me.

81. THE TRUEST BEING, MARK I AND MARK V

At home, a very uncomfortable junior lawyer in a suit inhabited the vestibule. The vestibule was howling as if the alarm system was overperforming. The lawyer was a little shorter than I am, and rumpled in the unmistakeable way of the airplane journey.

She had huge dark-brown eyes rimmed with red from sleepless-ness, and her suit was a size double-zero and seemed a little big on her.

The source of the howl was the carrier beside her on the floor, in which Micah the Fifth crouched, complaining to the universe. I knew it was Micah Five only because of the circumstances and Pris's e-mailed photos. We'd never met.

A further (pun unintended, but apt) source of the young lawyer's discomfort was the stuffed dead brown tabby cat sitting in a shallow box in her arms. That was Micah the Original: I recognised him, though he was looking — um, a little stiff (pun intended).

"Come in," I said, unlocking the door.

As soon as he saw me, Micah Five, an elegant Abyssinian, stopped howling. We went up to the apartment.

As soon as Micah Five saw Bunnywit, he began to purr.

So did Bun.

These are the end times.

82. SHADES OF SCHRÖDINGER

I have in the past introduced cats to each other, processes requiring days of negotiation. Sometimes months. Sometimes unsuccessful months. The case of Freda Goodholme vs. Babe the Gallant Cat did not end well for Freda, for instance.

When we came in with the carrier, Bunnywit ran to the door to meet me. He twined around my legs in his usual perfunctory manner, then got up on his hind legs in his gopher stance to peer into the kennel, from which was emerging a purr loud enough to trigger noise ordinance penalties. When he saw Micah Five, and smelled him, he began to rub against the bars of the carrier from one side, and Micah from the other.

This was astounding behaviour.

I decided to go with the consensus that seemed to be developing. Ready to referee, but curious, I opened the door.

Micah Five stepped elegantly out. Bunnywit circled around until they could touch noses. "Ne-ew?" he said tentatively.

"Ne-ew!" replied Micah Five, and looked around.

Before I could move, Bun leapt away from us, and Micah followed him, down the hallway to the bedroom. I followed, too, leaving the lawyer with her dusty armload of nostalgia in the entry hall, but I wasn't witnessing a cat fight. I was witnessing Bun introducing Micah Five to his second-favourite retreat, the space under the bed. His duck-tailed Manx behind and Micah's sleek tail were just disappearing.

I leaned down to see.

Bun lay down on his side. Micah Five lay down beside him.

They put their paws around each other and licked each other's faces as if they had known each other for years. They were both purring.

Bunnywit looked over at me. And purred louder. I'd swear the little devil was thanking me.

I give up. Never will I understand my cat.

Either cat.

Any cat.

Or, really, life in general, but that's another matter.

Shaking my head in wonder, I went back down the hall to the young woman waiting. I spread my hands in the universal gesture for "WTF?" and she said, quietly, "It made that noise all the way here."

"From where?"

"London," she said.

"London, England?"

"Yes." She had an English accent to prove it.

"Holy . . . toledo. You poor thing."

"I have cats," she said. "They love travelling. In the car. They hate meeting new cats."

"These are the end times," I said.

"No joke," she said. "Here, take this bloody thing too." She shoved the box of Micah (deceased) at me.

"Er . . . ?"

"I mean, here is the rest of your bequest. Ma'am."

"Oh, that's overdoing it the other way. Don't I at least have to show you some ID?"

"Um, you are, um, recognisable," she said. "I'm sorry, my cab is waiting. I have to catch my flight home. Here's the file with the cat's medical records. Here are instructions for the care of taxidermied animals. Here is the veterinary expenses claim form for importing a cat — all covered by the estate. Here is a photo album that comes with the cats. Please sign this receipt. Thank you."

And off she went. She was wearing four-and-a-half-inch heels much like Roma's, I noticed.

I was left holding a dead cat in a box. Shades of Schrödinger.

83. SCHRÖDINGER'S AFTERMATH

I imagine that in one of the universes just after Schrödinger's experiment, Schrödinger himself sat weeping, his cat dead on his lap, his heart broken. *Why*, he was thinking, *why did I open the box?*

I had no such recourse. It wasn't my hand that opened the deadly box, I wasn't the particle that time and fate had tipped the wrong direction. I wasn't even Schrödinger. I was just someone who had become involved after the particle started moving but before the box was opened. At least, where Pris was concerned. Maybe it had made a difference for Nathan's situation, for which I would deal with my guilt whenever it surfaced, but Pris had been on the precipice for a long time before she came back into my life.

Until that moment, standing in my hall with Micah in a box and Micah under the bed, two quantum states of the same pure character, I hadn't been sure who cut the rope. But in that moment, I accepted what I had known for a long time. Like Nathan, Pris had been innocent — of that, anyway. Her only mistake had been to love Lockwood Chiles and then try to leave him.

I moved into the apartment and put the box down on the couch. I lifted out Micah, the truest being in the young Priscilla's life, and placed his uncanny effigy on top of the tall bookshelf, up where even Bunnywit had not been able to leap. So far.

I took out the album and opened it to the first page. There was a photo where Pris and I and several other young (so young) friends surrounded the newly-dead, newly-preserved Micah One. Even Pris, who had been about twenty-five while we were barely twenty, looked like a child. Her fine aquiline face was unshadowed. She was laughing.

The photo blurred in the time-honoured way of all such artefacts.

I closed the album and placed it among the books below Micah. There was just room.

I am proud of myself. I had not hurled either Micah One or the album across the room. I had not made a noise. Later that night I would find myself playing the apposite murder ballad "Banks of the Ohio" and weeping. But that was then.

84. HEART-TO-HEART WITH BUNNYWIT

The cats came out for dinner. Of course. They are cats.

I separated them to eat, just in case. I put Bun's food in his usual place and Micah Five's on a chair nearby. Neither showed the slightest tendency to poach.

As Bunnywit ate, I told him about my day.

"Where did she go? Who did she see? Do *you* have any idea?"

"Niaow," mumbled Bunnywit through a mouthful of feline-appropriate mixed meats.

Gratifying. I didn't either.

Micah might have known, but he wasn't talking.

WHAT *IS* THE MATTER WITH MARY JANE?

85. THE FOLLOWING DAY . . .

After my place had been trashed the previous fall and my Mendelson Joe slashed, I had become security conscious and installed an alarm, but whoever had come into my apartment the following day was good, very good.

I only knew because my cell phone was gone.

"Bun," I said, "I have to go. Where the fuck is my cell phone?"

No answer. Where the hell was my cat?

"Maybe it slipped out of your pocket," said Roger when I called him from the land line.

"Nope," I said. "The place has been tossed. My underwear is in a slightly different order. And Bunnywit is lying on his new boots. Unless he has learned doorknobs, someone let him into the closet."

"He could have learned doorknobs."

"I can buy him figuring out how to get *into* the closet, but closing the door behind himself? It opens outward, you know." Micah was under the bed, but that proved nothing.

"I'll send Annette over."

"Perfect."

"Don't touch anything else."

"Duh. Except, too late, because it was a while before I was sure it wasn't just me forgetting where I put the thing. And then I had to find Bunnywit."

"She'll do the best she can."

"Thanks, Rog."

"I may even come over myself, after I finish this shitload of paperwork."

"Isn't that why you have an executive assistant?"

"Feeling freaked out, are you?"

"Not at all."

He waited.

"Well, yeah. I was only gone half an hour. We were out of cat food, so I went to get some before I came down to meet you. I could have surprised whoever it was . . ."

"Get out of there right now!"

"Too late. I looked everywhere for Bun."

"Which closet?"

"Hall. Why?"

"What was that cat's original name, did you say?"

"Fuckwit."

"As God made you he matched you. I'll be right there. Wait at your neighbour's."

"Too little too late," I said. "I'm not going anywhere."

It wasn't bravado. I was covered with cats. Micah was on the couch back, leaning on my head, a trick learned from Bun, while Bunnywit was pinning me to the couch by sitting on my lap kneading. Apparently he only likes the boot closet when the door is open and he chooses to retreat there, not when he goes in in good faith and then is imprisoned there.

"Why didn't you miaow?" I asked him. "I would have found you 'way sooner!" He closed his eyes and stuck his head under my arm the way he does at the vet.

That freaked me out too.

Bun is a pretty good judge of character.

86. THE END TIMES

That afternoon I had been scheduled to go into the foundation office, and I called Roma — on my land line — to say why I wouldn't be there. I told her about my stolen phone.

"No worries," she said.

"No worries? What the f—"

"I grabbed your numbers in my phone. We'll just grab you a new SIM and phone, and track the old one with GPS. Meet me at the mall in fifteen!"

That was fine, because Annette and her forensic team were getting pissed off with me being in the way of their smoothly oiled machine, and Bunnywit had gone back to the closet as soon as they appeared. When I peeked in at him, he was dividing his weight between the old red boots and his legacy from Nathan. His back remained firmly to me, Annette's team, and the world, and he ignored me saying his name. I knew how he felt. Micah was under the bed. It was pretty clear from the dust trails that only cats had been under there, so that was okay too.

At the mall, Roma ignored the line at the phone kiosk. She tapped on her high heels directly over to one of the junior scientists behind the counter and called her by name (Konni: it was on her name tag, so that wasn't a miracle, just an example of Roma's wit and wisdom in action again), and soon they were comparing tattoos.

"Can I grab your password?" said Roma to me.

"For the account?"

"For your phone. You don't have a password on your phone?" said Konni.

"No," I said.

"Fail," said Roma. I consoled myself that when she was in the nursing home, she'd still be using the same slang she learned in her youth and would sound ridiculous.

Of course, that's true of any of us. What-*evs*.

"Your phone's been used. Let's grab that call list."

I didn't recognise the more recent numbers. "Can you give me a printout of those?"

"No problem, I can grab that for you."

'Grab' was apparently the next portmanteau word. At least they hadn't mentioned having a nice day yet. Maybe that one is finally over.

She offered to e-mail the list to me, but I had her e-mail the list to Roger too. He could track them down.

In moments I had a new phone, all my data was back from The Cloud and/or Roma's phone memory — whichever was applicable — and I'd only seen Nathan or Pris once and Lock twice in the mall crowds. Progress.

More to the point, moments after that, Roma was behind the counter with Konni, and they were looking for the actual location of my stolen phone. The other tattooed techno-wizards at the kiosk were looking over their shoulders and suggesting things. It was the spookiest, most disquieting thing I'd seen in ages.

"Anyone could find where I am by tracking this?" I said, holding up my phone.

"Well, the old one," said Roma. "I got you a BlackBerry this time. Not flashy but the encryption on them is lit."

"These are the end times," I said.

"What?" they said in unison, their elven, unlined faces tilted in an identical expression of cluelessness and disapprobation.

"Never mind, children," I said. "Talk among yourselves."

"What?"

"Just carry on."

"Sure, let's grab that puppy's where," said Roma, and she and Konni went back to their conjuring.

I called Roger and told him that 'where' was now a noun synonym for 'location'. I also told him what they were doing.

"These are the end times," he said.

"That's what I said," I said. "Did you know they could do that?"

"Yes," he said. "That's how we track stolen vehicles now. But these are still the end times. I don't care. It's weird."

"I'm with you. In Ludd-ville."

"I thought you were in the mall."

"Ha fucking ha. What did Annette find at my place?"

"This stuff takes time."

"Unlike, apparently, surveilling the world for stolen mobile phones."

"Do you want to listen in to whoever has it?" said Roma beside me.

"Their calls?"

"No, I think Konni and Taffi here can activate the microphone remotely. We can record what's going on."

"Is that legal?" I asked.

"No," said Roger in my ear.

"I dunno, whatever," said Roma. "It's easy. We can record it."

"Sure, whatevs," I said. "Awesome. Record everything."

I hung up before Roger could sputter too much.

Turns out there was a form I could sign giving permission to record my calls. We didn't need to note that the phone was at the moment being used by someone who might not have been that willing to share data with The Cloud. I signed the form, and just to annoy him I gave the kiosk-bunnies Roger's e-mail as the 'where' to send the recordings. If I ever got out of this, I could easily change it online: they showed me how.

87. OTHER PLANS

Apparently my phone was in my apartment building.

"You sure you didn't just lose it?" said Konni.

"I've had a police forensics team in my apartment all day," I said. "I think not."

"Well, did you go to some neighbour's place and drop it there?" asked Roma.

"No," I said. I picked up my new phone and tucked it away in my pocket. "Thank you so much. Do I owe you anything else for the detective work?"

"Nah, no problem, it was fun."

Fun, I thought.

"Have an awesome day," said Konni.

"Thank you, dear," I said. "I have other plans."

WHAT IS THE MATTER WITH MARY JANE? SHE'S PERFECTLY WELL AND SHE HASN'T A PAIN,

88. "JUST PRETEND I NEVER HAPPENED / AND ERASE ME FROM YOUR MIND . . ."

When I got home, Lockwood Chiles was sitting in my living room.

Unlike my recent memory flashback visitations, he didn't go away when I blinked.

My old cell phone was on the coffee table. His coat was over the easy chair. Bunnywit, showing his true colours, had crawled into the lining and was trying to detach the fur from it from within. Lock paid no attention to him. Bun paid no attention to either of us. Some guard cat he was.

"Who the fuck wears a sheepskin coat at the end of June?" I said.

"I like that coat," said Lock, reasonably. "You, on the other hand, are a pain in the ass."

"You didn't have to come here."

"Oh, yes I did. You have the paper."

"I don't."

"He told me he was giving it to you. For the Homelessness Alleviation Whatever-the-fucking-hell. Left it to you in his will."

"Oh, that paper."

"Yeah, that paper,"

"Who knows you're alive?"

"Nobody. I have a whole new name now. I've been setting it up for years."

"Convenient."

"But I need the paper. I need those thumb drives."

"I don't have them —"

As I spoke he surged out of the chair and had my lapels in his fists before I finished. One of his hands was heavily bandaged. That would be the one missing a couple of fingers.

"— here!" I said. "I don't have them *here*! Geez, give me a fucking break."

He put me down more gently than he'd picked me up, and smoothed my jacket.

"Nice," he said. "One of Nathan's?"

"Yes, he left me half his best clothes."

"Too bad his shoes don't fit. You could be a little Nathan clone and nobody in the office would know the difference when you go in and *take over our company*!" His voice transformed on the last words into something damned close to a snarl.

"What are you taking about? I know nothing about your business! I don't want it! Are you nuts?"

"*I'm* not the one who's nuts. Who *wouldn't* want it? I want it."

"Why didn't you just come back from the dead?"

"With the marks of my hands on Priscilla's throat?"

"She was crushed in the fall. They were both mangled. Nathan's face was the only recognisable body part. For crying out loud, you could have read that in the newspaper. Nobody could prove a thing. Nobody even suspected . . ."

"Except you, and you were up there with that medical examiner bitch, making my life impossible. I couldn't go back without the face of Nathan Lockwood. Who'd believe Chiles, the puffed-up bodyguard?"

"Oh, give up the pity party. You own half and everyone knew it. And they knew you had half the brains too. Now it's more like half a brain instead. What, did you get a blow on the head in that accident?"

"That I did. Pris hit me with her climbing hammer. I was just trying to talk a little sense into her."

"Ah."

"And then she stabbed me, the bitch."

"Your light of love and life-mate — a bitch?"

"She could be . . . difficult. And she wanted to split up, anyway. I listened to her on the paper." Lock had indeed worked out his "security bug", in no one else's favour but his own.

"So you killed her. And Nathan."

"That was an accident. I just intended a little tiny rock fall. It got out of hand. Anyway, he was standing too close."

"How silly of him. All his fault, of *course*. Except, you had already cut his harness also."

"Yeah, well, I was mad. But I decided not to haul him up once Pris was dead. Without her, we could have started over. Well, there was you, of course."

Sure. Of course. I shivered. Even had Nathan suspected nothing, which wouldn't have been the case, how long would I have lasted?

"And now he's gone and you're here."

"Yeah. So give me the smart paper. With that I can start over by myself. And I may not even kill you, though I'm bloody tempted."

"No point now."

"Though I *have* told you 'way too much."

"There's nobody here with us except the cats. Who'd believe me?"

"Cats?" He turned as if to search the place for additional eavesdropping pusses and saw Micah One, at his eye level on the shelf. He jumped back and actually hollered.

"What is that thing doing here?"

"Pris. Left me Micah One and Micah Five. They were just dropped off a couple of days ago. Five is still hiding under the bed probably, especially after that yell. And the smart paper is in a vault."

"Get it." He grabbed his coat. Bunnywit fell out and howled indignantly. "I'll come with you."

"It's Friday night, Lock. Timelocks, remember? Impossible to bypass, even for the rich, which you aren't any more. Temporarily, of course," I added hastily. "I can't just go get it. It's not even under my name. It's a lawyer's. Come back Monday."

Astonishingly, he grabbed my first cell phone, shoved past me and stomped down the hall toward the door.

"I was never here," he said. "This never happened."

"I didn't know you liked Willie Nelson," I said.

He slammed the door after himself.

I would have run and locked it, but it had been locked and the alarm on when he got to it, both times, so I assumed it would do no good — if he wanted back in, he'd come back in.

He should have been called UnLock.

Well, in a way, he *was* Un-Lock. Lockwood Chiles certainly hadn't been his original name, and it wasn't his name now.

89. "YESTERDAY, UPON THE STAIR, / I MET A MAN WHO WASN'T THERE! . . ."

"He took a *shower* while he was waiting for me! In *my bathroom*!" I told Roger.

"He's probably been sleeping rough."

"Can you imagine if I'd come home while he was . . . never mind. And he didn't clean up afterward. He left towels lying around and shaving goo in the sink like it was a hotel and the staff was going to come in and shovel the mess out after him. First he threatens me, and then he treats me like a fucking servant? And I'm supposed to pretend it didn't happen?"

"At least there's some physical evidence. I'll get Annette back here. Good thing you *didn't* clean up."

"As if."

"You recognise that he's not really — um, firing on all cylinders, don't you? He has killed several people."

"I told him to come back on Monday. And he just *left*. I still can't believe I'm alive."

"Tell me exactly what happened. In order this time."

"It's all going to be in your e-mail in-box, if those mall rats did the job right."

"What?"

I explained. "And it's even legal."

"Hmmph. We'll see if that holds up. But I'm not at my e-mail, I'm here. So just tell me what you remember, will you?"

I did. As I recounted the time of maximum tension, that moment when Lock rough-housed me and we began to discuss Nathan's clothing, Roger began to laugh. He continued laughing periodically through the report. I glared at him.

"I could have been killed!"

"That's not why I'm laughing, kiddo. I seldom tell you how I appreciate you, do I?"

I stared at him. "Um . . . no . . . never, recently, actually."

"Well, I do. Whenever I have a dull day in future — assuming you survive all this — I am just going to think of you sassing a huge, dangerous murderer because he got in your face and wasn't being *logical*, and I am going to enjoy that image. The guy is six-foot-four, at least."

"At least. Probably six-five or six-six."

"And you're —"

"Roger, I know how tall I am! What am I going to do? He's coming back on Monday!"

"No, he's not," said Roger. "Right now he's kicking himself for leaving at all. He's thinking about you, and your character, and he's figuring out that you aren't pretending anything didn't happen today. He's either outside, fuming, waiting for me to leave so he can hold you hostage until Monday, or he's on his way to Timbuktu."

"What's in Timbukt— . . . oh, the generic one."

"Yes, O elevated one, the generic one. May I suggest that you find somewhere else to stay tonight?"

"I have cats to feed."

"And a life to lose."

"It's my life. For what it's worth."

"Fine," said Roger. "I hope you've made a will."

"I've left the cats to you," I said. "All three of them."

"I'll take the one that doesn't shit," he said.

90. ". . . HE WASN'T THERE AGAIN TODAY, OH, HOW I WISH HE'D GO AWAY!"

I knew I wasn't in physical danger from Lock yet. He didn't have the data sticks with the smart-paper formulae, or the samples, and until he did, I was relatively safe.

I know because he told me so.

He called me every two hours all weekend. Using my old phone, to my new phone with the unlisted number. He was the king of tech, and he had clearly earned all those millions.

"How ya doin'?" he said, each time.

The fifth time, in the middle of the night, I said, "Lock, it's still the weekend. It's still the middle of the night on the weekend. What the fuck? Let me sleep."

"I don't sleep, you don't sleep," he said.

"Why aren't you sleeping?"

"I miss Priscilla."

"You shouldn't have killed her, then."

"It was self-defence. She was coming at me with that knife."

"It had a four-inch blade."

"Neck's a vulnerable spot."

"And explain why again she was coming at you?"

"Well, I was kind of —"

"Strangling her. You mentioned that. Why, again?"

He hung up.

I turned off the ringer, put the phone under a pillow, and got four hours' sleep, but then Micah Five — thinking a vibrating phone was a great new cat toy, I suppose — clawed it out one time it rang. It showed two missed calls.

"You and this fucking cat of Priscilla's," I said before he could say anything. "What is it with you two? Are you in cahoots?"

"I hate that cat," he said. "Both of them. She thought it was a big joke, that stuffed cat. And she put catnip in my coat pocket one time."

"That explains why Bunnywit was trying to eat your coat. Look, I'm a little unclear on all this. I thought you loved Priscilla."

"I do love her."

"But, this strangling thing."

"I told you. She wanted to split up. And Mowbry was dead. Do you know how long it took me to prime him?"

"'Prime him'? You're kidding me, right?"

"Crazed fan. It would have worked. But he went a little too postal on us."

"'On *us*'? Priscilla was the one learning to walk again."

"That's what I mean. And then he got religion in prison or something, and was all sorry. He had to go."

"So you waited for him to leave. Did you push Nathan?"

"Yeah, he showed up while I was waiting for Mowbry."

"So you nearly kill your best friend, then you met Mowbry and did him in."

"Oh, it was better than that. I got Pris to slug him. Then I told her I prettied him up with the knife to confuse the scene."

Ah. Hence Priscilla's screaming fit.

"She thought she killed him. Didn't she see the blood?"

"She doesn't read a lot of mysteries."

God, he was fast. He knew I'd meant that the amount of blood showed that Mowbry had been alive when Lock had cut him.

Alive, but unconscious. That explained a lot. Pris would have been realising that after the conversation in the restaurant. I bet her desire to split up started right then, over rubbery lobster and a side of lies.

"He was unconscious — so you could make the scene look the way you wanted."

"It was fun."

Between the three of them, I had already widened my concept of fun considerably, but this was too much.

"Fun? You killed a guy just for *fun*?"

"Well, you have to admit," he said, "things were getting a little dull." I had my phone recording his calls. He knew it was happening, because I had told him. But he didn't seem to care.

"I think everyone could have done with it staying that dull."

"That's what Pris said. While we were climbing. She figured out the blood that day in that fucking steakhouse, I think." Ah, I'm good under pressure too. Somehow, though, I wish I'd never had to learn that.

"So, your blood on the gear?"

"I scraped myself on a carabiner on Nathan's climbing gear while I was working on it, and it kept oozing. I guess it set her thinking a bit more."

"And the strangling bit?"

"Well, that was more in the way of a warning. We were halfway up a rock face at the time. It wasn't like I intended anything serious."

"She clearly didn't understand your vocabulary."

"Her loss."

"Apparently. Well, she marked you, anyway."

"No, she didn't. I took her knife away easy and stuck it through her goddamn hand."

"So how did she cut your rope?"

"She didn't. It broke. It wasn't only the one, anyway. I had a safety."

"Come on, you know it was sliced. Just like you did to Nathan's. You must have meant to look innocent."

"Nathan was getting so boring. Giving away *our* money! But you're saying mine was . . . that bitch. That bitch. So *that's* what happened! She wasn't going for my neck after all. She was going for the rope! Clever, clever little Pris."

"Look, you know I'm recording your calls and e-mailing them to the cops," I said again. "Don't you care?"

"It doesn't matter," he said. "Lockwood Chiles is dead. Try to prove otherwise."

"You're six-foot-six for heaven's sake! Airport infometrics, even I know about that stuff. Besides, I have your DNA in my bathroom," I said.

There was a moment of silence.

He hung up.

91. "I'LL BE WATCHING YOU . . ." REDUX

"You two had a hell of a fine relationship," I said next time the phone rang.

"What?" said Roger.

"Oh, it's you."

"And you were expecting . . ."

"Lockwood Chiles has been calling me every couple of hours. Want to hear his confession? It's in your e-mail in-basket. A whole bunch of them, actually. About five minutes per every two hours. It's been swell. If I don't answer, he leaves voice mail."

"He must be nuts."

"Ya think?"

"Decompensating, it's called."

"Decomposing, more like."

92. THE NEXT DAY . . .

I had a mentor once who said, "Would you want Hitler to approve of you?" to teach me to care less about the opinions of people I didn't respect. I have valued her lesson for years.

Now I knew what it was like if, in essence, Hitler did approve of me. It was creepy.

On the other hand, I didn't have to answer the phone either. But I did.

"I'm not coming to meet you on Monday," said Chiles. "I may be crazy but I'm not stupid."

I had to laugh, briefly. "So you acknowledge that you are crazy."

"Several people I respect have told me so. It was one of the last things Pris said to me. So I have to at least take it under advisement."

Could he hear himself?

"So . . . so how does someone cause a climbing accident without being killed themselves, especially if an avalanche is involved?"

"Clever explosive devices. Good anchors for me. Bad anchors for them. A little more dramatic than I intended, but my gear was good. I made it out. The others didn't. Too bad."

"Too bad? You killed your lover and your best friend and several other people and you say 'Too bad'?"

"Well, I killed them, but . . . well, yeah, it is too bad. It's very bad. But I can live with it. And I have to say, it was a rush, when that ceiling went. A little encouragement in those cracks and . . . boom! One hell of a rush."

"But you almost bought it yourself."

"What makes you think that?"

"Small body parts at the bottom?"

"Pris did that. Well, Pris gave me the idea. I actually had to finish it myself. They had to find *something*. Good thing her knife was sharp."

"So let me get this right. You set up the accident, and while you guys were struggling in the air you cut your own fingers off?"

"That was after. I was actually trying to pull her up at that point."

"Oh. *That's* why your blood was on her gear."

"Yes. God, she was such a *bitch*!"

"So why not just go find someone you liked?"

"She was *mine*," he said simply.

"Ah," I said.

This time I hung up first. I really had had enough.

93. HOW THE HELL . . . ?

"Roger, how the hell are we going to catch this guy?"

I had asked Roger how a guy who is tall, handsome, bulky, and distinctive — and who seems to have a sheepskin coat fetish — could elude the law-enforcement might of an entire city police force plus the RCMP. How was that?

"With over a million people to choose from, some of them are bound to be tall," he had said, tall-ly.

"Easy for you to say," I said bitterly. "He isn't phoning you every two hours. Apparently in collusion with an Abyssinian cat, who always hears the phone no matter where I put it. For all we know, the damned cat was the mastermind."

"Probably thinks it's trying to help you catch its mistress's murderer."

"You don't know much about cats, do you?"

Roger was stretched out in the easy chair with his feet up on the new ottoman.

The ottoman was one of the posthumous gifts Nathan kept sending me.

The first delivery had come only two days after Nathan's death. It was a forest-green cashmere dress coat in an androgynous upmarket style. The accompanying card read, "Now you will quit borrowing mine." Bunnywit had been distressed by the commotion.

Next were the flowers. Nathan had left a standing order for new flowers every week at a local florist known for artful arrangements. They came with cards that said some variation of "I love you." After the third one arrived, I had to call them and put the whole thing on hold. They had been given fifty-two cards. I told them to hang onto the rest them and I'd resume the series, or at least pick up the cards, when I could manage it. They were sympathetic. They sent over an orchid — plant, not cut flower — as a condolence. So far, it was actually still alive, and apparently thriving on a western exposure and a random cycle of watering versus neglect.

Every now and then, something would show up in the mail or a delivery person would ring the bell.

They weren't big things. They weren't expensive. They were just there. There, as he wasn't.

Roger and I had been profoundly suspicious of the delivery guy who showed up that Monday, but he was a real UPS guy, and I even recognised him, because months ago we'd discussed his unusual name, Nachtigall, which means 'nightingale'. He had a bulky box on his dolly which turned out to contain an ottoman cleverly made to match my antique plush-upholstered armchair.

I could scarcely look at the thing at first, but it matched so well, and was so perfect, that within an hour it was as if I had always owned it. Thus proving that Alexander Pope was right in his "Essay on Man":

Vice is a monster of so frightful mien,
As, to be hated, needs but to be seen;
Yet seen too oft, familiar with her face,
We first endure, then pity, then embrace.

Apparently it was also true of surprises from beyond the grave and overstuffed furniture.

"Let's listen to the evidence again," he said.

He meant listen, not look at, because some of the smart paper had been set to audio recording so that it looked empty but wasn't. Some of that audio had been password-protected with words that meant something only to Nathan and me, like 'fun' and 'cashmere' and 'eavestroughing' and 'pomegranate'. So we went back to Spak's office and down into the boardroom in the basement where Spak kept the stuff in his safe.

"I'm gathering evidence," said Nathan's voice into the room. I'd gotten to the point where I could listen to it without wanting to scream, but it was nauseous. "But I am far from understanding yet. There are some imaginary people on the payroll, but that sort of thing happens in any large corporation. There is always someone trying to scam the system."

"I must be naïve," I said to Roger. "I had no idea that imaginary people were so common."

"We see 'em all the time," he said with no hint of humorous intention. I didn't laugh, though I felt like it, because I also felt sick and I wasn't vomiting, so.

"I see semi-imaginary people all the time, these days. I am afflicted with memory. I'm always seeing Pris or Nathan or Lock —" I broke off and stared into space.

"What?" said Roger.

"What if he wasn't semi-imaginary? He's alive, after all. So those memory flashbacks I've been attributing to PTSD — what if I actually saw him those times?"

"That is — awesomely logical, even for you." He didn't seem to notice that was a compliment, not an insult. "Okay, where did you see him?"

"The mall, last time. The mall makes sense. He was stalking me. The first time was — back in Jasper. Where's Horenko?"

"Tahiti, probably. Why?"

"I'm getting a bad feeling about this. The first time I saw Lock, I did a double-take and Horenko was standing there. What if . . . what if he actually was standing beside Horenko? What if he was working with Horenko?"

"Horenko isn't that stu— hmmm. Maybe. He could have been played."

"Can you find him?"

"Let me make a couple of calls."

It took him about half an hour, but he actually did track down Rodney's whereabouts, and Rodney wasn't in Tahiti. He was right back in his house. This required some thinking.

"Okay, is he in league? Because if so, Lock is there, and highly dangerous, and if not, Rodney may not outlive our interest in him."

"Point," he said. He hit a speed-dial on his phone.

"Lance," he said. "I need you."

He was silent for a moment. "Don't be a smart-ass," he said, "and tell Denis to quit laughing. I'm keeping an eye on our mutual friend, and I need you to meet me at the station PDQ."

Only after he had hung up and tossed his phone onto the table beside him did I think about Roma and her friends in the mall.

"Shit," I said.

"What?" he said.

"Won't being in water like that hurt your phone?" I said. I took it into the other room and closed it in the safe with mine. Then I unplugged Spak's boardroom extension line.

Then I told Roger why. "And it's too little, too late, girl," I said. "If the king of tech was listening."

"Well, if he was, we were hooped half an hour ago," said Roger. "I can't imagine how we'd avoid being heard. For all I know, your whole place is bugged in the traditional way."

He made me give back his phone and called Annette.

"I need you," he said.

She said something.

"Is everyone who works for me a wise-ass?" he asked irritably.

Apparently, yes.

He told her why he needed her.

She said something else, and he laughed and hung up.

"What?" I said.

"She said she spends more time in your apartment than she does at her own."

"Please assure her that I would rather it be otherwise," I said. After a pause I said, "Nothing personal."

"I'm sure she would take it in the best possible way," he said.

Then we went back to my place and waited silently for her to show up with her bug-sniffing team.

I have been in a lot of dicey situations in my life, some of them alone. But even with Roger sitting there, his nasty little cop gun on the end table beside him, I have probably never felt so unsafe.

Lock had money stashed. He had the kind of deep expertise that could make me and all my belongings disappear into cyber-oblivion. He could stalk me for life, the way he had stalked Priscilla. He could send evil minions to kill or maim me. He could do the same to Roger, Lance, Hep, Denis, Thel and her family, even Micah Five and Bunnywit — because they got in his way, or just to get to me.

"Niaow!" said Bunnywit.

"Nooaow," said Micah Five.

I listened. But even when Annette's crew decided the apartment wasn't bugged, I wasn't comforted. We all headed off to do the same to my lawyer's office, and then Roger and I took all the smart paper, for safekeeping, and went to the police station.

94. OUT OF THE CLUB FOR A THOUSAND YEARS AND FOUR DAYS

Rodney Horenko was not dead. That was also good news.

Roger got Lance to go out and pick him up — discreetly.

Ha. Lance wasn't exactly inconspicuous. The first time I met Denis's *beau-laid* main-squeeze, he had been masquerading as a drag queen, in five-inch fuck-me boots which made him about six-foot-nine. Without them, he was still usually the tallest guy in the room, taller even than Roger. But he and Lock were about the same height. Who knows which one of them would have won in a fair fight? I hoped we never had to find out, because Lock wouldn't fight fair. Mine you, maybe Lance was no Dudley Do-Right either. He'd worked undercover for years before transferring from Anti-Drug to Homicide.

You have to understand something about cops. Cops are genial and affable in social situations and meetings. Sometimes they're genial and affable when they come to your door too. They dress well, often snappily, once they get out of uniform, and can quickly lose that swagger that is the result of the uniform belt with all the equipment loaded onto it. In other words, they clean up pretty well.

But, as I probably have alluded to before now, up every cop's ass is the metaphorical broomstick of law and order. These days it's tempting to think that most cops became cops because it would then be legal for them to carry a gun and push people around, and the viral videos would back you up, but those assholes are still in the minority. Clichéd and Nathan-Fillion-esque as it may seem, more cops than not got into the biz because they really believe in Right and Wrong, Justice and The Law[26].

So when you're talking with a cop, you're cruising along just fine, sometimes joking and sometimes serious, but always with that little bit of social leeway that most people allow in order to make life pleasant, and all of a sudden you hit a rock.

The rock you hit could be when you refer to a friend snorting up at a party, or complain about a parking ticket, or tell a cute story about your friend's four-year-old copping some candy in the grocery store and having to go back and say they were sorry to the store manager. Suddenly your cop friend is asking for the friend's full name and address, giving a lecture about parking laws being there for all of us, or offering to give the pre-schooler a tour of the Remand Centre to scare him straight.

Mostly cops do draw the line when they're naked with you, and don't check to be sure all the positions you suggest are legal — but not always, and sometimes when a cop is naked, it's easier to see the broomstick rather than harder. (I'm told. Not that I've ever been naked with any cops except, long ago, Roger — and this little broomstick problem only manifested when we were clad. Nevertheless, it was the reason my relationship with him, while friendly, has been for many many years completely without nudity . . . but never mind that now.)

I say this to explain what came over the passel of cops (what's the collective noun for cops? "An enforcement of officers"? "A custody of cops"?) who surrounded Rodney as they brought him into the downtown cop shop. No vestige of a sense of humour

---

26. Canadian cops, anyway, so far. And by the way, the *good* cops? They fucking *hate* those assholes in the viral videos.

infected their faces. Horenko was still dapper, and even carried a thin briefcase, but he had probably used up his efforts at bonhomie in the first five minutes, and now an uneasy silence enclosed him and his former colleagues, and his Hugo Boss suit couldn't disguise the twitch in his shoulders.

It wasn't just that he had been warned that Lock might be gunning for him. It was more visceral. He had sold his former "family" out for a tabloid bonus — something they didn't appreciate and, in many cases, didn't understand. Now he didn't belong to the siblinghood of cops any more, and that knowledge was under his skin, making him jumpy.

He also looked confused by the feeling. From what I'd seen of him, I don't think introspection was his strong suit.

Roger had told me that he was only bringing me along because I wasn't safe at home. That was his story and he was sticking to it. I said if I wasn't safe neither were Bun and Micah, and he gave me a Look. "Count your blessings, and get in the goddamn car," he said. He had a point. After all, he wasn't saying "Stay out of it!" now.

As for the cats' safety, Roger absolutely refused to let me put them into their carriers and bring them along, so I left Lock a Post-it® note suggesting that any atrocities involving cats would be counterproductive, and hoped that being crazy hadn't made him too stupid to think that through.

"You're just afraid your cop buddies would call you a cat lover," I accused Roger.

"Think of it that way if you want," he said.

When he gets past grumpy toward icy like that, despite what previous anecdotes might indicate, I actually prefer not to bait him. I'm not a sadist.

So there we were, sans cats, in the cop shop, in that meeting room where they have the emergency lockdown equipment in case of nuclear threat, watching Horenko, who wasn't nuclear even in the family sense, it seemed, being brought in to face the music.

Roger pretended not to see Horenko's outstretched hand as he gestured to everyone to sit, a gesture that consisted of a curt sideways tilt of his head. Everyone sat but the young members who leaned against the wall to either side of Horenko, just at the edge of his field of vision if he craned his neck, which he did once each way before settling down.

"I won't caution you yet," Roger said bluntly, a fine meeting opener if you like that sort of thing. "That's on account of what you might call professional courtesy. Don't count on it carrying you very far."

"What's *she* doing here?" Horenko countered, and his head-jerk was combined with his trademark eyebrow lift. By "she", he didn't mean any of the female officers.

"Protective custody," said Roger. "And given the recent run of police misconduct in this case, Rodney, I'm keeping her in visual contact with officers I can *trust*." He made the emphasis particularly strong.

Rodney flushed. "I did right," he said. "I quit the job."

Roger guffawed. In someone more subtle, I'd have thought he did it for effect, but he was really laughing. His metaphoric broomstick was well in place.

"You're shitting us," he said. "I fired your fucking ass. Oh, and this conversation is being recorded. Any objection?"

One of the junior police members jumped up and turned to the wall of equipment, flushing slightly as he flipped some switches.

"This conversation *will be* recorded," Roger amended. "Tell us when you're ready, Constable Dahvay." Since I'd heard him address the constable as Prasan earlier, I saw no reason to revise the diagnosis that everyone here was in broomstick mode. Later I found out the name was spelled 'Dave', with no accent to signal pronunciation of the final *e*.

"Ready, sir!" Constable Dave was ready in record time. Oops, pun unintended. Really.

"This conversation is being recorded," Roger repeated. "Do you have any objections, Mr. Horenko." Mister. Oh, that was cold. I loved it.

"No," said Horenko. "No objections."

"I'll go around the table. Please state your name and rank. If any." Cold. Good.

We did that too. Despite now being, after several days of permanent high stress, in a resulting almost-permanent state of ironic wisecrackitis, I forbore from saying anything else but my name. The tall, upright throng around Horenko in the lobby had resolved into Lance, four constables (Dave, the two guards, and one other whose affiliation went unexplained), and an inspector and staff-sergeant from whatever-the-hell-buzzword they now call Internal Affairs. The last to arrive, coming from upstairs, turned out to be a deputy chief and Roger's boss, a compact blonde dynamo about my height who looked like she could battle her weight in bobcats — before breakfast and without messing up her hair.

"Normally," began Roger, "you would be interrogated like any other suspect would be. I'm giving you a chance here to speak up and make a voluntary statement. That won't absolve you of any prosecution if you have broken the law."

That didn't seem like much of an incentive to spill his guts, and indeed, Horenko was wily.

"Do I need a lawyer?"

"Call one if you want," said Roger in the same flat tone he'd used with me earlier in the cat discussion.

Horenko looked around. Everyone glared at him. I enjoyed doing my part.

"Fine. Okay. So I told the media, big deal. I thought she did it. Short cut the process, but hey, I was getting ready to retire. A little extra money . . ." He folded his hands complacently on the table.

"Perhaps you could —" Roger began.

I interrupted him involuntarily. "'Thought,'" I blurted.

96. THOUGHT

There was a split-second of silence, as Roger first snapped his jaw shut preparatory to growling at me, then belayed the growl and turned his gaze back to Rodney.

"'Thought'," he said. "'Thought'. So what changed your mind, Rodney? Why don't you still *think* that Priscilla Jane Gill was a psychopathic killer, as I believe you described her to the *Weekly World News*?"

"I really did think she did it," muttered Horenko. He put his hands in his lap, but we'd all already seen how his grip had tightened until his knuckles were pale.

"But." Roger leaned forward, as if about to try some empathy manoeuvre, then didn't. The result was a kind of cross-table looming. Very effective.

"He threatened my mother," said Horenko defensively.

"And gave you money," I said.

"Shut up, I've got this," said Roger to me, then turned to Horenko. "And gave you money. Right?"

"Er, yes." I had never heard someone say "er" before without humorous intent.

"How much?"

"He matched what the paper gave me. He did promise me more, but I don't expect to get it. Criminals aren't reliable." He managed to look scapegrace and smug at the same time. Rodney was a real bag of tricks.

Dave snickered. Roger made a tiny hand motion sideways, just a flicker, and there was silence again from the gallery.

"Who exactly are we talking about here?" The deputy chief had a notepad, but as far as I could see, all she had written was

Rodney's name and mine in full and the initials of everyone else there. She had spelled mine wrong, but there was very little downside to that, and my ego wasn't insisting on getting involved with that bit, anyway.

"Mr. Lockwood Chiles, a.k.a. Ambrose Bierce Chiles, a.k.a. Simon Locke, a.k.a. Ambrose Locke, a.k.a. Unknown," said Roger. "Correct, Mr. Horenko?"

"Fuck, Rog, don't bust my balls like this," said Horenko.

"You ain't seen nothin' yet if you dick around with us," said Roger.

"Language, fellas," said the deputy chief, and gestured toward the slug-like microphone in the centre of the table. Come on, I thought, way to inhibit a confession!

"Cripes, Ellie," Rog said to her.

But she had a point, and made it. "Horenko can swear all he wants; he isn't one of us any more. But I will not have the image of my clean police service tarnished on the record by casual, quotable profanity and implied threats." She then wrote 'Lockwood Chiles?' on her notepad.

"Okay," said Rog. "Let me be clear. My intention was to convey colloquially to Mr. Horenko, disgraced former member of this police service, a warning that we were treating him with courtesy and that he was not yet under arrest, but that this state of affairs could change. That is a statement of fact, not a threat."

"Very well put. Much clearer. Mr. Horenko, you stand warned."

"'Disgraced' is a bit much, Rog," Rodney said.

"We'll decide that after you tell us about Mr. Lockwood Chiles and his post-mortem contacts with you."

"He showed up at my hotel room. He had his hand wrapped in some grotty kerchief, and he was sweating inside that coat he wears. He told me Pris tried to kill him and she was in league with someone else, he suspected *her* —" he indicated me with his mobile eyebrow and a slight head-tilt. What is it with head expressiveness and cops? Do they learn it in their training? A special module in micro-tasking? I rolled my eyes.

"Shh," Roger said to me before I could say anything, although I hadn't planned on saying anything. "Go on, Rodney."

"So he had to hide out, basically, until he figured it out."

"Was this before you gave the news conference, or after?"

"B— after, of course! What do you mean, before?"

"So he knew to come to you because — ?"

"He dealt with me over the body in the alley. He was an arrogant sonuvabitch. Sorry, ma'am." (Not directed at me, of course, but at Deputy Chief Ellie.) "But after, he needed someone on his side. He read the papers, said he could provide extra proof. I helped find a doctor who kept quiet because it was a police matter. I still had my badge."

"And you didn't come to us because — ?"

"She was in every meeting! She knew what you knew. I couldn't take the risk. We decided I'd investigate alone. I've got a dossier," he said proudly.

"Where?"

Rodney reached down to his briefcase. His guards tensed, perhaps in case he came out with some sort of ceramic knife or plastic gun the X-ray at entry couldn't detect, but all he seemed to have there was paper.

I borrowed the deputy chief's underused notepad and pen and wrote a note to Roger, *When did he give you his badge? I'm sure right after news conf. He's lying!!! Lock came BEFORE news conf!!*

"I've got this," Roger murmured to me, but he kept the note. Turned it over, pulled out a pen of his own, wrote something in his little squinchy scrawl that I, due to prior acquaintance with said scrawl, could decode as *badge*. I gave Deputy Chief Ellie back her gear.

She grinned at me. Grinned! Then stifled the grin before anyone could see it: back to broomstick mode. And she was in uniform, I should mention. Senior-management version, which means a white shirt and no gear belt, but crisp as can be. I knew people who would have been on their knees before her at this moment. But it was me she grinned at.

Alas, I don't really have a uniform fetish.

She pulled the top half of the pad off and pushed the rest toward me with her pen, which had the police service crest on its plastic barrel. "Carry on," she whispered, managing to sound kick-ass even in a whisper, and pulled another, identical pen out of her shirt pocket for her own use.

This was a real cop.

Being in a roomful of real cops was reassuring. Lock would have to work pretty hard to get at me or the paper here.

With enough planning, he could, but Roger had chosen his meeting room carefully. This was the room designed to help the city's brass run things in case of major catastrophe. It would take some doing to get past the security perimeter into the cop shop and through these bomb-proof walls.

97. TASKING

Rod had finished fussing with his paperwork, an untidy file in a brown folder. He opened it on the table as if he were still leading an investigative team. Old habits die hard.

"Okay, first contact. June nine," he said.

I told you so, I mouthed to Roger. Rodney showed no sign of realising he had contradicted himself.

"Subject showed me his wounded hand. Clearly a sharp knife, a single blow, lack of hesitation marks suggested that it wasn't self-inflicted. His story was that he was holding onto the rope when Priscilla Jane Gill sliced through rope and fingers. His DNA was on the rope so I had no reason to doubt his version of events."

"Except that we didn't know th—" began Lance at the same time as Prasan Dave said, "There are so many explanations for his DN—" Roger shut them both down with that nifty homeopathic little hand movement. I would have to practise that at home.

"Discussion later. Next?"

"I got him to a doctor. He was ranting a little, sounded a bit like a conspiracy theorist, to be honest, but that could have been the infection. He didn't trust the police. I badged the doc and he agreed to keep it quiet. I don't think he knew who he was treating. Lock had some ID —"

"His ID was all at the hotel," said Lance.

Roger's hand was getting a minimalist workout, but nothing deterred Horenko now. His shoulders had bulked up to fit his suit, and he was acting like he was a senior cop again.

"Be that as it may," he said, "he had ID with him."

"In what name?"

"Er . . . I didn't notice."

"Pull the other one," said Roger. "In what name, Rodney?"

"Nate Bierce."

"He used *Nathan's* name?" I said. "My god. He's going to try to get money out of the company somehow. Backdoor."

"Yours," Roger said to Lance, who nodded and made a note. "But wait. Rodney, any more names that you've seen him use?"

Rodney looked into each corner of the room, his gaze darting diagonally until he had exhausted the possibilities of the ceiling tile, and lingering in one corner long enough for one of his guards to look up there involuntarily. The rest of us watched Rodney. He must have figured out his little show of studiousness wasn't working because he snapped to grid and said gruffly, "Gil Preston. Bierce Dalziel-pronounced-Dee-all. That one goes with an English accent. Janeway Rogers."

"He's fucking with us," I said. "He's using all our names, or names that relate to us, with a touch of *Trek* just to spit in our eye.

But he'll have another one that came first — the one he told me he prepared a long time ago. Not Nate Bierce, though why the hell he used something real —"

"Happened to have it. ID he stole from Nathan," said Roger. "I bet it was a throwdown. He never used it again, right, Rodney?"

"He threw it in the garbage right at the ER."

Roger sat back and steepled his fingers.

"What else have you got in that file?"

"Some paper he left there. Nothing on it though. I kept it for fingerprints. And recordings — on this thumb drive. I tried to record our conversations. If it was safe. After all, this was evidence. Against Pris, I thought. I was going to turn it over to the investigation, when something conclusive came out of it."

Sure he was, I thought.

"But nothing conclusive did," said Roger.

"Well, nothing that wasn't hearsay. I kept pressing him for more information but he —"

"How long did he stay at your house?" Roger interrupted roughly.

"About three w— . . . how . . . never mind. You got me there, Rog."

"Don't call me Rog. We're not friends. Let me see that paper you're talking about. He left it with you for safekeeping, I assume."

"Er . . . yes, that's what he said."

"With his trusted ex-cop buddy."

"With a trained investigator."

Rodney had carefully clipped the paper Lock had touched between two sheets of typing paper. Roger pulled a pair of latex gloves out of his inner pocket. Cops. Maybe they were once Scouts. Always be prepared. I knew what Roger was going to do, so I kept my gaze on Horenko. Mr. Trained Investigator hadn't figured out the card, and his treatment of it showed that he hadn't figured out this paper either.

When Roger tapped the sheet and the text lit up on it, the surprise and chagrin on Rodney's face would have been the basis for a great viral video on YouTube™. I laughed aloud, and he turned and glared, also very funny.

"Trained investigator," I murmured into the air. The deputy chief heard me and I thought I heard her make a sound, but when I turned slightly she was still calm and poker-faced, her hands clasped around her pen and resting on her yellow notepad, on which there was still nothing new written. She was a professional.

Roger made one of those hand motions, and suddenly Constable Dave was pulling on gloves. Rog handed the paper and thumb drive to him, and with two tiny movements (one cut of eyes and one tilt of head), Rog included Lance in the party and sent them both out the door, evidence and tablet computers in hand.

I was definitely going to have to practise my tasking.

98. WHERE'S WALDO?

"So where is he?" Roger's voice suddenly had an edge I'd rarely heard. He whipped his head around and leaned forward.

"Pardon me?" A brave front. Rodney *had* worked with him for years. But he flinched.

"You don't believe he is innocent any more, right, Mr. Horenko? So where the . . . where is he, Rodney? I *can* call you Rodney, after all these years, can't I?"

Roger had heard the recordings Lock had made, on his smart-paper card, of every interaction Lock had had with Rodney on that first night of April Fool's Day, and he was doing this on purpose. Rodney didn't know that, but he flushed anyway. Roger had him on the run.

"Not only where is he, but *who* is he, now? What's his name now, Rodney?"

Rodney took my pen and paper without permission. He hunched over the page in that defensive-looking way of the left-handed, but this time it really was defensive, not just a function of how hard it is when we write from left to right with a left hand.

"There," he said, ripped off the page (unevenly, I noticed), and sliced it across the table to Roger.

Roger was cool.

He reached out one finger and stopped the page in perfect alignment in front of him.

He picked it up.

He read it.

He folded it and put it in his pocket.

"You're under arrest, Rodney," he said. "In recognition of your co-operation, you can go down to the cells under your own steam. Dan here will caution you. Lawyer, Charter, blah blah. Have a nice life. Book him, Dan-o."

"Oh, Inspector, you know I hate it when you say that," said one of the guardians. "I am *so* not Hawai'ian." She wasn't, at all.

"Get out of here," said Roger.

99. TASKING RODNEY

The deputy chief broke her silence. "I'll have my pen back, Mr. Horenko."

Rodney had pocketed it. He handed it back to me as if he didn't dare face her, which was probably true. I refused it, and gave a minimalist little twitch of my head in the deputy chief's direction. Horenko obediently gave her the pen.

Hot damn. It works.

100. THE SEARCH FOR AMBROSE BIERCE

Ambrose Bierce was a famous disappearing guy. It's an accident, I'm sure, that he had the same last name as Nathan, but it was typical of Lock's sense of humour that he had pretended to me, the first time we met, that it was his name: the name of one famous disappearing guy was — ta-da! — the name of another famous disappearing guy.

Chiles had an entire history under that other, non-Biercian name. At least one, but this was the one we could find.

"Don't they call that a 'legend' in books?" I asked Roger.

"Maybe the kind of books you read. The kind I read, they call it fraud," he said, and ruined his comedic timing by adding, "and possibly even identity theft." After a moment he made it worse: "And total bullshit."

He was waiting for his guys to go arrest Lock. He had sent out the Serious Incident Team under Lance's direction.

He paced. "What the fuck is taking them so long?"

"I told you you'd hate this promotion," I said.

"What?" He wasn't even listening to me. That was bad.

"Roger!" I said, sharply.

"What?" he said in a much more present tone.

"Sit down! You're making me anxious. Either they get him or they don't. If they don't . . ."

"What? For Chrissake!"

"If they don't, I know where he'll be."

And I was right.

101. ENTER, A MURDERER

Six hours later, when I came into my house, Lockwood Chiles was standing in the angle of the window embrasure, half-hidden by the curtain, looming.

It would have been more menacing if it hadn't been the longest day of the year, thus the sun was still high, so the room had a pleasant glow and he wasn't yet backlit. It was still plenty dramatic. I noticed that Micah Five and Bunnywit were well out of the way, but Micah One was angled on the shelf so as to get a good view.

"Oh, for fuck's sake," I said irritably, throwing my bag down on the sofa. "Will you stop that! Just knock on the door like a regular person, would you?"

"But I'm not a regular person, am I? I'm your murderer."

I opened my mouth to beg for my life, and this is what came out. "If we're going to have the fighting-for-my-life scene, can I move a few ornaments first?"

What? I thought.

"What?" said Lock.

"And that rug. I just got it cleaned from the last time I bled on it. It was bloody expensive. Oh, sorry, pun unintended."

"You won't need your fucking rug."

"You never know. I fight dirty. I could win."

"As fucking if."

"Lock! Language."

"I'm a foot taller than you —"

"Like that matters!" I interrupted.

"— and I . . . what?"

"Nothing. You were saying, 'and'?"

"And I have a gun."

"Oh, damn," I said. "That takes all the fun out of it."

He did have a gun. Oops. "Fun?" he repeated, as if he thought *I* was the crazy one.

"Before you shoot me," I said desperately, "which I wouldn't recommend because my neighbours are particularly sensitive about sound, they even speak to me if I make love noisily, and as for the one downstairs, you should hear him talk about

Bunnywit, but anyway, before you shoot me, would you mind confessing?"

"What?"

102. TASKING LOCKWOOD CHILES

"If I'm going to die," I explained, and was astonished at my ability to put a tone of aggrieved patience into my voice, "I want to know why. So far I don't exactly know why you have this hate on for all the people who like you."

"My psychiatrist says I'm conflicted about self-esteem," he said. Really.

And I didn't laugh. Really. Not out loud. I only kind of snorted. "You told him you like to stalk and attack and kill people who trust you, and he said you're conflicted?"

"Told her. I didn't exactly tell her about the killing part. But I'm making progress on allowing love to enter my life."

"Starting with killing Pris, Nathan, Mowbry, me, and a few other people?"

"I'm starting fresh. She only knows my new persona."

"You're not trying the old multiple-personality scam? That is so old!"

"No, of course not! That's just stupid. I have none of the . . . Wait. You did that on purpose."

I tilted my head slightly in agreement.

"You shouldn't annoy me if you want me to talk to you."

He was right. I bit back all the things I felt like saying. I rejected a number of smart-ass remarks in favour of "True. So go on." If I got out of this alive, I planned to make Roger and all my other friends commend me for this restraint. If.

"I told you everything on the phone, anyway."

"Not everything. Like, I'm really curious where you came from."

"Nowhere."

"Not today, doofus. I mean when you were a kid, and met Nathan."

"I was never a kid. Certainly not when I met Nathan. But if you look young enough, you can be a kid as long as you want."

He let his face go a little blank and swung his hands down as if awkward and helpless. He looked about twenty-five for a moment.

"So how old were you? When you said you were fifteen?"

"I think about twenty-two. I'm not entirely sure any more. I've been a lot of ages. And it's not like they registered my birth."

"They."

"Parents. I did have them. For a while."

"Did you kill them too?"

"Unfortunately not. In retrospect, I wouldn't have minded, but I lacked the confidence at the age of seven, which is when I became a foster child. How do you think I knew how the system worked?"

"You're not pleading 'I was abused in care' either, I hope."

"Of course not. I was, but so what? It's a fucked-up world."

"So . . . you graduated, and then voluntarily came back and put yourself in care again somehow?"

"I had some reasons for needing a place to lie low. And I'd met Nathan online. We didn't call it that then, of course. Bulletin boards. I knew where he was living. But he didn't know how old I was. It was such a great surprise to him that we met so fortuitously."

"So, no scion of a wealthy family."

"No. It was fun to make up stories for Pris because she knew it was a game."

"What *was* your birth name?"

"That's a secret. Even Pris didn't know. I'm sure as hell not telling you."

"But you're about to kill me."

"Even so."

"Okay, fine, be that way. So why Pris, now . . . why did you have Mowbry attack her in the first place?"

"She thought she could do without me and my protection. She broke up with me. I needed someone to show her that she needed me."

"He almost killed her. He stabbed her feet, for fuck's sake! Wasn't that a bit extreme? Couldn't you have just sent her roses?"

"Why do you think I had to deal with him when he showed up at the bookstore? First he gets carried away, and then he's going to confess that it wasn't even his idea? The hell with that. The best part was convincing Priscilla she'd helped me."

"Why would you do that to her?"

"Then she could never leave me."

"But she tried."

"Well, yes. But I stopped that, didn't I?"

"Would you like to sit?" I said.

"I'll stand, thanks."

"Well, I'm sitting." And I did. The armchair was at an angle to Lock's position, though he didn't seem to notice. If he wanted to shoot me I wasn't going to make it easy for him. "Don't you care that you actually killed people? Don't you feel bad about it?"

"I don't, actually. I know how to pretend, but we're past that, aren't we?"

"So you're the classic sociopath, the kind we were talking about that day we all had dinner and discussed your house issues?"

"I suppose so. I find it hard to align that description with myself."

"You read the same information I did. Nature sets the brain up, lack of nurture sets it off. Classic. I bookmarked it; I can refresh your memory . . ." I reached for my tablet, on the table beside the chair, hiking the chair a little more to the left as I did so.

"Never mind, for cryin' out loud," he said. "I remember it just fine." He had to turn his head now to talk to me, and he did. On

the spot, I was inventing a new life-and-death type of tasking. I
didn't like it. But it was working.

103. JUMP

"Quit jumping around," he said.

As if I was being compliant, I swung the chair around a bit
more by shifting my butt. Now, though I was facing him, I was
also another two inches further away, in the angular dimension.
He didn't seem to notice that part.

"You killed your best friend."

"He was giving away our money to charity, for heaven's sake.
Homeless assholes. *Our* money." He moved the hand with the
gun to try to follow me, and it brushed against the curtain, behind
which was the corner where the wall bent into the bay window
embrasure. His hand rebounded reflexively from the hard edge,
and he made an involuntary moue of irritation, but it didn't seem
to impinge on his conscious mind. But the net effect was that the
gun wasn't easy to aim right at me any more. "And he didn't want
to live in our house any more. And then there was you, you bitch!"
He gestured with the gun, and twitched his hand away from a
second collision with the wall edge.

"I loved him," I said, "and he loved me." I pretended more fear
than I felt — no, let's be honest, I allowed my fear to show —
and with feet flat on the floor, pushed back another inch or two.
Or three.

But I also pushed back verbally. "He didn't want to live in
your house because it was like you. Cold, amoral, un-giving.
He wanted to be with me, and he wanted to do some good in
the world. More than you, you asshole." It would have been
more impressive as a denunciation if I hadn't started crying.

"Oh, he would have gotten tired of you. *I'm* tired of you. Get
up and turn around."

"So you can shoot me in the back? No way!"

"Oh, come on, get up," he said. Coaxingly. "You'll get blood on your upholstery if you stay there. You won't like that. You said so."

"Go fuck yourself," I said, elegantly, and stayed where I was.

Lockwood took one impetuous step toward me. It brought him off the rug and onto the hardwood floor. More importantly, it brought him out of the awkward angle of the window embrasure.

I ducked and rolled out of the chair and behind it in one urgent motion, then scooted back as far toward the kitchen as I could, keeping the chair between us.

He should have shot me then, of course. The chair would have been no barrier at that distance, even if his little grey handgun was low-calibre.

But he didn't.

He took one more step toward me.

Then Roger stepped out of the hall closet and shot him in the leg.

104. "... WATCHIN' THE DETECTIVES ... AND THEY SHOOT, SHOOT, SHOOT ..."

And that, as they say, was that.

Who are "they", anyway?

Anyway: and that was that.

While Chiles rolled on the floor screaming and hugging his bleeding leg, Roger and Lance stepped out of their ambush locations, and suddenly the place was full of cops. They'd been there for hours, in the apartment and next door in the empty suite. Before I got word from the Serious Incident Team guys that the trap was set, I had led Lock around some public places, while being guarded by Lance and some other ostentatiously big cops, and then on a pre-arranged "call to Roger" — to his cell phone left at the cop shop — I insisted that I wanted the guards to stay outside and leave me alone in the apartment. Privacy and all that.

The reality was that I would have allowed any number of cops to follow me everywhere — to help me brush my teeth and to scrub my back in the bath — if it would have kept me safe while they caught Lock.

But I didn't trust him not to be smarter than them, and skate off around the world in a protective haze of money. So we did all these public theatrics, while I assumed my cell phone calls were accessible to him.

All to set the hook in Lockwood Chiles's jaw. To convince him that the only place to get at me was my apartment. And back in my place, the trap was carefully prepared.

And it worked.

Luckily, being shot is a hell of a shock to the system, so Chiles was relatively easy to cuff despite his size and craziness. He only required one Taser shock and four cops sitting on him.

Soon the place was even more crowded, with paramedics and firefighters and even more cops. I had hoped there was a red alert on and the paramedics would be late so Lock would hurt a lot more, but they were distressingly prompt with their field dressings and morphine or whatever the hell glazed his eyes and calmed him down as they carted him off strapped to a stretcher.

Roger hugged me.

"I can't believe the way you lipped him off, but it was perfect! You were bloody brilliant!"

But "bloody" didn't apply. The blood was all his. This time, I hadn't shed one single drop.

I'd had my heart cut out, but there wasn't a single drop to show for it.

The heart grows back, they say.

But it takes a while, and there's always a scar.

AND IT'S LOVELY RICE PUDDING FOR DINNER AGAIN! —

105. "TO ALL INTENSIVE PURPOSES . . ."

After the climax comes the denouement — it's a principle of narrative structure. I studied it in high school.

Even then I had some inkling that there was an analogy to sex, but until I started having Adventures in Real Life I didn't know that these rules apply to just about every Big Job.

The denouement is by nature — anticlimactic. Pun unintended. The story is for all intents and purposes (or, as Konni had put it while fixing my cell phone, "to all intensive purposes"[27]) over. But there is litter all over the landscape that needs to be cleared up. If you weren't well trained, you just leave your tools out in the rain and go home. If you have some kind of work ethic, you may be dog-tired but you keep cleaning up until the worksite is spic-and-span.

I was beyond dog-tired. I was cat-tired. I was perhaps even dinosaur-tired, in that I was the left-over of a mass extinction

---

27. Thus proving again that, for all intents and purposes, these *are* the end times.

event and I felt like I also had died. Since I hadn't, I was doing the conceptual equivalent of creeping around the aftermath of the meteor impact tidying what I could and watching others tidy what they could.

106. ᏏᏢᴁᎢ.

For instance, I tried to find out, again, where Pris went.

I actually spent a lot of time on it. I hired a real detective too. Still, I wasn't successful.

But one day, after the big bolus of media coverage exonerating her had hit the *In Depth*–type feature sections, I got a phone call.

Yeah, I was answering the phone, even though I'd had to block the number of the prisoner line at the Remand Centre. I was, apparently, Lock's new best friend. That worried me some, when I could summon the energy.

So, "Hello?" I said, hoping I didn't again hear Lock voice-stalking.

"Hello, um, I hope I have the right number. This is Mattie Groves[28]."

Who? "Yes?"

"Um, you don't know me, I guess. Groves is my married name. Really I'm Mattie Gill. I'm Prissie Gill's sister?"

She didn't sound certain. Prissie?

"How can I help you, Ms. Groves?"

"Call me Mattie. I'm her half-sister, really. I just wanted to thank you? For what you did for Prissie?"

Prissie? "I'm sorry, I didn't know she had a . . . half-sister."

---

28. Later I will tell you why I assigned this transparently false and narratively inappropriate name to Priscilla's sib. Because false it is. Try to really find her. I dare you.

"No, we like our privacy. But you know, I never thought she would do what they said in the paper? So thank you for proving it. I know Prissie would appreciate it too."

Appreciate it, I thought. As if I'd given her a nice gift. "Um, you're welcome, I guess."

"Because, you know, when she came to see me that time in the winter, she didn't mean there to be all that fuss. But never mind, I just wanted to say that it will make a big difference to us, you know . . . Well, I'll let you go; I don't want to bother you . . ."

Wait. "Wait! Don't hang up! Priscilla came to see you? Wait!"

Hwæt (Ƕᵽæt) is the first word of *Beowulf.* It's usually been translated as "Lo!", but to most scholars it means, basically: Shut up and listen up! Witness this! Wow, do I have a story for you! Lookit! Yo! Or just, *Wait!*

I get that. Think about it. It's the ye-olde-English version of what happens on a grey day when you've ordered in pizza and everyone's bored with what's on Netflix™, so you propel the endless round of distractions with that word, staying in motion through repetitive and competitive pausing:

"Wait, guys, this is a good one. Remember that time when Daly drank so much she puked all over her dad's Escalade and we had to wash it at five a.m.?" "Come on, wait! You think that's bad? Remember when Walt rolled his car? And walked away?" "No, wait! When Bobby snagged his hair in that drill press? Man, he almost scalped himself! He still has the scar!" Eventually you end up — wait! — in the Lover's Lane with the Hitch-hiker's Thumb, or — wait! — tying a lawn chair to some helium-filled balloons to try out for the Darwin Award . . .

. . . or listening to Pris's sister provide the end of a thread, the pulling of which would unravel the last knot of mystery, the loose end that we had all been — hwæting for.

"Wait! Will you tell me what happened? Why she came?"

There was a long pause.

"Maybe you should come and see me too," said Mattie Gill.
So I did.

107. "COME HOME WITH ME, LITTLE MATTIE GROVES . . ."

Priscilla Gill's invisible sister lives in an auto suburb which shall remain nameless. Possibly not in my city. Probably not, in fact. In fact, I've changed all the hard facts about this part of the story so that she can't be found. Her name isn't Mattie Groves at all — I took that name from a bloodthirsty old ballad about a jealous husband, Lord Arlen (or Lord Donald — his name varies), who kills his wife, Lady Arlen, and her boy-toy Mattie Groves. It seemed appropriate, in a weird and gender-switched way, even though in this story, Mattie is the sister of the doomed lover.

Roger came with me. I can afford to treat a friend to these little weekend jaunts now, from time to time, if I don't have them very often. People think Nathan left me a fortune, you know. But he knew I wouldn't want that. So what I have is just enough. Enough, as one of his notes slyly suggested, that I won't have to eat fish sticks again. Unless I'm foolish enough, too often, to buy full-price same-day air tickets to distant places. This trip would mean a few more Kraft Dinners™, for sure.

We rented a car and followed the brittle, oddly-accented voice of its GPS to a sub-suburban crescent of the sort always named after an ocean, a mountain, or a river that is a figment of a developer's imagination, and dubbed a Mews or Close or Drive when really it's just an excuse to face some monster garages onto a small circle of pavement venting onto a winding access road. Outside the house stood one perfect mid-size sedan and one perfect mid-size tree, the first in the enormous driveway and the second in the postage-stamp lawn. Shackled to the tree with an expensive lock was a shiny state-of-the-art bicycle, the only thing in the entire crescent that wasn't factory-clean. It looked like it was ridden often on real streets. Kid in the house.

Otherwise, the whole suburb looked like it came out of a Hasbro Easy-Bake Oven™.

Mattie — we'll pretend her name was Mathilda and she hated it, and everyone called her Mattie, and that's a version of the reality, anyway — greeted us at the door. She looked like a quieter version of Priscilla. Pris Gill Lite. A little shorter, a little paler, a little plumper, a little older, and probably only someone who knew Pris well would have been able to detect the likeness in ears and hand shape and elegant curve of skull.

I introduced myself, but she said, "Yes, I recognise you from Pris's photos. And the news, of course."

"Pris's photos?"

"From university days."

"Ah. Of course." Photos? I had a few of those, myself, now.

"You look just the same, really."

She ushered us into a cathedral-ceilinged living room — oh, wait, they call these The Great Room these days, don't they?: people do their living in what used to be called the rumpus room, which now is labelled the family room, and nobody who lives in a house like this ever has a rumpus, anyway. The room had a pale floor and was furnished in shades of porcelain from almost-white to almost-beige. It was lovely, and restful, and quiet. And so Not-Pris.

She recognised Roger too, of course, from the media nonsense.

"But you brought . . . the police?" She was alarmed — seemingly slightly, but if her range of emotional expression matched the rooms, she could as easily have been in a panic and I wouldn't have recognised it as such. My friends and I tend to live out loud, and Pris was one of the most flamboyant of us all.

"Roger's here as my friend. I've known him for almost as long as I knew Priscilla. He helped me clear her name, and he was curious."

"I guess . . . I can understand that."

"Nothing official," said Roger. "Unless it's illegal as hell, of course. Small lies can be overlooked."

She looked at him sharply. He was grinning. But I know Roger.

I could see her decide he was joking, and she gave a small laugh. "Please, sit down," she said. "Would you like something to drink?"

I was about to say no when Roger moved in, in a rather scary Rog-is-Charming style I'd never before seen in him. "Do you have something cold? It's been a dry journey and the taxicab was warm."

"Juice? Soda pop? Kiwi water?"

When we'd picked, she bustled out to the adjoining open plan kitchen, and I heard her getting ice cubes from the ice-maker in her refrigerator.

"'The taxicab was warm'?" I whispered to Roger.

"When in suburban Rome, do as the Romans do," he said quietly, then, more loudly, "Lovely room, isn't it? So airy."

The Pod People aren't plausible, so I had to admit I was seeing Roger channelling Helen Mirren. In her character of Inspector Tennison, though perhaps as The Queen. "Lovely," I said, and pulled a fold of my sleeve more securely over my tattoos.

Mattie came back into the room.

"Isn't it," she said. "We saw it for sale, and it suited us so."

Roger and I had drifted over to the marble mantel, which hosted several tastefully-framed family photos. The one of Pris and her sister was also from university days, and they both looked like other people than the ones they had become. Both wore Indian cotton skirts and shirts (that's what rendered Mattie into another person), both had tangled long hair and the sun in their eyes so that squinting changed the shape of both their faces — and the glare turned Pris's dark hair almost silver-red. She was unrecognisable.

Mattie and her family were pictured in a conventional grouping. I picked it up and looked closer. The husband looked stolid and safe and gentle: swarthy and earnest, and a little too zaftig for my tastes, but not fat exactly, just — comfortable. And bland. Like his house. Wearing fixed smiles and colour-co-ordinated outfits, he and Mattie perched on stools with their children around them, the two oldest standing behind and the youngest in front. Mattie's hand was on the youngest child's shoulder. There was about a ten-year age difference (second honeymoon, perhaps?) between the mousy-haired young man and pleasantly-pretty, dark-haired young woman behind them and the lanky, awkward kid crouched in front. Of all them, she, or he, I couldn't tell for sure, looked the most interesting, but also spotty, with bad glasses and an uncomfortable smile.

"That was three years ago," she said, coming up beside me. "That's my husband Tom, and behind us that's Bobby and Sarah, and of course that's Kim."

"Of course, that's Kim"? There was a world of forbearance, or something else less obvious, in that "of course". I put the frame back in the exact spot I had found it and turned to find a glass of lemonade thrust into the hand still raised in front of me.

"Thank you," I said. My patience lasted as long as my first sip. "Please excuse me," I said, "but I've been waiting for a long time, over a year, to find out where Pris went that time, and I was completely gob-smacked, er, surprised by your call. So please forgive me if I ask you why . . ."

"Please, let's sit," she said. "It's rather . . . difficult . . ."

Her difficulty was short, however, for somewhere in the back of the house, a door slammed, and a young voice shouted, "Mom! Mom!"

108. FOOTPRINTS ON THE SAND

A stampede of adolescent feet resolved itself into a youth I recognised instantly, though we had never met. Into the room issued all the rumpus this house would ever have, or ever need.

"Mom, can I go over to Destiny and Soleil's place?" Kim said, fortissimo, before seeing us and stopping with a clatter of heels, dropping a backpack and swinging a cell phone and headphones from one shapely hand.

"Kim, dear, say hello to some friends of Auntie Jane's."

Auntie Jane?

"Hello," said the kid, blushing. "Sorry, I didn't know anyone was here. Mom?"

"Just a moment," said Mattie. She turned to us with only a ripple across her sang-froid, and told the kid our names.

"Pleased to meet you," said Kim. "How did you know Auntie?"

"Would you like some kiwi water, dear?"

"I'll get it," said Kim, and zipped back to the kitchen. The air seemed to settle and relax in her — his? their? — wake.

Six feet tall, beautiful, dark, vivid. Same raptor-like nose, same intense stare.

"Does Kim take after her —"

". . . er, his?" murmured Roger, behind me.

"— mother?" I asked quietly.

"Yes," Mattie said calmly.

"Does Kim know?"

"No," she said. "Everyone thought it best, given the circumstances. Tom and I wanted a third child, and Priscilla was . . . um, wasn't —" She didn't trail off. She stopped, knowing we would finish the sentence.

"Yes, she was," I said. "And wasn't."

"Kim knows in a general way, of course, that Prissie wrote those books and so on. But we call her Auntie Jane because Prissie wanted privacy when she was here. Off duty, she used to say. Civilian life."

Her lips twisted slightly. I could see we would never get the real and complete story of this half-sister's complicated feelings for Pris. "Kim knows that. Kim is very . . . sensible, really. A bit of a handful, but sensible."

"I can imagine."

"We love her very much," Mattie said. Her. Take that, Roger. Not that one could tell, either way. "Her Auntie Jane has left her a large legacy and, you know, the usual letter, which a lawyer will send her when she is of age."

"She's not — Lockwood's?"

"Oh, definitely not. Pris didn't meet Lock until after she was expecting, and she went away to have Kim. Lock never knew. Kim might be, you know, she might be . . ."

I looked through the archway into the kitchen, at the dark head bent over the telephone, the slim fingers texting.

"Nathan's?"

"I have always thought so," said Mattie. "But she never told. Us, or him. She said the father could never know. They met first, you know, and were together for a while before she went with that Chiles."

She paused, and her fingers clasped even more tightly around her glass of kiwi water. "When Prissie came here last winter, it was to urge us, beg us really, never to try to guess. Never to tell, if we did guess. She said that Lockwood wasn't safe. If he ever found out . . . She said . . . Kim wouldn't be safe."

"That's true," I said. "Even now."

Mattie nodded. "She was right. He mustn't know."

"He won't find out from us," said Roger.

I was still speechless. I had thought Nathan and Priscilla's children would have been beautiful. I had been right.

WHAT *IS* THE MATTER WITH MARY JANE?

109. LONG DARK TEA-TIME OF THE SOUL

Smart paper doesn't burn. It doesn't melt at any temperature I can muster at home. The rest of the oven smokes, but the damned stuff just lies there. It sparks a bit if you microwave it, but still works. It barely creases, and it certainly doesn't tear. It can be cut with scissors along certain lines, twice per sheet, and you get two or three or four smart pieces of paper. Otherwise it resists cutting.

Nathan's smart paper has his voice on it. I try not to play it too often. It sits in that box and metaphorically calls to me. I tried leaving it in Dafydd Spak's lockup but that was worse. Finally I had to bring it home.

Lockwood Chiles's smart paper can be convinced to decommission itself if it feels the situation is too dire. But that is hard to convince it to do because sometimes it signals home base as soon as it feels threatened, and asks for help. The first time it happened and armed SWAT-type security guards showed up I was shocked. Eventually, if I was fiddling with the stuff and it got nervous, I would just phone the guys and say, "False alarm, don't worry." Someday I'll figure out how to turn it off.

I really hate the stuff.

110. OKAY, OKAY.

Okay. Okay. I eventually had to reveal what my smart paper love letter said.

It said it for real: because it was smart paper it spoke in my dear dead Nathan's voice, in my dear Dafydd Spak's office; it spoke out loud into the air of the cop shop, because it was needed as evidence of motive and of Nathan's intentions; it spoke out loud into the air of the boardroom of our Own Domains housing initiative, because it was needed to convey Nathan's intentions and the fact that he had meant me to be a key player in Own Domains; it would later speak up in court, at Chiles's trial, and eventually I'm sure it will end up having something to say to the media, too, damn their eyes.

It says, in the present tense because it will say it again and again, any time I ask it, in Nathan's beautiful voice that it kills me to hear, many things, but among them, this:

"My dear, my beauty, my brilliant love . . . if you hear this, the usual is true, blah blah dead. If I die young, I am pretty sure I know who is going to kill me. But Pris may surprise me and be the one instead. I doubt it though. She's too fastidious, and she likes her alligators with rubber bands around their snouts.

"But I don't plan to die young. I plan to spend the rest of a very long life with you, and we are going to have such fun. It will be fun to show you what money can do, things we can approve of, and it will be fun to invent stuff together, because I am sure we will. We will be partners one hundred percent of the way. You will listen to this with me fifty or sixty years from now, when we are so old that everyone has begun to underestimate us at last, and we will laugh at our young and happy selves, and we will chuckle at what really happened during our long and happy life together, and then we will hold hands and smile at each other, and the young people who will be working at the nursing home will say in their incomprehensible future slang that those two centenarians are making love again, and they will think it's gross. Too bad for them.

"If I don't get a chance to say it, or alter my will again, I'll say it here. Holograph *and* spoken word will, what will they think of next — it should be in poetry or something.

"With all my worldly goods I thee endow. Or as many as I think you will accept.

"Just sayin', my love.

"And I promise that by the time we have finished with Own Domain, and the other things we've been talking about, my worldly goods will be about equal to yours. And not because you invented your version of smart paper either. Rather, because we were smart enough to give it all, all of it, to places where it should go. Legally and happily. Just keep enough to live on with a bit of freedom and comfort, no fish sticks.

"My lawyers started to tell me it's not possible. I am going to be getting new lawyers. If career criminals can manage to launder their money, surely career honest people can do it better. For something that stays, not nose candy and yachts. Lock can have his yachts. We are going to have far more fun than that."

Then there was a whole stack of spreadsheets and instructions. He had had it worked out, in every brilliant detail, how.

Lockwood Chiles isn't allowed to profit from a crime, but Nathan Lockwood World, or Incorporated, or whatever, has lots of lawyers working for it too. Jail is semi-permeable, after all. Nathan's family have teamed up with Lock's legion of lawyers and a few competing, ambitious wannabes, and the whole thing, Own Domains and all, is stuck in a limbo from which it may never recover. Even after Lock got killed in jail the palaver went on, but that's another story, and one too complicated for a denouement chapter.

Every now and then I have tea with Gary, the mayor, and we think about what almost happened to the east of downtown, and occasionally I'm not the only one with tears in their eyes.

But that's later, in the inevitable, evil denouement. After the weeks when I tried to figure out how to turn Nathan's voice off all day, only to obsessively listen to it all night, until finally I achieved some sort of stasis.

That was all in the future.

111. AS THE NAIL HEAD BEND, SO THE STORY END.

So let's go back to that moment. That, right there, the minute after I was nearly killed, and Roger was hugging me, and Lock's blood was staining my hardwood in a most gratifying way.

I debriefed with the whole of cop-dom, it seemed.

Then I came home.

I weathered the media storm.

Then I came home.

I explored the subplot of Pris's disappearance-that-wasn't, which I can only tell you about above, even in this general and disguised way, because of that other shit-storm that arose: to wit, Lockwood's death.

I demanded to see his corpse, you know. I wasn't going to believe that a guy with his skills, and access to more money than God, hadn't bought himself out of jail. But it was him, and although police withheld his manner of death for investigative purposes, I imagined him painfully gouged into oblivion with the usual brand of jailhouse shiv, and thought that it couldn't have happened to a finer person.

I have to admit to my karmic debt that along with my revulsion, I suffered both that vengeful satisfaction and also a huge wave of relief. He couldn't come after me and mine — or Kim and Kim's. And just in case of good Hollywood F/X, the DNA evidence, an evidence chain Roger and I shadowed all the way, really did bear up. I think that Rog and Dave and Lance kept a twenty-four-hour vigil in the lab until the test was done. Lockwood Chiles, whoever he had been, was, as far as we could confirm it, dead.

I spat on his grave[29]. Then I came home.

I spent hours with Denis, and Hep, and even with my cousin Thelma, her husband and new baby, and Vikki the caregiver.

Then I came home.

I took a holiday and followed the Cirque du Soleil for a dose of my friend Jian's practical love. I told her the whole story, cried in her arms, she consoled me, and even made me laugh a little, when I forgot for a moment.

Then I came home.

Home was two living cats and one dead one, and, on the top shelf of the closet, a hand-carved box that whispered to me in the night.

"Sometimes I wish it had never happened," I said to my audience of two. I patted Bunnywit. "If I'd listened to you when you said 'No' . . ."

But I was glad I hadn't listened, because of the time I'd had with Nathan.

I left unexamined, for now, the weird existential tree-in-forest question of whether if I'd listened to Bun, I'd have even known what I was missing. And if I'd listened to Bun, would they all still be alive? Was Nathan loving me, and Pris having someone to talk with, the tipping factor? Had I, by being there, observing the system, actually been, despite my stubborn denials, a kind

---

29. Sort of. He was cremated. But I spat on his paper coffin before it slid into the furnace.

of Schrödinger's-observer, causing the whole destabilization, opening the box, triggering the outcome of that fatal electron that killed the cat?

That way lies rump of skunk and madness.

One day I re-arranged the living room so that the easy chair didn't face the window but instead covered the unremoveable last of the bloodstain, and the couch was out from under the shadow of Nathan. It was too easy to see ghosts. Nathan had never been in this newly-configured living room, though Bun's cashmere pillow still adorned the couch, and a bespoke ottoman still twinned my favourite chair.

When I was done, although shoving the furniture around had only taken ten minutes, I was exhausted. Pushing back against the weight of the past takes a lot of energy.

Bunnywit climbed into my lap. He walked up my chest until we were nose to nose. He licked my nose, then put one paw up and patted my face. He spoiled his unprecedented conciliation somewhat by licking my tears off his paw, but redeemed himself by patting again with no following lick.

"Niaow," he said.

"You're right, I said. "Forget the emotional cowardice. I'm glad I met him. You see? Sometimes I listen."

From the bookcase, Micah One glared his cross-eyed, moth-eaten glare, which had been made worse when one of his glass eyes had temporarily been replaced by the police webcam. Because it was in my apartment, and I'd signed the permission document, all the evidence from it was in the end fully admissible.

Priscilla's elegant cat climbed up beside Bun and they butted my face with their heads, one on either side.

It was a lovely moment of solidarity.

"And I'm glad I re-connected with Priscilla Jane. 'And it's lovely rice pudding for dinner again'," I said aloud.

Mistake. I had mentioned dinner. End of solidarity.

Bunnywit purred and jumped down.

M5 purred and followed him.

They ran to the kitchen.

I noticed one of my finger picks on the floor, half-under the couch. The colourful little claw-substitutes had become, whenever they could steal one, a favourite toy of the Terrible Twosome.

"Leave those alone," I muttered. I was going to have to find a worthy container to keep those particular treasures safe from my disrespectful little four-footed twerps.

I picked up the little yellow fingernail and absently put it on, thinking of the day Nathan and I had made them, and the evening at the Little Flower open stage when I first used them, and the song we had sung.

Poor Nathan's dead and gone
Left me here to sing this song

I sat there for a moment longer, tapping my forehead with the finger pick as if I were smart paper and something else would emerge.

Perhaps my forehead would split and Nathan would rise, like Athena from the head of Zeus.

But apparently not.

"Now! Now!" M5 said.

"Nioaow!" said Bun.

From the bookcase, Micah One still stared. He would always stare the same way. Dead means you can't move, forward or back. Dead means you can only hope for justice. And if you get it, justice only comforts the survivor, so even then, it's a cold comfort.

My mind ran on relentlessly, in parody of ancient storytellers:

My friends are as dead as the cat on the shelf
If you want any more you can tell it yourself.

I got up and fed the cats.

-30-
[a.k.a.]
finis
[a.k.a.]
... the end.

RICE PUDDING
("WHAT IS THE MATTER WITH MARY JANE?")
— BY A. A. (ALAN ALEXANDER) MILNE

What is the matter with Mary Jane?
She's crying with all her might and main,
And she won't eat her dinner — rice pudding again —
What *is* the matter with Mary Jane?

What is the matter with Mary Jane?
I've promised her dolls and a daisy-chain,
And a book about animals — all in vain —
What *is* the matter with Mary Jane?

What is the matter with Mary Jane?
She's perfectly well, and she hasn't a pain;
But, look at her, now she's beginning again! —
What *is* the matter with Mary Jane?

What is the matter with Mary Jane?
I've promised her sweets and a ride in the train,
And I've begged her to stop for a bit and explain —
What *is* the matter with Mary Jane?

What is the matter with Mary Jane?
She's perfectly well and she hasn't a pain,
And it's lovely rice pudding for dinner again! —
What *is* the matter with Mary Jane?

ACKNOWLEDGEMENTS

The original Bunnywit was named Kitty Vendetta, a tiny cat who could make large dogs (in the plural) cower, just by giving them A Look. I learned a lot from Kitty V.

My partner and I live just down the street from our nameless hero. Of course, the Epitome Apartments are down a street of the mind, but throughout this book I've relentlessly name-checked our neighbourhood of east downtown, and spoiler alert, it will get worse in book three. That's because I love our neighbourhood, despite everything. (By the way, why is it always the East Side that gets the bad reputation?)

Living near our homeless and underhoused neighbours as we do, it's small surprise that I began to yearn for a billionaire fairy-godparent who wanted to build harm reduction villages Right Now and knew Dr. Gabor Maté (who is a real, very smart guy whose book *In the Realm of Hungry Ghosts* you should all read!). Alas, I know that it's not that easy — but wouldn't it be great if it were? If we just got out there and got those villages built, right now, using Housing First to really get rid of most homelessness?

When I wrote the first line of this book, I had no idea where it would go, and the day I discovered that there would be no happy endings was a traumatic one.

Each of these books takes on different mystery/crime tropes, which I learned from reading a lot — a *lot* — of crime and mystery novels over the years, so thank you to all the authors I've admired, collected, and in some cases gotten to know, to my great edification. Also, and again, I want to thank all the people I've name-checked, quoted, parodied, and used as inspiration in whatever manner while writing this series. Dear Reader, I hope you have fun tracking down as many of the references as are not so completely personal as to be opaque: I enjoyed salting the mine with them. Even though the social justice issues I deal with are real and urgent, and even though this one was surprisingly sad, I'm still enjoying Nameless's sarcastic take on life. I want to thank all the first-readers over the years who read these books, both for fun and to check for mistakes in structure, typing, and assumptions. For any of my expert witnesses, any deviations from their advice are for the sake of story and Aren't Their Fault.

Thank you to the Alberta Foundation for the Arts and the Edmonton Arts Council, who at various times provided funding for this series. Thank you to my agent, Wayne Arthurson. Thanks to all the wonderful people at ECW, whom I only don't list because, as proven in the last book, between when I write this and when the book comes out more people will pop up and make my lists obsolete before they even see the light. Just know that I see you and appreciate everything you do to make the books happen — for me and everyone else you publish. I am so glad Wayne brought me to your door.

I have never had the chance (as Nathan, Lock, Pris, and Nameless did with mixed results) to prove that wealth wouldn't spoil me (I'm still willing to try — hint, hint, Universe!), but as many people (not just working creators) learn the hard way, poverty can be dangerous too and make one mean. I am grateful to everyone who helps me stay generous, keep an open heart, and continue to appreciate a sometimes-challenging world. I dedicate this book to my friends, neighbours, and family, living and departed — and in particular, to the late Betty Gibbs, my dear friend and chosen sister, who would have been tickled that I am writing mysteries. Also to my Pomeranian dogs, Gracelyn and Joffrey, who are distracting, annoying, adorable cats-in-drag, and, as always, to Timothy, who is neither a dog nor a cat, but the best human partner a person — well, this person, anyway — could have.

Our nameless friend will be back in *He Wasn't There Again Today* (October 2022).

© P. J. GROENEVELDT

CANDAS JANE DORSEY is the award-winning author of *Black Wine*, *A Paradigm of Earth*, *Machine Sex and Other Stories*, *Vanilla and Other Stories*, *Ice and Other Stories*, *The Adventures of Isabel*, and *The Story of My Life Ongoing, by C.S. Cobb*. She is a writer, editor, former publisher, community advocate, and activist living in Edmonton, Alberta.

This book is also available as a Global Certified Accessible™ (GCA) ebook. ECW Press's ebooks are screen reader friendly and are built to meet the needs of those who are unable to read standard print due to blindness, low vision, dyslexia, or a physical disability.

Purchase the print edition and receive the eBook free!
Just send an email to ebook@ecwpress.com and include:

- the book title
- the name of the store where you purchased it
- your receipt number
- your preference of file type: PDF or ePub

A real person will respond to your email with your eBook attached. And thanks for supporting an independently owned Canadian publisher with your purchase!

Printed on Rolland Enviro.
This paper contains 100% post-consumer fiber,
is manufactured using renewable energy - Biogas
and processed chlorine free.